# EMILY ANTOINETTE

# SPACE FOR LOVE

## A SWEET & SPICY SCI-FI ROMANCE

Copyright © 2023 by Emily Antoinette

ISBN 979-8-9883161-0-7 (paperback)

Cover art by Fires

All rights reserved.

No part of this book may be reproduced in any form or by any electronic or mechanical means, including information storage and retrieval systems, without written permission from the author, except for the use of brief quotations in a book review.

No generative artificial intelligence (AI) was used in the writing of this work. The author expressly prohibits any entity from using this publication for purposes of training AI technologies to generate text, including without limitation technologies that are capable of generating works in the same style or genre as this publication. The author reserves all rights to license use of this work for generative AI training and development of machine learning language models.

This book is a work of fiction. Names, characters, businesses, places, events and incidents in this book are either the product of the author's imagination or used in a fictitious manner. Any resemblance to actual persons, living or dead, or actual events is purely coincidental.

*To all my fellow horny geeks who think holodecks should be sexier.*

# CONTENT NOTES

Hello there, fellow sci-fi romance lover! Hope you're excited for some alien dick and kinky spice. If not...well, this might not be the book for you. Otherwise, get ready to meet your new space boyfriend!

Tropes/elements in Space for Love include plus-size romance, alien/monster love interest, pleasure sims/VR, secret identity, mutual pining, misunderstandings (due to anxiety and cultural differences), fish out of water, groveling, and size difference/will it fit.

CWs include discussion and explicit depictions of sex and kink-based activities (rope bondage and dominant/submissive dynamics), alien genitalia, ingestion of alien fluids, explicit language, and accidental intoxication. Due to the hidden identity aspect of the story, some of the scenes can be interpreted as dubious consent, though all characters involved are consenting to the best of their ability.

There are also depictions of anxiety and negative self-image (worries about attractiveness to alien species). Characters use profanity and explicit language throughout the book. There are brief, minor references to stalking, slut-shaming, and food-shaming from background characters.

If you have any questions or need more details about the content of the book before diving in, please feel free to reach out me at emilyantoinetteauthor@gmail.com.

# GLOSSARY

**Aespians (ay-spee-ans):** An insectoid, bipedal species with a chitinous hide that covers most of the body and long legs that bend much more prominently than humans. Aespians have vestigial translucent wings and large, prominent eyes, thin noses, and antennae-like protrusions on their foreheads.

**Ankites (an-kites):** A humanoid changeling-like species that can alter their features to look similar to other alien races. When not catering their appearance to look more appealing/welcoming to other alien races, their forms are more amorphous, with less defined features. They can't change their limb configurations or skin shade. They are typically slender and tall, though they can become more or less curvaceous or angular as desired. Ankites don't have hair, but can make a facsimile of it that looks like tentacles or a solid drape coming from their head.

**Coalition:** The main human governing force formed from the various human colonies and starships.

**Cycle:** One full day. On Spire, the artificial environmental systems create a day-night cycle that lasts 26 galactic standard hours.

**Esh'et:** Seladin curse, closest human curse is "shit".

**Fa-shar:** Seladin curse, closest human curse is "damn".

**Fa'sli:** Seladin slang, translates to "eager slut".

**Flesstra:** A large rodent commonly kept as a pet in the Xi Consortium.

**H'spith:** Seladin social class of merchants.

**Jefl'ka:** potent nexxit liquor with a sweet aftertaste.

**Kha-shar:** Seladin honorific, translates to "master".

**L'thris a talla:** Seladin term (antiquated), translates to "most beloved" or "keeper of my heart".

**Mslep:** A cabbage-like, sickly gray vegetable eaten by nexxit.

**Nexxit (neck-sit):** A humanoid species that has four arms. Their skin ranges from dark pink to light pink skin. Nexxit tend to have black hair, large dark eyes, thin noses, and pointed ears that rest flat against their heads. Most nexxit have a slight build and they are shorter than humans.

**R'hbis:** Seladin social class of artists.

**Seladin (cell-ah-din):** A humanoid species characterized by their dark gray or midnight blue skin, glowing pupilless eyes, and luminescent skin markings. They have long pointed ears, sharp angular facial features, large noses, and sharp, fanged teeth. Typically, they have white or gray hair and brow ridges with skin markings instead of eyebrows. Their bodies are tall and broad shouldered, with long arms and legs.

**Shikzeth (shik-zeth):** A humanoid species with volcanic, magma-colored skin under rougher slate-colored outer skin/plating. They are typically broad and muscular, with large, blunt features and narrow eyes. They have horns and either no hair or coarse red, black, or orange hair. Some Shikzeth wear a breathing apparatus to allow them to breathe oxygen, however most that leave their homeworld have respiratory implants.

**Spire Station:** The largest and most technologically advanced space station created by the Xi Consortium. The station is broken into three habitation rings/districts—Orion, Sagittarius, and Perseus. Often shortened to Spire.

**Vash-ka:** Seladin curse, closest human curse is "fuck".

**Vuloi (voo-loy):** A humanoid species characterized by their hulking, muscular bodies. Vuloi have dark green skin with a lizard-like texture. They have two rows of eyes, with the top row smaller than the bottom row.

**Xi Consortium:** The united governing force for Xi space, which borders humanity's local sector of the galaxy. Comprised by representatives from each of the Consortium species—aespians, ankites, nexxit, seladin, shikzeth, and vuloi.

**Y'thir:** Seladin social class of second-born seladin those who leave the seladin colony ships or Sela II to learn from other cultures and provide for their families.

# PRONUNCIATION GUIDE

Fina (fee-nah)

Breks (brehks)

Maerlon (mare-laan)

Mezli (meh-zli)

K'thress (kuh-thress)

Jezrit (jeh-zrit)

Dezlon (dez-laan)

Grespran (greh-spraan)

# 1

## ✦FINA✦

"Just one more stop, I swear!" Mezli shouts at me with unflagging enthusiasm, leading us to our next destination. My feet ache and I wobble in my absurdly tall heels as a pair of her long, dark pink arms tug me past the line at the club entrance.

This is the fifth nightclub we've been to in our whirlwind tour of nightlife on Spire—the largest space station in the quadrant. They're all blending together in a haze of garish neon bodies pressed together on dance floors, and outlandish, overpriced drinks.

A sign that translates to "Epiphany" hangs above the entrance, cycling rapidly through the colors of the rainbow. It illuminates alien faces as we pass, some eyeing us with frustration as we cut in line, and others gawking at us.

Well, probably just me—the purple-haired human in a too-tight, blindingly fluorescent outfit Mezli insisted I wear. When I showed up at my friend's apartment in a cute black dress, a pair of sensible boots, and my hair pulled back in a neat bun, she scowled at me and proclaimed there was no way I'd go out with her dressed like that for my introduction to Spire.

After an hour spent quick-dyeing my chocolate brown hair to a vivid purple and raiding her closet to find something suitable, my excitable and vastly more fashionable friend found my appearance satisfactory. I'm not as convinced. Mezli is nowhere near as curvy as me, nevermind that she's a nexxit and has two sets of arms. The sides of my breasts peek out of the extra holes in the ridiculous hot pink crop top and the matching shorts keep riding up into my crotch.

As we head to the front of the line, I tug my translucent coat closed, as if that will somehow hide me from the curious stares of the aliens surrounding me. A wide, muscle-bound bouncer with reptilian green skin—a vuloi, my mental catalog of alien races reminds me—nods at Mezli as she pulls us past. She runs a free hand playfully across his beefy arm and he winks with his left column of stacked eyes in return.

The flamboyant, bubbly nexxit yanking me along is my only friend on Spire. We've only recently met in person, but she's the reason I'm here and my sole lifeline on this space station. So I can at least try to pretend to be fun for one night. I just didn't realize when she said we were going out for the night, she meant *all* night.

We pass through a set of thick chrome doors, the forceful blast of rumbling club music almost knocking me off balance. Mezli squeals in delight, pulling me after her through a throng of dancers, straight up to the circular bar in the center of the club. She slips past a group waiting to order and leans over the bar, her low-cut top catching a bartender's attention. An ankite with smudged black eyeliner and a prominent nose ring eyes her up and down appreciatively. Their brow creases in surprise as their eyes land on me, but the bartender goes back to smoldering at my friend after their initial shock at seeing a human.

"Two shots of *jefl'ka* and...what do you want, Fina?" Mezli looks back over her shoulder at me.

I've already had too much to drink tonight and there's no way in hell I'm doing shots. "Maybe just some water?" I shout over the music.

She purses her lips and crosses both sets of arms over her chest, ready to argue with me.

"I've had a blast tonight and while I'd love to get wild with you, tomorrow's my first day at the new job. Can't show up with a raging hangover." I feel bad about letting her down, but I've reached my limits for tonight.

Her face softens a little. "Ah, I keep forgetting about your human metabolism. I understand." Mezli fishes through her cluttered purse for her credit tab as the bartender pours the shots and my glass of water. They watch us impatiently as she pulls out a crumpled list, a datapad, and a condom in a glowing wrapper—but no credit tab.

"Don't worry, I've got it." I hold my credit tab out for the ankite to scan as Mezli struggles with her mess of a purse.

"Are you sure? I've got the credits, just have to find my tab..." she says, still digging around in her bag.

"It's the least I can do for you after you've given me such a vigorous intro to Spire nightlife."

The bartender scans my tab, and I suppress a wince when I see the total—5 credits for water?! Not exactly how I wanted to spend the meager savings set aside for my move to Spire, but I suppose it's unavoidable if I want to get the full experience of station life.

Mezli tugs me into a tight hug. "Thanks, Fina! I'm so glad you're finally here."

"Me too!" I try to match her enthusiasm and squeeze her back. I really *am* happy to be here, even with my overwhelming anxiety.

Mezli tried for years to convince me to leave my job working for the Coalition's ambassadorial office to get a taste of life in this part of the galaxy. When a human cultural consultant position at her marketing firm here on Spire opened up, I couldn't say no. It was time for a change. I just didn't realize how intense of a change it would be.

Mezli gives me one last squeeze and releases her hold on me, then grabs the shots and downs them with no reaction. Just watching her makes my throat burn. I sip my water and try to push back the surge of nerves that flooded me at the mere thought of work tomorrow.

She scans the crowd, looking for someone to grind against on the dance floor. A few moments later, her eyes light up and she digs around in her purse again. She probably found someone to use that condom with.

I admire how easygoing and straightforward Mezli is about sex. I'm more the "watch from afar, never make a move" type of girl. Hopefully, some of her confidence will rub off on me. It's been way too long since I've been on a date. Or been intimate with anyone besides myself.

"Found it!" She pulls a small silver tab out of her purse triumphantly. "Repayment for the drinks. But you have to use it tonight. It's the perfect way to end your Spire initiation! I can't believe I didn't think of it sooner." She passes over the shiny tab and I look at it in confusion. Etched on it are the words "SimTech."

I've never heard of SimTech, but Mezli seems to think it needs no explanation. "How am I using this, exactly?"

"It's a gift credit! I kept forgetting to use it and it expires at the end of this cycle." She glances at her wrist comm. "So, in fifteen minutes. It's just across the walkway. If you go now, it shouldn't be too late to use the credit."

"I should call it a night..." A prickle of embarrassment creeps up the back of my neck. I hate feeling clueless about everything on Spire. Even though I am.

"No way, I insist! Trust me. This is the perfect end for your night." She gives me a knowing grin. If only I could read nexxit facial micro-expressions to get some sign of what's in store for me.

My reflexive urge to decline rises, but I stop myself from saying no. I came here to try new things. *I'm a brave, badass babe.* My mantra for the new me seems dumb, but maybe if I keep saying it over and over, it will eventually be true.

"Go on. Get out of here and have fun! I'll see what the bartender is up to after their shift." Mezli nudges me and turns back toward the bar. As I weave my way toward the club exit, she shouts at me over the heavy beat. "Ask for number 39! It's one of my favorites."

Pretending like that makes sense to me, I give her a nod and wave goodbye. She's already leaning across the bar to whisper in the bartender's ear by the time I turn away.

As I exit the club, passing aliens' eyes latch on to me.

*Ugh.*

I know there aren't many humans in this part of space. But I'd hoped I wouldn't be such a novelty on an enormous station like Spire. I pull a small cloth square out of my hip pouch and, with a touch, it expands into a plain black hooded cloak. Throwing it over my shoulders, I move away from the light of Epiphany's glowing sign.

Tonight has been a *lot*. All my remaining energy drained away as soon as I left Mezli's bolstering presence. I should go home and sleep, but Mezli will grill me tomorrow about this SimTech place. If I knew what the heck the gift credit was for, I could pretend I went. I'll just stop in and find that out and then go home.

With a yawn, I head across the walkway toward an illuminated "SimTech Suites" sign before I fall asleep on my feet.

# 2

## ✦BREKS✦

Things are as quiet as they get in this district of Spire. The constant cacophony of a myriad of aliens bartering, partying, and fighting mixed with the blaring holoscreen ads calling out to any passersby has faded away as the late hours of the night cycle set in. I pinch my brow, attempting to fight off the headache that's been building all night from looking out at the neon signs and flashing lights that fill Sagittarius district. I stare out at the walkways outside and tense as I see a young nexxit couple approaching, two pairs of their long arms entangled as they unsubtly caress each other over their revealing club wear.

"Oh great," I mutter to myself. With less than ten minutes before closing, the last thing I need is a pleasure sim booking that will end far past my shift. The pair chatters and pauses for a moment outside the entrance to our lobby. I give them a polite smile from my spot at the welcome desk.

Well, rather the handsome ankite holo-receptionist I'm controlling does. No one wants a harsh seladin face like mine scaring off potential customers. My teeth alone are enough to frighten some of the gentler species.

The shorter nexxit giggles and wraps another set of spindly arms around their partner and they move away, heading across the walkway and into the line outside Epiphany, one of the many nightclubs in the district.

I let out a sigh of relief as they leave and tap the comm device on my wrist. A small screen appears in the air and I swipe through my incoming messages despite knowing I'll find nothing there. It's been almost ten cycles with no word from my partner—*no, ex-partner.* I keep having to remind myself that we're not together anymore. For our anniversary, K'thress canceled our dinner plans I'd booked months in advance, brought me back to their dingy apartment, and broke up with me almost immediately after I went down on them. In their exact words, "we wouldn't work out because my parents won't approve of me dating a seladin."

*Fa-shar.* They could have mentioned that before I wasted two years on them. Still, I can't stop hoping that they'll change their mind and I'll get a message proclaiming how they were wrong and how they want us to be together, no matter what their parents think of me. Pathetic, isn't it? But I still care about them. Another stab of heartache pierces me at the thought.

I refresh my messages again, then close the comm screen with a sigh. Only five minutes left in my shift. Then I can get a break from these thoughts. I took a job at SimTech Suites to keep my mind from obsessing over my broken relationship. To stop imagining what I could've done to make K'thress love me more. The logical part of me knows if I have to convince someone to love me, then it isn't a good relationship. But the pain of losing that chapter of my life—of losing the person I thought I would soul bond with someday—doesn't care what logic says. Once I shut things down for the night, I'll get a few blissful hours in a custom sim to drive out any thoughts of K'thress.

The loud beep of a cleaning bot scouring the walkway outside of the shop snaps my attention back to the holo-receptionist's visual feed. I almost fall out of my chair in surprise as I see a short, hooded figure standing in front of the welcome desk, shifting nervously.

"Sorry, I didn't see you come in!" The entryway motion sensor must be malfunctioning again; its annoying chime didn't go off when they entered. The figure takes a startled step back from the welcome desk, stumbling on their platform heels.

I smooth my hair back and the ankite holo-receptionist follows my movements despite not having any hair. "Welcome to SimTech Suites—where we bring your fantasies to life. How may I assist you?" I keep my tone even and friendly so I don't startle the customer more. I don't need a complaint filed against me after less than a week on the job.

"Oh, um hi, hello?" The figure's voice is tentative as their eyes track over the holo-receptionist, almost as if they're not sure where to focus. Have they never interacted with a holo?

I boot up the customer protocol interface and do a quick scan, suppressing a small gasp when the word "human" pops up.

Stars, what's a human doing way out here? It's rare for humans to travel to Consortium space. I can count the times I've seen one on Spire Station on one hand. Our technology can be strange to non-Consortium species, so if they're a human...no wonder a holo is odd to them. Intrigued, I attempt to zoom in on the human's face through the visual interface, but the hood obscures most of their features.

"So, I was looking to...I have a gift credit. But I know you're about to close, so I'll come back another time." A flash of white, blunt teeth accompanies their apology.

I'm tired, have a rotten headache, and waited through my long shift to escape into a sim afterwards. However, I shouldn't turn away a customer. Especially not one as unexpected and unique as a human. "I'm happy to assist you," I say in a feigned upbeat tone as I suppress a yawn.

The human looks up and their hood falls back slightly, revealing a sliver of purple hair and a hint of skin as pale as the moons of Sela II. They shift their weight back, hands clasped together in front of them as they survey the holo-receptionist.

"Are you sure? I don't want to inconvenience you. I wouldn't have come so late, but my friend insisted and the credit expires tonight and...you don't need to know any of this. Sorry, I'll just go!"

I resist chuckling at their nervous energy. Some things span across cultures. Like how awkward first-time sim users are. Most act like they're getting caught doing something wrong or inappropriate. The giant ads that feature lithe, scantily clad ankites offering to fulfill your every desire don't help.

I give them a warm smile—the expression would be off-putting to most species as it exposes my pointed teeth, but it looks charming and smooth on the holo-receptionist's delicate ankite features. "No trouble at all, don't worry. Scan your ID and gift credit and we'll get you into a suite and ready for your sim experience."

"Right...my sim experience. Wait, you need my ID? Does this go on some kind of record?" The human's voice pitches higher as they dig through their hip pouch.

"Everything that happens on Spire goes on some sort of record."

I barely keep my amusement out of my voice. They must really be new here. "But SimTech doesn't provide any illegal services and doesn't share any private data from our customers."

"Oh? That's reassuring, I guess." The human holds a gift credit tab and their ID toward the holo-receptionist and I reach out and take them both, swiping them against a reader on the desk. It's awkward with the size differential between my hand and the holo's, but I manage with minimal fumbling.

Their data profile pops up on my interface. *Serafina Kress. Human. She/Her.* Followed by a long string of numbers and other bio-data on her that's irrelevant at the moment.

"It's a pleasure to meet you, Serafina. I'm Breks and I'll be assisting you with your sim experience. There are no restrictions on your choice of simulation, and your credit is for an hour." I press a few buttons on the system control panel. "Please follow the illuminated path on the floor to your sim suite and we'll get you set up and ready to go."

For a moment, Serafina hesitates, then mumbles something to herself and nods. She follows the path from the lobby, through a narrow corridor lined with numbered doors, and into her room. I switch to that suite's holo, one identical to the holo-receptionist.

She startles, flinching and taking a step back as I appear in the empty, white chamber. "Ah! Didn't realize you could just pop up like that."

I wince and step backward as well. "Apologies for startling you."

"No, it's fine! It's all part of the experience, right?" She peers around the room. "Well, this is...stark."

"Yes, it's fairly clinical when a simulation isn't active. I think they make the rooms white so that you can see they are sterile, since..." I trail off, not wanting to be indelicate in case humans don't enjoy talking about excretions and fluids.

She looks confused but says nothing. The door slides closed and disappears into the wall and she appears nervous again.

"Now you're trapped in here with me," I say, trying to cut the tension.

Her eyes go wide in fear.

"I'm so sorry! Please don't be frightened." I deactivate the holo-technician in her room and switch to audio-only. "Excuse my pathetic attempt at humor. Nothing here can harm you and you are free to leave at any time."

"It-it's fine! I know you were kidding; I'm just a little nervous. You can come back."

I re-activate the holo, attempting to make my posture non-threatening. "You truly are safe. Once I activate your simulation, you can move around, and interact with stuff or touch anything you'd like. Things will feel real, but they have no ability to cause you actual harm. If you need to stop the simulation, you can say 'aquamarine'."

"Why 'aquamarine'?"

"It's not something that you're likely to say in most...scenarios." I don't tell her I chose that word because of the intriguing shade of her wide eyes watching my holo intently from under her hood.

"Right." The human nods and her hood falls back a bit more. I can't help thinking about what the rest of her looks like. As if hearing my thoughts, she presses a button on the clasp at her neck and the cloak retracts into a small bundle she places in her hip pouch.

I inhale sharply as I see what the drab cloak was hiding. She's a burst of color, wearing an electric pink top and shorts that do little to conceal her body. A body which is...*fascinating*.

Everything about her is thick and curved, and I swallow hard at the sight. I didn't know humans could look like that. Her stomach and hips are rounded and her breasts strain against the fabric of her top in the most delicious way, with cut-outs on the sides showing even more skin.

*Stop staring at her breasts!*

I snap my gaze from her chest and thankfully she doesn't seem to have noticed any gawking from my holo. Now focused on her face, I'm lost in her delicate, alien features. The human's—Serafina's—tiny nose upturns at the tip, her full lips have a sensual curve, and her eyes remind me of crystal clear ocean waters. She has her thick purple hair pulled back, but a few stray strands hang down along her neck. I have a powerful urge to tuck them behind her small, rounded ears. Not that I would be so bold.

*Vash-ka*, get yourself together! I'm acting like I've never seen a beautiful alien before. Though I can't remember ever feeling such an immediate, disorienting attraction. Not even to K'thress.

I shake my head, trying to clear my senses. With a placid smile, I hand her a datapad listing the available sims. "Here's our library of simulations. Just let me know the number you want when you've decided, and I'll start it up."

She takes it from me and gives me a nod of understanding.

Before I start staring at her again, I make myself deactivate the holo in her room and give her some time to select a sim. As soon as I'm out of her suite, I run a hand across my face with a heavy exhale.

*That could have gone better.*

Only a few moments pass before I hear her voice over the audio comm. "Um, I think I already know which one I want."

That was fast. "Perfect! Which one would you like?"

"Number 39?" she says, almost like it's a question.

I choke at her words. That simulation involves a lot of bondage, whips, and domination. My pants grow uncomfortably tight at the thought of her naked and tied up.

*Vash-ka*, what's wrong with me? I do my best to be professional and disinterested in what goes on in our sims, but here I am getting hard thinking about a customer. A gorgeous, far too intriguing customer.

"Of course, running that simulation for you now." I desperately try to sound composed and load the sim into the suite, then set it to run.

A small gasp issues from the audio feed and I consider peeking in to make sure everything's running smoothly. Pushing that impulse aside, I set the audio to only go to my comm if she says the shutdown word, then turn away from the control interface.

She's fine. I don't want to violate her privacy and I've got to get my unprofessional reaction to her under control.

This is going to be a long hour.

# 3

## ✦FINA✦

I close my eyes against the blinding light that fills the chamber and a rush of dizzying sensation washes over me. When I open them, all I see is darkness. There's something obscuring my vision. A blindfold?

Cool air pricks against my bare skin and I shiver. Wait, how am I naked? And why am I naked?! I go to remove the fabric covering my eyes but can't move my arms. Silky rope binds my wrists.

I hear movement behind me, and my heart pounds furiously as my mind races in panic. The word Breks told me almost escapes my lips, but I freeze when something trails down my arm.

"Mmmm, you look so good, pet. I can't wait to play with you."

My whole body tenses and I struggle futilely against my binds. Am I in some kind of horror simulator? Mezli is obsessed with horror novels about people getting kidnapped by serial killers and having to use their wits to escape. With her twisted sense of humor, I wouldn't put it past her to prank me with a scary survival game. If that's what this is, I'm going to kill her.

"Before we start, the safeword is 'crest'. Be a good pet. Say it for me." The finger runs down the side of my breast and to my waist, leaving a trail of goosebumps.

Oh. *Oh.* Not a fucked up escape sim, then. The pieces slide into place in my mind and I feel foolish for not realizing sooner that it's a sex simulation. A kinky one. God, Mezli *would* think this is a good way for me to end the night. Especially after I confided in her I've had a long dry spell. A tiny laugh bubbles up in my throat at the absurdity of the situation.

A hand grabs my chin, and the husky, sensual voice speaks again. "You think this is funny, pet? *Say it.*"

*Wow*, okay. We're jumping right into it then. "C-crest." I stumble a bit over the word.

"That's a good pet," the voice purrs, the warmth of their breath caressing my neck.

Suddenly, I'm overheated despite my lack of clothing.

They release my chin and trail their hand down to rest between my breasts. "You're already panting for me. What do you want me to do to you?"

I should say "aquamarine" and end the simulation now. In the past, I would've. But tonight is the start of my new life. I told myself it's time to be braver and bolder. Besides, I've fantasized about being tied up before. Though imagining it while alone in the privacy of my bedroom is a far cry from acting it out without warning.

"Is untying me and giving me my clothes back an option?" I smile weakly, trying to stay calm.

"Say your safeword if you want that. But I think you want something more interesting, don't you?" Their hand slides down to my stomach and rests above the juncture of my thighs.

"I...wow, this is happening."

The hand moves down further and cups me between my legs. "Do you want me to slip a finger inside you and see how wet you are? *Tell me.*"

*No!...Yes?* I'm so confused. "I-I don't know what I want," I murmur in response.

The hand pulls away. "I don't know what I want, *master.*"

"W-what?" My words come out as a nervous laugh.

"If you laugh again, I'm going to punish you," they growl in warning.

"Punish me?" I giggle again. This whole situation is absurd, and my mind is still a little fuzzy from fatigue and multiple alien cocktails.

Strong hands spin me around, my binds twisting but still holding my arms in place. They push against my back so that I bend forward at the hips. I almost lose my balance, but they hold me in place, nudging my feet apart.

"Such a disobedient pet. You need to be taught a lesson."

Something tickles across my ass and then lashes against it in a stinging strike. I wince against the pain. "Oh fuck. Sorry!"

A fist tangles in my hair and the flogger cracks against my ass, harder this time.

"Sorry, *master,*" they hiss at me.

A wild part of my mind imagines that the person controlling the holo-receptionist is watching me. Breks stared at me before they left, though I'm not sure if it was in interest or distaste. What would they think, seeing me like this? Would it turn them on?

My cheeks heat as I grow slick between my thighs. I'm not seriously getting off on the thought of some pervy alien voyeur, am I?

"Sorry, master." The words are unexpectedly breathy as they come out of me.

"That's better." They rub my ass and give it a firm squeeze, letting their nails dig in where the skin is tender. A slick tongue runs up my neck and then their teeth nip at my ear. "Now, be a good pet and tell me what you want. Beg me for it." The hand on my ass slips dangerously close to the yearning heat between my legs.

Another wave of arousal washes over me, but it's immediately shut down by the part of my brain screaming with embarrassment and anxiety.

This is too much. I'm not ready for it. "I'm sorry, crest. Please, untie me...I can't."

The binds on my wrists release and a gentle hand on my hips keeps me from toppling over. "What can I do to make you more comfortable?" The voice behind me is soft now.

They remove the blindfold, and a low-lit room comes into focus. I stand up and turn to see a latex-clad ankite holding a flogger, looking down at me with mild concern. Their lithe, amber body stands almost a foot taller than me, and I can see why they use this holo for the simulation. Everything about their appearance screams sex and power.

Seeing them, I'm keenly aware of my much more ample form still on display. "Clothes would be good."

They nod, and a robe materializes in their hand. I slip it on, relaxing somewhat now that I'm no longer completely naked.

"Can I get you anything else, pet? Would you like to try a different scene? We still have playtime left."

"Let's just sit here for a bit or...I don't suppose you have any cute animals I can pet? That's more my speed."

The ankite holo blinks in confusion. "I don't think animals are appropriate for this setting, do you? But I can pet *you*." They lick their full lips lasciviously and take a step closer.

Guess that's a no on the cute animals.

I step back to increase the space between us again. "Uh, can you answer some questions, then? Like...are you sentient? How are you so real?" My thoughts go back to the idea of the holo-receptionist watching me. "Shit, are you Breks?"

"I'm an advanced holographic simulation generated using proprietary technology from SimTech. I'm not 'Breks', I am known as 'Master'. Or you can call me 'Daddy'." Their voice drops low and they give me a heated stare.

Damn, not Breks. Wait, why am I disappointed?

Pushing that ridiculous thought aside, I consider what to do next. My stubborn side wants me to stay and wait out the remaining time so I can truthfully tell Mezli I had the complete experience. I yawn and glance around. Maybe I can lie down and rest until the time is up.

I direct my attention back at the holo still prowling around the room, watching me with disturbing intensity. "Could I have a bed?"

"Mmm, of course." The ankite waves their long, elegant hand and a four-poster bed appears next to them. They stroke down the silky sheets and then beckon me. "Come over here and I'll tie you to the bedposts until you're begging—"

My cheeks heat and I shake my head, cutting them off. "Never mind, I'm good." With a sigh, I lean against the wall and close my eyes.

A moment later a small chime goes off and I hear Breks' voice. "Ms. Kress—Serafina? I'm getting a reading that there may be a malfunction. Is everything alright?"

Oh thank god, an excuse to get out of here.

# 4

## ✦BREKS✦

I'm wearing a groove into the control office's floor, pacing to keep myself awake until Serafina's simulation ends. There's no way I'll have enough energy to enjoy my own sim tonight, though I'm not that disappointed. Meeting a human has been distracting enough.

A ping goes off at my customer interface terminal. *Vash-ka, don't tell me the sim is malfunctioning.* I read the notification with a frown. *Deviation from normal simulation parameters.* That alert only happens when a bug pops up or when a customer tries to get a pre-programmed sim to deviate from its original intent. Or do something illegal.

I need to check on the issue, but hesitate. The human chose a very sexual sim and as intriguing as I found her, I don't enjoy violating anyone's privacy. But the insistent alert continues to flash, so I push my reservations aside and bring up the visual feed of the suite Serafina is in. Just in time to see a flash of bare skin before she wraps a shiny robe around her body. She says something about animals, but I'm too distracted by that glimpse of herself to hear what.

"I don't think animals are appropriate for this setting, do you? But I can pet *you*," says an ankite holo dressed in full bondage gear. They move closer to Serafina, who looks wary of them and backs away.

I'm not an expert in this kind of sex play by any means, but this doesn't seem like it's following the simulation's base programming. Unless seeming nervous and talking a lot is foreplay for humans.

"Um, can you answer some questions? Like...are you sentient? How are you so real? Shit, are you Breks?!" She sounds upset at the idea that I could be in there with her.

They continue their conversation, with the ankite holo suggestively leading her back to a scenario that fits the simulation's programming. But Serafina keeps changing the subject. She asks for a bed and when the ankite suggests they use it together, her pale skin reddens.

Is she unwell? I recall flushing can indicate fever or illness in some species. She leans back against the wall and looks unsteady.

"Miss Kress—Serafina? I'm getting a reading that there may be a malfunction. Is everything alright?" I call out over the comm, worry building in my chest.

Her eyes open and she reflexively tugs her robe tighter. "Breks? Yes, I'm alright. I just...it's late, and I got what I needed, so I should get going."

She got what she needed...The image of her writhing as the ankite touched her, making her cry out in pleasure, pops into my head. My cock stiffens as I unsuccessfully attempt to shake the thought away.

"Breks? Are you still there?"

"Oh, right—yes, I'm here." With a few button presses, I end the simulation and the ankite holo and dark room disappear. Serafina is back in her tight clubwear and she startles at the sudden change. The empty white chamber's door slides open and I illuminate her way back to the lobby. She follows the path, and her steps look as fatigued as I feel.

Part of me thinks I should go out in person and help her to the transit station, but I don't wish to upset her more with my frightening appearance. Instead, I bring up the holo-receptionist and give her a polite smile as she returns to the lobby.

"Thank you for visiting SimTech Suites, Serafina. I hope you had a pleasant experience."

"It certainly was an...experience." She looks a bit dazed as she moves toward the exit.

I feel guilty. It's obvious she didn't get what she expected. "Wait! Before you leave, I want to apologize," I call out after her.

She turns back over her shoulder, and her smooth brow furrows. "Apologize?"

"It's clear that you did not enjoy your experience tonight. I should have done a better assessment to find out your needs. It's just...I'm a bit tired."

She takes a few steps back toward the welcome desk and squints her eyes at the holo-receptionist, then laughs to herself. "A tired hologram, that's a first."

I open my mouth to explain that an actual person is controlling the holo, but she holds a hand up.

"Yeah, I know. I'm not a completely clueless human. You're there. Well, not *there*." She gestures at the desk.

"You should be glad I'm not. There's a reason they keep me hidden behind a holo." I follow my words up with a self-deprecating laugh.

"Oh? Is it because you're too attractive and customers would get distracted by your beauty?"

"Hah! I wish. Let's just say I'm not as appealing as an ankite. Especially to a delicate human."

"Hey, I'm not delicate!" Her plush lips downturn, but there's still a hint of humor behind her eyes.

"My mistake. I just assumed from how...soft you appear." Just imagining that softness arouses me even more.

"Is that some kind of dig at my figure?! Now you *should* apologize." Her arms cross under her chest, pressing her ample cleavage together even more.

Stars, what I wouldn't do to run my tongue across the swell of her breasts...*focus*! "I didn't mean it as an insult. Far from it, in fact."

"O-oh..." A deep pink flush washes over Serafina's cheeks.

Real smooth—I'm making her ill with my terrible flirting.

"Anyway, if you are willing, I'd like to make it up to you. I've put another credit on your tab. Come back another night and I'll help you pick out a simulation that you'll enjoy. I have a few fun ones I can recommend."

The reddening of her pale skin creeps down her neck and she rubs at her ear like she didn't hear me correctly. "Did that translate right? Y-you'll help me pick out a sex simulation?" Her words come out high pitched—she's clearly alarmed at the thought.

"No! If that's what you wanted, I could..." The idea of helping her choose the best form of pleasure is far too appealing. "No, there are many options besides pleasure sims. That's what I meant."

"Oh god, of course. Now I really am acting like a dumb human."

"No, not at all." I rub the side of my head in frustration. "I'm just making this worse, aren't I?"

"No!" Serafina shakes her head vigorously. "It's a very generous offer, thank you. I'd like to try something you'd suggest. Not sex! At least not..." She trails off, looking away from the holo-receptionist.

Not sex. Of course not sex. Nothing she's done showed that she has any interest in that. And that's with me presenting as a much more attractive ankite. I'm just a sex-starved fool, apparently.

"It would be my pleasure," I say, attempting not to betray my dirty thoughts.

She looks back up at the holo-receptionist and smiles. "Well then, it's a date. Wait, no. Not a date!" She reddens again. "I-I'm going to stop talking now. And leave." She scurries toward the exit.

"Have a good evening, Serafina."

I watch as she almost trips in her hurry to get away. The doors close behind her, and even though I'm exhausted, I wish she stayed longer. I doubt she'll come back, but if she does, I'll do everything I can to show her a good time.

# 5

## ✧ FINA ✧

"Soooo, how's it going?? Is it everything you've dreamed of?" Mezli's giant eyes glimmer with excitement as she sits down across from me and passes over a mug of something that smells like a mixture of coffee and dirt. I have no idea how she's just as bright and energetic now as she was last night. If it's an alien thing, I'm jealous.

"Pretty good so far. Minus the sleep deprivation and the purple hair that won't go away even though *someone* promised me it would fade back by the morning." I mock glare at her as I pull at one of my curls for emphasis.

"That's how it's always worked for me! Must be your weird human DNA or something. It'll come out eventually...I think. Purple looks amazing on you, though, so I don't see the problem."

It may not look bad, but it's eye-catching, and I'm already sick of standing out. I roll my eyes at her comment. "Oh great. Another way that I'm abnormal here."

"Not abnormal, special! Everyone's so excited that you're here, Fina." Mezli pats my hand reassuringly.

I choke back a scoff at her unflagging, unrealistic positivity. "That's good to hear. I just hope that once the novelty wears off, they won't get sick of my 'special' qualities."

"Nonsense. No one could ever tire of you. We've been friends for almost twenty years and I'm not tired at all!"

Most of those years of friendship were digital rather than in person. We met by chance through a pen pal program called OneGalaxy back when we both were awkward preteens. We bonded through our shared love of cheesy alien romance vids, but the friendship grew to be one of the most important things in my life. She helped me through my breakup with my ex, Paul. She's the impetus for my brave new life on Spire station. But in the back of my mind, I'm worried that she'll think I'm lame in person.

"Nothing could make you tired, Mezli. But don't worry, I'm tired enough for the both of us." I realize that my words came out wrong. "Tired in general, not of our friendship!"

Mezli chuckles. "I know. That's why I brought you some *latra*. Drink up before it gets cold!"

I peer down with suspicion at the contents of the mug. It looks like hot mud, but if it's caffeinated, I can choke it down. By the time I got home from last night's madness, I only had three hours before I had to drag myself out of bed and get ready for work. I close my eyes and take a hesitant sip. Ugh, definitely an acquired taste. I tip back the rest before I have time to think about the strange flavor.

Out of the corner of my eye, I catch a few of my new coworkers watching me with interest, so I pretend I enjoyed the drink. It's exhausting being a representative of humanity. Aliens scrutinize everything I say and do. Now I know why the ambassadors I worked with were so stressed all the time. And I only need to impress a few curious aliens, not negotiate treaties and trade deals.

"I should get back to work," I say, wanting to make sure that I get through all the training and orientation tasks I have on my schedule. I *have* to make a good impression. If I fail at this job, then my exciting new life on Spire will vanish before it even has a chance to begin.

"Don't work too hard! Seriously. Work should be fulfilling and enjoyable, so if you're stressed, it means something's wrong."

I almost laugh, but her straight face makes me realize she isn't joking for once. If someone had said something like that back when I was working with the Coalition fleet, they'd get chastised for not having a good enough work ethic. As much as I like the thought of not needing to bust my ass to prove myself, I can't relax. Maybe in a few years, once I've established myself at CiaXera. I just hope I don't exhaust myself before then.

The rest of the day and work week go by in a blur. There's so much to learn and adjust to. I work late just to keep up, but no one else stays past the end of work hours. Some even spend the latter part of the day just wandering around the building, socializing. I pray I get faster soon, because right now I feel incompetent if they have time to spare and I don't.

Mezli keeps bugging me to go out for drinks with her after work, but by the time I get home each night, my brain is fried. All I can do is grab a quick meal from my food synthesizer and curl up with my datapad, reading silly romances until I pass out.

How many more times will she be okay with me declining her invitations before she decides I'm a waste of effort?

Will I ever be able to keep up with this new job?

My inner anxiety gremlin knows just where to poke at me to make me worry everyone hates me, so I say my affirmations over and over until it shuts up. I refuse to let that voice rule my life.

On the last day of the work week, I'm in the shower when my comm dings with a notification. I peek my head out to see who it's from. The message icon shows an image of a stoic, periwinkle ankite. Zandra, my boss at CiaXera.

My stomach sinks. Why are they messaging me when I'll be in the office soon? Crap, I've done something wrong. I'm not doing a good enough job and I'm fired. I knew it seemed too good to be true. I jump out of the shower and pick up my comm, ignoring the water I'm dripping all over the floor.

> Zandra: Ms. Kress, I must inform you we will not be needing your services...

*Oh fuck. Shit. Fuck.* Acid rises in my throat as I expand the message.

> Zandra: Ms. Kress, I must inform you we will not be needing your services today. We've noted the effort and dedication you've shown in your first week at CiaXera. However, I must insist that you take the day off. I understand human working habits may differ from ours, so I do not mean to cause offense. You will adjust to our practices in time.

I re-read the message twice to make sure I didn't misunderstand. They're giving me the day off because I worked *too much*? I type out a hasty reply, trying not to get my comm wet.

> Serafina: Thank you, Zandra. It's foreign to me, but I will do my best to adjust to this new work culture.

A trail of shampoo suds runs down the side of my face and I realize I didn't rinse out my hair in my panic. When I glance in the mirror, it's still as bright purple as before. Great, guess I'm stuck with this indefinitely. Unless I want to try dyeing it back to brown, but I'm wary of alien hair dye now.

I'm back in the shower for all of thirty seconds when another notification pings my comm. Then another ping a few seconds later. I sigh and finish up, since my brain is still on high alert.

> Mezli: Drinks tonight. Don't say no, I know you have the day off.

> Mezli: Check your mail. I got you a few new outfits. Your wardrobe is very mundane. No offense. I'm sure it was perfectly fine for a dull Coalition ship.

As I'm reading, another message pops up with a program attachment.

> Mezli: Oh! Install this before we go out. It's mandatory for life on Spire.

She's demanding today. Honestly, I don't mind it. She knows I need to be pushed out of my comfort zone a little. Though sometimes her pushing is more like being shoved off of a cliff.

> Fina: Okay, FINE. I'll be there. But seriously, thanks Mez.

I tap on the program to download it and then realize my potential mistake.

> Fina: If this is one of those erotic chat VI's you've told me about, I'm going to kill you.

> Mezli: I would never! But…if you want the link for those, I can send them too.

> Fina: No thanks. After what you subjected me to at SimTech, I'm good.

> Mezli: I forgot to ask about that! You didn't like it?

> Fina: You could have warned me it was a sex sim!

> Mezli: I thought that was obvious. Forgot that humans are prudes.

> Fina: Just because I'm not into bondage simulations doesn't mean I'm a prude.

> Mezli: Yes, it does! But we'll work on that. Got a meeting, talk later.

> Fina: See you later.

A minute passes and I see she's messaged again a bunch of times—all program attachments I'm definitely not downloading.

# 6

## ✦FINA✦

The bar Mezli's chosen for us tonight is more intimate than the previous ones we've visited. There's no packed dance floor or bone-rattling club music. Instead, low, sensual music mingles with soft conversation. Dimly lit, plush booths line the walls and a long chrome bar sits in front of an enormous viewport that displays the glittering stars and ships coming and going outside the station.

I grab an empty booth as Mezli goes to the bar to get our drinks. With a quick scan of the room, I notice I'm not getting the typical stares from the aliens here. The lighting in here is low enough that no one seems to have noticed the purple-haired human in a ridiculously low-cut jumpsuit. Tension eases from my shoulders as I'm able to sit back and enjoy the atmosphere in peace.

After a few minutes of watching people mingle and pretending to check my comm so I don't seem too awkward and lonely sitting by myself, Mezli returns with a drink in each of her hands. She flashes a toothy grin and sets two of the drinks down in front of me.

I raise an eyebrow at her. "Trying to get me drunk already?"

She laughs and takes a big swig from one of her glasses. "Nonsense. A kind gentleman at the bar wanted to buy me some drinks after I'd already ordered and I never say no to free drinks." Her gaze lands on a graying nexxit in a well-tailored suit. He locks eyes with her and raises a glass.

"I didn't know you were into older men."

"Oh, not particularly! But it would be rude to refuse such a generous offer." She gives him a coquettish smile and then turns away, as if dismissing him. He looks unfazed by her rejection and goes back to chatting with the hulking vuloi bartender.

I take a sip of my radioactive-looking, viscous drink. "You're sure this is safe for humans?"

"Only one way to find out," Mezli says with a dismissive shrug.

I spit the liquid back into the glass with a sputter. "What?! I can't take that kind of risk!"

She holds my shocked gaze for a moment before breaking into a laugh. "You should see your face! Like when my parents found out I'd run away from home. It's totally safe. I triple checked with Grespran." She gestures over to the behemoth alien tending bar.

With a long-suffering sigh, I take a tentative swig of the drink. It hits me almost immediately, making my limbs tingle. But the taste is pleasant—like a mix of tart green apple and lemon. Once it's clear that I won't go into anaphylactic shock from the strange drink, I quirk an eyebrow at my friend. "You're on a first name basis with the bartender?"

"Yeah, we went on a few dates. Nice guy!" Mezli downs the rest of her drink and glances back over at the bartender with a dreamy sparkle in her dark eyes.

The image of Mezli's pixie-like frame paired with the vuloi as wide as an air taxi is hard to picture. I doubt I'd want to know how that works, though I'm sure she'd be more than happy to illuminate me.

She smirks as she watches the confusion and mild concern cross my face. "Speaking of dates, did you check out the app I sent you?"

"I already told you, I'm not lonely enough to download an erotica VI!" Not yet, at least...

"No no, not those. Syzygy!"

"Oh, that? Not yet. What is it?" I downloaded it on my comm, but got suspicious after she sent all those other apps and didn't open it.

"Damn, I keep forgetting you're new in this sector of space. It's only the hottest dating app!"

I take another sip of my drink to stifle my groan. I've been here for little more than a week and she thinks I'm ready to date? When I can find my way around the station without getting lost, I'll consider it.

Though...the limited dating pool was one reason I wanted to move off the Coalition ship. When I broke up with my ex, I knew my chances of finding a partner there were slim. And god, I want a partner. Or even just someone to make out with.

Wait, do aliens kiss? From what I've read, I think at least some do. But I doubt the alien erotica Mezli shared with me was the most reliable source. I need to research Consortium cultures more before even considering going on a date.

"I don't know if I'm ready to date yet..."

"Oh, come on! It's not like I'm asking you to find your bride or whatever you humans call it. Just to have a bit of fun. You said you wanted to learn more about the aliens here. What better way than with some hands-on experience?" She waggles her thick black eyebrows at me.

She's got me there. But dating aliens seems like a cultural minefield. I barely understand how to date humans.

"I'll take your silence as agreement! Here, I'll help you set up your profile."

⋅✦⋅

BY THE TIME I've finished my drink—and Mezli's had the other three—she's coerced me into setting up a Syzygy profile. Not without a lot of arguing over what it should say, though.

Mezli's idea of a good bio is *"Hot, lonely human desperate for close encounters with aliens."* No way I'm using that. I change it to *"New on Spire and looking for connections to help make the station feel like home."* It's not great, but I'll fix it when she's not hovering. Or just delete the whole profile. I'm already overwhelmed by the prospect of using it.

Mezli grabs the wrist my comm is on and adds a few vids from our night out last weekend. My profile now features me stiffly holding a shimmering drink and nodding my head to club music while Mezli shouts in delight and pans up and down my body. At least it does a good job of capturing my appearance. And my general awkwardness.

"Now, let's fill out what you're looking for...Fun, check. Romance, check. Freaky sex with hot aliens, double check!"

"God, don't put that!" I try to pull my comm back, but she holds tight and grins at me.

"Don't pretend like you're not hooked on alien smut—excuse

me, alien 'romance'. You're the one who started our book club!" She pokes an accusatorial finger at me across the table.

My cheeks heat as I glance around the bar to see if anyone heard her shouting about my love of alien erotica. A tall, hooded figure seated at the bar looks back over their shoulder at us. All I can make out in the low light are glowing eyes. They immediately lock onto mine and I dart my eyes away, praying they don't take the eye contact as an invitation to come over.

"Fine, fine. I'll just say that you're interested in casual dates but open to longer-term relationships. The ones that are looking for life mates can be super clingy and intense, but they're incredible in bed, so we don't want to rule them out completely."

"You know my anxiety is way too intense for me to hook up with random aliens."

"Didn't you come here to conquer your self-limiting beliefs? You've done the hard part. You left your old life behind and you're here on Spire. Now it's time for you to let your inner freak out!" Leave it to Mezli to translate my desire to be brave into me needing to sleep around.

I pull my comm back to check what she added to my profile, then delete where she said my interests include "sensual massage" and "pleasure sims". Even if I were interested in casual hook-ups, that's *way* too forward for me.

A sudden squeak of excitement from Mezli pulls my focus away from the profile and I glance up. Right into the luminous eyes of the hooded person from the bar.

"Ahh!" I flinch in surprise, shaking the table. The empty glass in front of me wobbles, but a dark gray hand with long, talon-tipped fingers darts out and stops the glass before it can fall over.

"Oh my gosh, Maerlon! What are you doing here?" Mezli leaps

up from her seat and wraps both sets of arms around the stranger in a crushing hug.

"...Hi, Mezli." The figure's voice is deep and rough. They stand there stoically and wait for her to stop, their eerie eyes still locked on me over her shoulder.

When she finally releases them, Mezli reaches up a hand and tugs back their hood to ruffle their hair, pulling their attention back to her with a huff of indignation. Their sleek, bone-white hair hangs down over their shoulder on one side but is shaved on the other. It contrasts sharply against their slate-colored skin that's dotted with minuscule, dim glowing markings across their brow and down the sides of their neck. It looks like some kind of makeup or ceremonial paint. Their features are sharp and angular, with a prominent nose and jaw.

Everything about this alien's appearance screams danger to some deep-seated instinct inside of me. I can't take my eyes off of them.

They peer at Mezli, unblinking as she steps back, and then turn their light-filled, pupilless gaze back on me again.

Shit, I'm staring.

Mezli looks between the two of us and I try to focus on her instead of her intimidating and fascinating friend. "Maerlon, this is my best friend, Fina! She just moved here."

I stand up, realizing I'm being rude just sitting here gawking up at them. My hip bumps the table and I cringe at my lack of grace. I go to reach out and shake their hand and then pause mid-movement. Crap, will that be offensive? I can't remember anything about seladin. At least I'm guessing that's what they are. Or possibly shikzeth?

The alien—Maerlon—watches me like a hawk as I'm frozen, waiting for my brain to give me some kind of helpful information.

Instead, I get distracted when I realize that the bright markings I thought were makeup are part of their skin.

*Say something. Anything!*

I give them a weak, awkward smile. "Hi! Maerlon, was it? It's nice to meet you. How do you and Mezli know each other?"

Maerlon gives me a tight-lipped nod, not returning the smile.

Mezli replies before they can say anything. "He works at CiaXera. Though he's in the design department."

He gives me once over, and it doesn't seem like he appreciates what he sees from how his brow furrows. "You work at CiaXera? What do you do?"

I blink back up at him, attempting to ignore his intimidating presence. God, he's gotta be at least six and a half feet tall. "Y-yeah, I'm the new human cultural consultant."

"Ah." He continues to stare down at me with such intensity that it makes me unsteady on my feet.

Mezli gives his arm a playful tug. "Come sit and have a drink with us!"

He frowns at her and I can see a hint of sharp teeth poking out behind his lower lip. "Sorry, I was leaving."

"Noooo, stay! It's still early and I'm sure Fina wouldn't mind your company. She's looking to *get to know* aliens better." Mezli drags through the words "get to know" to make them sound suggestive.

Maerlon's dotted brow raises, and he turns his intense gaze back on me. It feels like he's boring into my soul with his incandescent eyes, and my stomach flutters. Whether it's with nerves or attraction, I'm not sure.

"She means that I'd like to learn more about other cultures," I say, cheeks burning.

"Yeah, we just set up her Syzygy account for *cultural research.*" Mezli cackles as I glare at her to stop.

Maerlon's expression closes off even more and he shakes his head. "I have a prior engagement and I'm sure your friend has no need for my company."

"Ugh, fine. Get out of here, broody," Mezli says, directing a frown at him.

He gives us a cursory nod and then strides away, the measured movement of his lean form keeping my focus locked on him as he leaves. Once he's gone, I release a heavy exhale. It felt like I was waiting for something to happen when he was near. Like I couldn't catch my breath in his presence.

Mezli shrugs at me. "Sorry about that. He's shy sometimes."

That didn't seem like shyness to me. More a distaste for gawking humans. "No worries." I try to keep my tone light and unbothered, but I can't quite manage it.

My comm pings and Mezli claps her hands together in excitement, all thoughts of her scowling friend evaporating. "You've already got matches!" she squeals. "Looks like everyone's horny for humans."

Not everyone. I think about how Maerlon stared at me and am oddly disappointed.

# 7

## ✧MAERLON✧

Esh'et, that was not ideal. But when I saw the human, I panicked.

There's no way that there are two identical humans with purple hair and full, curvaceous bodies on Spire. I couldn't help gawking at her from the bar, but then she noticed and couldn't look away from me fast enough. Any thoughts of introducing myself—SimTech confidentiality be damned—went out the airlock.

Then Mezli stopped me before I could leave. When I looked down into Fina's wide eyes, my chest felt like it was crushing in on itself. I could make out details on her delicate face that I didn't catch through the holo interface—a small healed scar on her forehead and a dusting of the faintest pigmented dots on her nose and cheeks.

A small part of me hoped that she'd recognize my voice. But she just peered up at me in fright.

Of course, she didn't recognize me. I gave her the name Breks at SimTech, but Mezli introduced me by my first name, Maerlon. Plus, she doesn't know what Breks actually looks like or that the holo's interface filters my vocals to make them sound less harsh.

Fina's wide-eyed stare dashed any hope of making a good impression. She was clearly terrified of me. I get that reaction a lot, so why am I surprised? I'm not attractive to most species. Not like ankites whose features adapt to be attractive to their companions. Or small, willowy nexxit. She even became flushed with illness when Mezli implied she was interested in being intimate with aliens.

*Vash-ka*, why do I even care? I've become so accustomed to the trepidation most non-seladin have around me that it barely even registers any more. But it hurt that Fina found me frightening.

I must be desperate for validation after K'thress broke things off. They told me many times that I looked intimidating, so I worked to soften my natural facial expressions and posture while we were together. A small part of me hoped that practice would make me more desirable. Or at least less off-putting. Stars, it's pathetic how much I changed just to please them. Especially since it didn't even end up mattering.

I check my comm for messages from K'thress, despite that cheerful thought.

Nothing.

I don't even want them back. I've had time to think about how bad our relationship was. But I still fantasize about them begging to get back together, so I can be the one rejecting them.

I shake out of my petty thoughts right before colliding with a grimy-looking aespian holding a greasy bag that reeks of cheap walkway food.

"*Sslsk*! Watch where you're going, seladin." Their translucent wings flutter in annoyance.

I apologize, but they're already striding away in a huff. At least they seemed more annoyed than scared of me.

As I make my way through Sagittarius district's crowded walkways, I try to focus more on my surroundings. I shouldn't let myself get so distracted or I'll end up getting pickpocketed like a clueless tourist. When I first arrived on Spire, I was so dazzled by the ceaseless noise and activity that I got my credits stolen at least ten times. I should tell Mezli to warn Fina about that. A lone human is an easy target for thieves.

Wait, why am I still thinking about her? I'm sure she doesn't need help from someone like me.

My shift at SimTech starts soon, so I speed up my steps as I weave through the bustling walkway toward my destination. Throngs of people are out tonight, so work will be busy. Normally, I'd dread so many customers during my shift, but at least that means I won't have time to think about K'thress. Or Fina.

## ✦FINA✦

AFTER TWO MORE DRINKS, Mezli wanders over to the bartender to flirt with him. I watch them with fascination from our booth, attempting to not make accidental eye contact with anyone else in the bar. Not after the way Mezli's friend reacted to me.

When she leans over the bar to lick the giant vuloi's neck, I take that as my sign it's time to go. I send her a quick message on her comm letting her know I'm leaving and to have fun. It's weird heading out without saying goodbye, but there's no way I'm interrupting whatever's going on over there.

Sagittarius district's nightlife is in full swing when I exit the bar. It's daunting being surrounded by so many aliens while I'm alone.

I surreptitiously tuck my credit purse into my cleavage when no one's looking my way. Better safe than sorry. My mom's repeated warning to stay vigilant because thieves are lurking everywhere echoes in my head. I know she's trying to protect me, but it seems a little xenophobic to assume the worst of aliens.

As if on queue, an insectoid-looking alien with sickly yellow skin and grease stains on their ratty shirt bumps into me. The sack they're holding falls apart and spills what looks like cooked hamburger meat covered in a purple sauce all over my feet.

*Ugh*, gross!

They angrily mutter something at me that my translator doesn't pick up. As I attempt to wipe off the mess, I feel their spindly hand brush against my hip where a credit pouch might be. But they're back on their feet and scurrying away before I can protest.

Damn, I hate that Mom was right. Even more, I hate that my new boots and my hands are now covered in stinky purple goo. So much for my plans to explore. Time to go hide in my apartment for the rest of the night cycle.

As I walk toward the nearest transit station that will take me back to Orion district, I'm on high alert, ready to slip out of the way of anyone that eyes me too intently. I don't want any more handsy aliens trying to swipe my credits. Because of my vigilance, I notice a pair of ankites following me. At first, I think they're just heading in the same direction as me. But when I stop to check my comm for directions, they stop too. I move a little faster, but they keep trailing me.

My mind starts to race in panic. God, what should I do? Keeping my credit pouch in my boobs may prevent pickpockets, but it won't stop me from getting mugged. Or worse. All the news vids my mom "helpfully" sent me about crime on Spire flash through my head. She shared them as a scare tactic, trying to get me to stay with the Coalition. At the time, I thought it was ridiculous, but maybe I should've listened.

The thought pisses me off. Fuck that. I'm so tired of being scared. I'm here now and I won't let some alien jerks intimidate me. Though I can't lead these people back to where I live. I scan my surroundings as I move with purpose, looking for anything that might help. Across the walkway, my eyes land on the illuminated sign for SimTech Suites.

That might work. I make a beeline to the entrance, almost tripping as some of the sludge on my boot slides under foot. I wasn't planning on coming back here after the fiasco last weekend, but it looks like I'm taking Breks up on his offer to give me a free simulation after all.

# 8

## ✦MAERLON✦

The first hour of my shift goes by quickly. With all the suites booked in advance, there's not much to do until those simulations end. Most nights I'd be thankful for an easy shift, but tonight I hoped to have something to distract me.

Instead, I'm sitting in the cramped control office, absently monitoring the suites for any notifications and scanning through a message my sister, Dezlon, sent me a few cycles ago. I've already read it many times, but it helps with my feelings of isolation. I haven't seen her in over a year and the rest of my family for much longer.

Not that I'm complaining. It's my job as the second child to provide for my family and learn from other cultures. That way, when I return to the colony ships, I can contribute to seladin knowledge and societal enhancement.

The entrance's motion sensor pings, snapping me out of my thoughts.

"Hello?!" an agitated, breathless voice calls out.

I shift myself into the holo-receptionist and plaster a fake smile on, ready to turn the customer away as politely as possible. My smile widens seeing who is in the lobby.

It's Fina. She's breathing heavily and keeps looking over her shoulder toward the walkway.

I take a deep breath to calm my nerves at her sudden appearance. "Hi there, welcome back to SimTech Suites. Ms. Kress, right?"

"Breks? Oh, thank god." She steps closer to the holo-receptionist and leans forward. Her ample breasts threaten to fall out of the front of her low-cut jumpsuit and it looks like something's shoved between them. How odd.

I tear my gaze back up to her face and force myself to maintain eye contact, despite the tempting sight.

"I need your help," she whispers near the holo's ear. My skin prickles as if I can feel the warm caress of her breath against my face. "Are they still there?"

Are who still there? I follow her eyes as she looks out onto the walkway again and this time I spot two ankites loitering nearby. They're pretending to be chatting, but their eyes keep darting back toward Fina. Anger boils inside me. Did they follow her here?

"Yes, I think I see your...admirers."

She pulls away and grimaces. "Shit, I hoped I'd lost them."

"Is everything alright? Do you need me to contact station security?" I'd go out and use my frightening appearance to "persuade" the ankites to back off, but I can't leave while sims are still running.

Her eyes widen, alarmed by the idea. "N-no, I don't want security involved!"

"Are you certain, Ms. Kress? I'm concerned about your safety."

"Positive. I don't need to end up on station news as the paranoid human who couldn't handle aliens looking at her." She sighs and runs a hand over her face. "I was thinking...could I cash in that sim credit you gave me? Hopefully, they'll lose interest when I show no signs of leaving."

"Of course!" I say, wanting to do anything I can to help. Then I remember all the rooms are full. "Wait, no. I'm so sorry. Our suites are all booked for the next few hours."

Her expression falls. "Oh, okay."

"But you can stay here and talk to me, if you'd like." I can't send her back out into a dangerous situation.

"Really? That would be wonderful. You're a lifesaver." She smiles, and it's so lovely that I smile back like a sap.

"Not a problem. I can't think of a better way to spend my time than getting to know you."

"O-oh?" A tinge of pink rises on her cheeks.

"Yes, I've never met a human before you and I'd welcome a cultural exchange between us." I'm backpedaling so that she doesn't think I'm coming on too strong.

"An exchange means I get to learn more about your culture too. I have to admit, I'm curious about you." Fina flushes again. I'm not sure what to make of her reactions to me. She seems pleased, but then her face reddens with discomfort.

"I'd be happy to tell you about the rich and proud heritage of holo-sims."

She laughs and rolls her eyes. "Fine. Keep your secrets."

"Trust me, the intrigue is part of my charm. Once I stop being mysterious, you'll realize just how incredibly dull I am."

She laughs again, the sound warm and bright. Just like her. *Fashar*, I'm hopeless around this woman.

⋆✦

Fina runs a hand through her unbound hair and sighs. "I hate to admit it, but my mom was right about needing to be careful. I guess I naively hoped that the people here had risen above things like petty crime. That the Xi Consortium is so technologically sophisticated that it's also utopia compared to where I'm from. That's silly though, isn't it?"

"Not silly at all. I wish I'd had someone like your mom to warn me. When I first came to Spire, I was so starry-eyed that I may have gotten my credits stolen. Multiple times."

"Multiple times?" Fina laughs and shakes her head.

"We don't all have ample breasts to hide our credit pouches in." I gesture down toward the pouch sitting in her lap. It fell out of the neck of her jumpsuit when she went to sit down earlier.

She looks down at her chest and laughs harder. "Finally, my oversized tits are good for something! Here I thought they were here to hurt my back and disgust aliens."

Don't look at her breasts. Don't do it. *Esh'et*, too late. My eyes have already followed hers, allowing me to enjoy how enticingly they jiggle as she laughs. Alright, I looked. Stop talking about her breasts.

"Disgust definitely isn't the reaction *this* alien had." My mind yells at me as the words escape my mouth.

"Oh?" She places her hand over her chest, covering some of the exposed cleavage. Her smile becomes shy and her teeth worry at her lower lip.

"Yes." I pause for a moment and allow myself to stare at her chest, as if considering it. Her eyes widen. "I would call it more of a mild distress than disgust."

"Ass!" she says, giving me an insincere scowl.

"True, your ass elicits the same reaction as well."

"What?! And here I thought you were a kind, respectful sort of alien, Breks." Fina's voice sounds angry but the amused smile on face betrays her.

"Mmm, that was your first mistake. My thoughts are not nearly as respectful as they should be." My voice comes out a bit more husky than I intended. I'm not usually this forward at all, but there's something about her that makes me bold. It's been effortless talking to her tonight and I'm starting to think that my attraction may not be entirely one-sided. Though, her attraction is toward the attractive holo version of me. I doubt she'd give me those same shy smiles if I were out there in the flesh.

"My mistake." Her words sound soft and breathy. The tension between us is palpable, and I'd give anything to be the ankite sitting in front of her so that I could pull her in and press my mouth to hers. Kissing isn't common for seladin, but my ex taught me how to and I've seen human vids that show how much they like it. Her soft, pink lips part as she looks at me, and I wonder if she's also thinking about kissing.

I'm startled when the alert signaling the end of the simulations goes off. Have we really been talking for hours? Time melted away in Fina's presence.

"Looks like the simulations are ending. I'll need to put the holo-receptionist on idle, so I hope you can survive without my wit and charm for a few minutes."

"Hah, I think I'll manage. Actually..." Fina turns around to peer out the entrance and scans the walkway. "It seems like those ankites lost interest, so I could head home now."

"Yeah, they left about an hour ago. But you were telling me about your work with the Coalition and I didn't want to interrupt."

"Oh god, that makes me sound like I was babbling. You could have told me to shut up!"

"Why would I do that? I enjoy listening to you." I could have listened to her talk all night. She's fascinating, intelligent, funny and...*esh'et*, I like her far too much.

The simulation end alert goes off again. "Stay for a bit? You still have that sim credit and I think I know just what you need."

"If you insist." There's a hint of reluctance, but I can tell she likes the idea. My pulse races thinking about spending even more time with her.

# 9

## ✦FINA✦

**W**ow, the holo-receptionist is creepy when Breks isn't controlling it. It sits there with a vacant smile, blinking at random intervals. That reminds me I have no idea what the person I've just spent hours talking with looks like. Other than his insistence that he's much less attractive than the ankite holo he's using.

Oh, I suppose I know that he's male. During our conversation, Breks said that he's the only male in his family. That means that he isn't an ankite, as they don't have a gender spectrum. But otherwise, it doesn't tell me anything about what sort of alien he is.

While I'm waiting for Breks to return, I go through my mental list of aliens that live on Spire. Aespians, ankites, nexxit, seladin, shikzeth, and vuloi. Out of all of those, many consider ankites the most attractive species since they have changeling-like abilities to adapt their appearance. But that's already ruled out.

It's possible he's a nexxit, but it seems strange he'd be so concerned about his appearance if that's the case. Nexxit are the most "normal" looking aliens to a human eye, minus the pink skin and extra set of arms.

The seladin I met earlier tonight instilled a strange combination of attraction and fright when he towered over me. His glowing eyes disconcerted me, but that only added to his dark allure. However, I've only seen a handful of seladin on Spire, so it's unlikely Breks is one.

That leaves an aespian, a shikzeth, or a vuloi. None of them is my top choice for the sexiest alien race in this sector.

Aespians remind me of insects with their carapace-like skin, antennae, and enormous eyes. If one had a personality like Breks', I'm sure I could grow to appreciate the insectoid vibe.

Vuloi are behemoths with lizard-like scales and tails. Mezli obviously sees some merit in them, but I worry I'd get crushed.

Shikzeth look like a golem crossed with some sort of demon. And not in a sexy, gargoyle-y way. More of a volcano turned into a person, complete with magma-like skin under rocky outer plating. Another alien that would probably crush me if we tried to hug. Please don't be a shikzeth, Breks.

I'm being unfair. Shikzeth might be the most tender and proficient lovers in the galaxy. Not that any of this matters. Breks is incredibly easy and fun to talk to, but nothing can come from it. Sure he flirts, but it's from behind a holo. I doubt he'd be interested in me if we were interacting face-to-face.

In my own twisted way, it makes sense that I'd have a crush on someone who's unavailable. Forming a romantic connection terrifies me and the potential sting of rejection often stops me from making an attempt. Knowing that there are no stakes to my flirtations with Breks makes it much easier to be bold. He can't reject me or break my heart because he isn't available to me to begin with.

I'm so wrapped up in my thoughts that I barely register when a string of customers exit through the lobby and the holo-receptionist bids them goodnight.

"Fina? You still there?" asks Breks, taking control of the holo-receptionist again.

I hop up from my chair and almost collide with a very relaxed looking nexxit as I move to the reception desk. "Yes!"

"Great. Come on back, I've got everything set up." The holo smiles at me and gestures toward the branching hallway of suites. A path on the floor illuminates and leads me to a blank white room identical to my previous time here.

My gut clenches as I recall what happened that night. At least this time I don't startle when the door disappears behind me.

"Trapped once again," I mutter to myself.

"And completely at my mercy." Breks' holo appears in the room with me.

I jump slightly at his sudden appearance and then smack the holo's arm in frustration.

He pretends to wince in pain. "If you're going to do that, at least give me a safeword." He lets out a throaty laugh that makes my stomach tighten.

"Ugh, don't remind me."

"What, you're not into being tied up and disciplined like a naughty girl?" His tone sounds teasing, but the idea sends a little thrill through me when he says it.

I cross my arms over my chest and scoff at him. "In your dreams."

"Absolutely." Breks gives me a wicked grin and now I'm blushing like a schoolgirl again.

"I'm not sure if I trust you to pick out my simulation, after all."

He laughs again, and the warm sound sends heat right to my core. "Don't worry, I have something much more tame set up. If you're ready, I'll hop out and leave you to enjoy. Oh, and just tell me you want it to end if you don't like it. No safeword needed for this one."

Okay. My palms start to sweat like I'm about to jump off a cliff instead of enjoy a recreational sim. He's promised it won't be like last time, but damn, I'm still nervous. I should just go if I'm going to make myself miserable with anxiety. Why did I want to do this again?

Oh. Right. Because I wanted to keep talking to Breks. I bite my lip, considering if asking him to stay would be too weird. "Is there the option to have you join me in the simulation? Using your holo, since I know you aren't comfortable with me seeing you. I just...I'm kind of anxious and I've enjoyed spending time with you so..."

The smile leaves his face and there's a very long, awkward pause.

"Never mind! Forget it. That's probably a super inappropriate thing to ask."

He places a hand on my shoulder, and I stop talking. It's still mind-blowing how solid and realistic the hand touching me is. I wonder if he has any sensation on his end.

"I can do that for you, Fina. Whatever makes you comfortable."

I search the holo's face, looking for any sign that he's just being polite. But he just looks endearingly earnest. "Really?"

"Yeah, just let me close up so no walk-ins interrupt us."

"Are you sure? I don't want you to get in trouble!"

He places a reassuring hand on my shoulder. "Positive. This time of night is always dead."

"Well, okay. As long as you're sure. Thank you."

Breks nods and his holo disappears.

I pace around the chamber, wringing my hands together as I try to calm my breathing. I belatedly realize that I should have seen what the simulation was before asking him to join me.

The room fills with blinding light, and I shut my eyes against it. When I open them again, I gasp.

I'm standing on a beach looking out over a glittering turquoise ocean. The sky is dusky pinks and purples as twin suns set on the horizon. Waves lap at my toes as I stand on bleached white sand and a gentle sea breeze tousles my hair.

"Not too much, I hope?" Breks appears beside me, his ankite form wearing a tight pair of swim shorts. He searches my face for my reaction.

"It's incredible!" I beam back at him. "Where are we?"

"One of the beaches of my homeworld. The beauty of it has always stuck with me, so I thought you might enjoy it."

I want to ask for his homeworld's name, but he omitted that for a reason. That won't keep me from searching for homeworlds that have binary star systems as soon as I get home.

"Thank you for sharing this with me, Breks. It's beautiful."

"It's not entirely altruistic. I get to see you in a swimsuit." He does a quick sweep over my body with his eyes.

I glance down and realize that I'm wearing a bikini. "Ah!" I wrap my arms around my exposed stomach and splotches of heat bloom on my cheeks and chest.

His expression shifts from a roguish smile to concern. "Are you unwell?"

"What?" I blink back at him in confusion.

"Your face is very flushed. I know that often indicates a fever. I apologize if my flirtations made you ill. That wasn't my intent at all."

I would think he's joking again, but he appears genuinely worried about upsetting me. How do I explain blushing? "I'm fine. I uh, when my skin turns red, it means I'm embarrassed. Or sometimes I'm, um...excited by the thought of something."

"Oh." He thinks for a moment, then a grin creeps onto his face. "So you're excited by me looking at you in your swimsuit?"

With the way he's studying me, *now* I am. "What? No! I'm embarrassed that I'm so exposed."

"Right." He continues to grin at me.

"So, are we just going to stand here and watch the sunset while you tease me? Or is there another element to this simulation?"

"If that's what you'd like, I'll be happy to oblige. However, the original simulation has options for a beachside massage or an...intimate companion."

"Oh boy, now I'm *really* turning red."

"You are. I like it now that I know what it means." His gaze drags across my face, then dips lower. "So, which option do you choose?" He takes a step closer to me.

Now my face feels like it's covered in flames. I know he's still teasing me. There's no way he's suggesting that we get intimate. "You're ridiculous!" I turn and go to move away, but his fingers gently circle my wrist.

I stare down at his hand and he runs his thumb in a small circle against the inside of my wrist. Who knew such a small touch could be so overwhelming? My heart feels like it's about to burst out of my chest as I turn back to him.

"I'm serious. I'll do anything you want, Fina." My palms tingle at the low, soft tone he uses.

I shouldn't do this. This isn't really even him.

"I-I'm not sure what I want."

"That's okay. Maybe we start with this?" He slowly closes the space between us, giving me time to move away or stop him.

Instead, my body moves on its own, pressing up against him.

He takes my hand and places it on his shoulder, then wraps his arm around my waist. "Is this okay?"

God, *yes*, my body screams. Instead, my reply comes out as a breathy "yeah".

The hand on my back rubs gentle circles along my skin and my nipples stiffen, scraping against his firm chest through my bikini top. My mind continues to marvel at how real he feels. "Can you even feel this?"

He chuckles, and it reverberates against my body. "I can feel enough. My imagination makes up for the rest of it."

Oh. I guess that's better than nothing. I wish he were actually here with me, though.

"So how would it feel if...if I kissed you?" My eyes dip to glance at his holo's mouth.

"Let's find out." He lowers his mouth to meet mine.

Sparks dance across my skin at his achingly tender kiss. He kisses me like I'm something meant to be savored. When our lips part, I'm breathless and he's looking at me with such desire it makes my legs wobble.

# 10

## ✦MAERLON✦

*Fa-shar*, if only I could actually feel her lips on mine. There's a bit of pressure feedback against my mouth from the holo sensors, but it's a ghost of a touch. I wish I could smell her scent mingled with the ocean breeze. Feel her breath caress my cheek as she pulls her face away from mine. I'm so hungry for her that my imagination fills in some blanks for the sensations, but it isn't enough.

"Well?" Fina looks at me shyly, waiting for my response to her kiss.

"That was...I need more." I pull her back against me and press our mouths together again.

She gasps and her lips part, allowing me to slip my tongue into her mouth. Her needy little sounds of pleasure make me want to devour her, even with only a hint of the sensation. Her tongue slides against the holo's and I notice how it's much shorter than mine.

Just another reason she wouldn't like the real me.

That depressing thought vanishes as she rubs her lush body against me. When I imagine how soft she'd be, my cock twitches, begging to be released from the confines of my pants. I can't touch it though—she'd notice my holo palming their crotch.

Our mouths part, and she gasps, looking up at me with a mixture of surprise and arousal. "Wow, that was…wow."

I couldn't agree more.

Her pale skin is flushed a lovely shade of pink and her violet curls dance in the breeze. I reach out and brush a strand out of her face, tucking it behind her ear. Her eyes close and I cup her cheek, running my thumb across her lips, trying to commit their shape to memory for when I think of her later.

The sky fades to a swirl of dark purple and gold as the twin suns continue to sink beneath the horizon. The dim golden light makes her even more captivating, and I yearn to see her through my own eyes.

She shivers as I reluctantly pull my hand away.

"Are you cold? I can adjust the temperature of the simulation or change the time of day."

"No, not cold. Just very…alert."

"Oh, like the flushing? Who knew human arousal was similar to the signs of a fever?"

"I didn't say I'm aroused!" Fina's skin turns an even deeper red.

"My mistake. It appears I have much more to learn about humans." I let my eyes rake across her figure to show what kind of learning I'm interested in.

She places a hand on my chest. "I'd be interested in learning about you, too."

She wouldn't say that if she knew the real me. I saw the way she looked at me when Mezli introduced me to her as Maerlon. Stars, I need to cool things off. I'm being a fool and letting my attraction to her run away with me.

"Oh! I have many fun facts about ankites. Did you know it takes a not insignificant amount of concentration for them to make their features appear defined? If you ever see one when they're tired or have just woken up, they're more amorphous." I shift the holo's appearance to illustrate this.

She rolls her eyes at me. "Fine, don't tell me. I understand you need to be professional."

I breathe a sigh of relief when she doesn't press me more about my true identity, despite my guilt for not being forthcoming.

"Oh yes, I'm the pinnacle of professionalism." I slide the hand on her back to rest just above her bottom.

"Ha! Well, in your *professional* opinion, what's the best use for the rest of my time in this sim?"

"Speaking strictly as a professional? I'd recommend the standard setting, which is a beachside massage." I use the sim controls to conjure a massage table and give her hip a gentle squeeze.

Her eyes narrow, and she crosses her arms, regarding me with skepticism. "Are you a trained massage therapist, as well as a sim technician?"

"No, but what I lack in experience, I can make up for with enthusiasm."

"I bet," she says with a chuckle. "Alright, just don't get too handsy."

"Never. I'm not a nexxit."

She groans at my terrible joke but moves over to lie face down on the massage table. I move to her side and materialize some massage oil in my hands. All of my bravado dissipates as I look down at her. What if I do the wrong thing or she doesn't enjoy my touch?

"Let me know if anything is uncomfortable or you need me to stop. I want to make you feel good."

"O-okay." She sounds as nervous as I am.

I start by pressing both hands into her shoulders and then drag them down her back in a slow, firm motion. They catch on her bikini's ties, so Fina reaches an arm back and undoes them for me. She sighs and relaxes as I stroke down her back again without impediment.

She might be relaxed now, but every nerve in my body vibrates with arousal, seeing her lovely form beneath my holo's hands. Each time I drag them down her back, I venture a little lower until my fingertips brush against the waistband of her bikini. She releases a tiny groan that goes right to my cock.

*Vash-ka*, I'm hard as a rock. I rub my palm along my length, trying to give myself even a small amount of relief.

With a shuddering breath, I try to calm myself and move down to her lower legs. I can't even think about touching her rounded bottom and thighs right now. She sighs as I massage her legs, but when I touch one of her small feet's strange, stubby toes, she twitches away and giggles.

"Sorry! I'm ticklish there."

"And ticklish is bad?" I can't resist caressing her other foot and watching her squirm again.

"Ah! Not bad, just not relaxing."

"Got it. I should only touch your feet if I want to excite you."

"What? No! God, you've got a dirty mind."

I move my hands back to her legs, chuckling softly at her reaction. "Apologies. I'm going back to professional mode."

She snorts and relaxes again as I massage her legs.

I reach the swell of her bottom as I work my way up her thighs. When I hesitate, her legs fall apart slightly as she lets out a deep, contented exhale. I let my hands slip up to work her inner thighs, my fingertips dipping dangerously close to her core.

She makes a sound that is undeniably a moan and parts her legs a fraction more.

My own choked groan escapes when I see that the fabric between her thighs is damp with her arousal. Reluctantly, I pull my hands back before I allow myself to get carried away.

Fina lies still for a moment, then rolls onto her side and sits up, one arm holding her bikini top against her chest.

"Sorry, was that too much?" I ask, worried that I did something wrong.

She shakes her head and stands up. Her free hand reaches up, and she places it on my shoulder, pulling me closer. I'd give anything for her to wrap her other arm around me and let her top fall down to the sand. Her eyes shine with desire, and she presses a kiss to my neck.

"Can...can you come in here, Breks? Like, actually come in?" Her question comes out in a husky whisper.

"I-I..." My brain freezes, wanting to do as she asks but panicking.

I can't. But there's no good reason I can think of right now that isn't, *"I've already met you and you were terrified by my appearance."*

Fina pulls away and steps back. My heart sinks as her expression falls. "I'm sorry. You've already told me no multiple times, but I just can't take a hint, can I?"

"No, Fina! That's not—I want to, believe me, I do. I just—"

"It's okay, I understand," she whispers, not meeting my eyes.

*Get up from your desk! Go in there and kiss her for real!* I scream at myself internally, but the anxiety and fear of rejection win out.

"I should go home. It's late and I'm sure you don't want to be stuck here past your shift." Her voice wavers and she looks out over the water instead of at me.

"Fina..." I don't know what to say to make this better.

She turns back with a shaky smile plastered on her face. "Thanks again. I really appreciate you letting me hang out here tonight."

That fake appeasing smile gnaws at me. I didn't mean to embarrass or hurt her. "It was my pleasure. Truly."

I end the simulation and she exits the room in awkward silence. When she gets to the lobby, she gives the holo-receptionist a weak smile and holds a hand up in a slight wave goodbye.

"Will I see you again?" I blurt the words out before she can go.

"I don't know, Breks. I need to think about it." Sadness flashes across her face.

I watch as she exits and heads across the walkway toward the transit station, aching to run out after her. *Vash-ka*, I've made a mess of this.

# 11

## ✦FINA✦

"Any big plans for the weekend?" My mom stares at me through the vid screen as I carefully pour flour into my mixer. She called me right in the middle of stress baking my favorite cookie recipe—the one my dad taught me when I first discovered my love for baking.

Mom's gotten into the habit of calling me almost every day as soon as she wakes up. It syncs up with when I get home from work and even though she insists that it's because it helps her not sleep through her alarm, I know she's doing it so that I don't get too lonely.

"One sec, I need to scrape the sides of the bowl..." I turn away from the vid holoscreen for a moment, but can still feel her watching me. Silently judging me.

"I'll never understand why you and your father insist on hand-baking things instead of using a food synth that takes a fraction of the time and improves the nutritional value." I catch her shaking her head at me as I look back up at the screen.

Because it tastes better.

Because I like how it gives my stressed mind a moment of serenity.

Because I like the freedom to make my own food choices after years of her guilting me to eat only the healthiest options.

Not that I'd say any of that. I've tried before and she just doesn't get it.

Deciding to ignore her comment, I forge ahead with answering her question about my plans. "I think I might check out the shopping in Perseus District this weekend. I could use some decor that doesn't scream 'utilitarian chic' and apparently the best second-hand shops are down there. Plus, I'd like to get Mezli a thank-you gift for helping me adjust to life here."

She frowns. "During the day, I hope?" If she had it her way, I'd do nothing but lock myself in my apartment when I'm not at work.

Dad wanders onto the screen and rolls his eyes at her behind her back. "Our daughter is thirty-five years old, Alessandra. She can go out whenever she wants." He shuffles over to their food synthesizer and punches in a code that I know is for his face-melting version of coffee.

I haven't gone out at night on my own since the incident the other week, but there's no way in hell I'd tell my mom that. She's already worried and looking for any excuse to tell me to return to a Coalition ship.

Dad gives me a smile, eyes lingering on the bowl of cookie dough I'm mixing with envy, then waves before leaving the room. When he's gone, Mom's eyes dart around, checking to see if anyone's listening in on us. "Speaking of going out, did you get the package I sent you?"

Why is she being so secretive? "The inhalers? Mom, you know I don't need them anymore. I get that you're a medic and want me to be prepared, but other meds control my allergies."

She leans in closer to the camera and I get an up-close view of her pillow-creased cheeks. "They're not inhalers," she says in a furtive whisper.

"What? What do you mean, they're not inhalers?"

"They're stun spray, sweetie. I disguised it as inhalers so you could carry it and no one would question you."

"You what?!" Oh my god, my mom's going to get me arrested. Stun spray is illegal on Spire. And in Coalition space. How she got her hands on it is beyond me.

"Shh, your father will hear." She backs away from the camera and glares at me.

"Mom, I can't use them!" I hiss through my teeth.

"You've seen the articles I've sent you. I won't have my only child wandering around a dangerous alien space station with no way to protect herself. Take an inhaler with you when you go out. Do this for me. *Please.*"

"Okay, fine. I'll do it for you. But if I'm thrown into an alien jail, you better come bail me out!"

"What's that about alien jail?" Dad asks in bemusement as he comes back into the room, slipping on his uniform's jacket.

"Just Fina promising me she won't do anything too reckless." Funny, coming from a woman who sent me illicit substances through interstellar post like it was no big deal. Mom's tense smile tells me not to mention her "brilliant" idea to my dad.

I scrunch my face up in disbelief at her behavior, but nod back.

Dad absently chuckles and goes back to his preparations for the day. He knows better than to ask questions when my mom gets like this.

"Alright, gotta go get ready for my shift. Have a good night, sweetie. Don't do anything I wouldn't do!" she says, relaxing now that I've agreed to do what she asked.

"Bye, have a good day."

I hang up the vid call with a sigh and glance at the box with the "inhalers". I should throw them away. But I've been too nervous to go out at night without Mezli. It'd be nice to not feel scared when I go out—Mom might have a point.

I carefully scoop rounded balls of dough onto a baking sheet and set them inside my food synthesizer, using a custom setting I programmed into it earlier. With a timer set and everything used for cookie prep set into the auto-washer, silence fills my apartment once more.

Getting off of a call with my parents always brings my relative isolation into sharper focus. God, I miss them so much. I haven't been on Spire long enough to get through the adjustment period, but it's tempting to give up and flee back to my old, safe life.

*No. Stop that kind of thinking.* There's a reason I left that life behind. I was suffocating, trapped in the meek, unfulfilling identity I'd unintentionally taken on. Spire is my chance to be someone else. Maybe even my true self—whoever she may be.

With that in mind, I open my comm to message Mezli and see if she's free tonight. I pause before sending it, a hint of anxiety nagging at me. She's spent practically every weekend night with me since I've arrived, and I need to stop relying on her for everything. The last thing I want is for my only friend on the station to get sick of me.

I need to branch out. I've put no genuine effort into making new friends since I got here. Well, there's Breks, but...

Great, now I'm thinking about Breks again.

I tried to get him out of my mind after our awkward encounter, with no success. I've spent an embarrassing number of nights touching myself to the thought of how he kissed and what would have happened if I'd let the massage keep going. My proverbial panties would have slid right off—I was already so turned on by his touch. I should have begged him to slide his powerful hands all the way up between my thighs and touch me where I needed it the most.

That was the sexiest night of my life. Pathetic, I know, but there weren't a ton of opportunities for sexy encounters living on a small Coalition ship. I ruined it by asking him to join me in person, even though I knew he couldn't. That he wouldn't. Flirting through a barrier of anonymity isn't the same as wanting to actually be intimate. It was silly to think that he'd want that.

*Stop obsessing over him.*

With a tap on my comm, I open the dating app Mezli made me download. Each time I've checked it, I get overwhelmed. So many messages are from obvious alien fetishists, asking about how small my hands are, what my hair feels like, or—my least favorite—what holes or appendages I have on my body. Ugh, no thanks.

There's a new message from a nexxit named Craik. We've been talking occasionally, when I work up the nerve to use the app. He seems friendly and hasn't asked any creepy questions. Plus, he reminds me a lot of what Mezli would look like if she were a guy, so he seems somewhat familiar.

> Craik: Hope you've had a pleasant week, and they didn't kick you out of the office again for working too hard.

I smile to myself as I read his message. This was the first week my boss didn't tell me to stay home and rest.

> Fina: Hah, they didn't! I'm getting better at doing less, though I still feel weird about it.

A few minutes pass and I get a reply.

> Craik: So, would that mean you're rested enough to grab a drink with me tonight?

My anxiety immediately goes into overdrive. He wants me to meet him in person? *Tonight?* My stomach clenches painfully.

I flop down onto my bed and take a deep breath. *Fina, you can't live your new life in this tiny apartment.* I drag in another slow inhale through my nose, then run my affirmations through my head as I exhale. I can do this. Time to be spontaneous and brave.

As I focus on my breathing, the logical part of my brain comes on board despite the static fuzz of my anxious thoughts. Drinks tonight means that I only have an hour or two to freak out. Plus, I can tell him I have plans later tonight, so there's a set cut-off time for the date.

I can do this. Before I can talk myself out of it, I message Craik back.

> Fina: Sure! I have plans later tonight, but can meet up for an hour or two.

His reply is almost instantaneous.

> Craik: Wow, I was sure you were going to turn me down! Guess I'm not as hopeless at dating as I thought. Meet me at Parallax in an hour? It's near the synth gardens in Sagittarius district. If you have time, we can take a walk in them.

In an hour?! I glance at my ratty sweatpants and threadbare shirt covered in flour. Shit.

> Fina: Sounds good, see you then!

The baking timer buzzes, pulling me away from the chat. I set the cookies out to cool, dropping more than one in my haste. I scramble out of my clothes in a frenzy, hopping into the shower and yelping when the cold water hits my skin. It'll be a miracle if I can make myself presentable and get there on time.

After a quick scrub, I'm back out of the shower and vid calling Mezli in a panic. She answers right away, and I see an image of her standing by her apartment sink, shoveling soup into her mouth. "Hey Fin—whoa...is this a sexy call? I didn't realize you thought of me that way." She waggles her eyebrows at the sight of me wrapped in a towel.

"Shh, I need your help!"

"*Sexy* help?" She gives me a salacious grin.

"No! Well, kind of? I agreed to meet a guy from Syzygy for drinks in an hour and I have no idea what to wear." My stomach roils with nerves at the mere mention of the date.

Mezli narrows her eyes at me. She sets her bowl down with a loud clatter. "Who are you and what did you do with Fina?"

"I know, I don't know why I said yes! Please help me. I'm going to throw up."

"Oof, he's that unattractive?"

I rub a hand across my face in frustration. "Mezli, you know I love your jokes, but I'm running out of time to get ready."

Her expression sobers. "Sorry! I'm just surprised. Where are you going? What kind of alien is he?"

"We're going to some place called Parallax. He's a nexxit." I brace for her inevitable glee that the first alien I'm choosing to go out with is the same species as her.

"So I *am* your type!"

This was a bad idea. Time's ticking away. "I'm hanging up."

"No, wait! Wear the silver dress I got you with those shiny boots you borrowed," she says, like she already had a date outfit planned for me, just in case I got the nerve to go on one.

I pull the dress she's talking about out from the back of my closet with a frown. It's far more revealing than something I'd ever pick for myself. "Are you sure?"

"Positive. Wear your hair up. Nexxit think necks are attractive and yours is beautiful."

I pause, touching my neck self-consciously. "Wait, really?"

"Have you read *any* of the smut I've been sending you since we were teens?? Yes!"

"I did. I just didn't realize they were based on any sort of fact. Wait, does that mean that seladin...packages are that big?" I think back on a very graphic story I *may* have re-read multiple times.

Mezli cackles, her black eyes sparkling with delight. "Oh girl, you have no idea."

"Wow, okay. Wow." I'm blushing just thinking about it.

"Focus! You're going on a date with a nexxit. This is no time to be thinking about seladin dick."

My gut clenches. "Ah, god. I'm doing this. I'm actually going on a date. I can't do this, can I?" My breath becomes shallow as the panic rises again.

She locks eyes with me and gives me a decisive nod. "You can and you will. Now get dressed and go show that lucky guy just what a *brave, badass babe* you are."

I should never have told her about my affirmations. She uses every chance she can to quote them back to me. At least it's helping this time. "Okay, yeah. You're right." I exhale and try to believe the words.

"Message me as soon as it's over! Even if it's in the middle of the night." She winks at me before ending the call.

I hastily slap on some makeup and get dressed. The dress is way too short, so I slip on a pair of dark tights underneath—Mezli's fashion sense be damned. I pin my still-purple hair up in a loose bun in case she wasn't lying about nexxit liking necks.

With a glance at my comm, I see the time and curse. I grab my purse and head toward the door, then see my mom's inhalers resting on the counter. I sigh, remembering the promise I made to her.

Alright you win, Mom. I'll bring one with me. I shove the inhaler into my purse.

Better safe than sorry.

# 12

## ✦ FINA ✦

A crowded transit ride and a brisk walk later, I'm approaching Parallax with only a few minutes to spare. I stop to catch my breath and a bead of sweat slides down my temple. As I wipe it off, I realize with horror that I forgot to put deodorant on after my shower.

*Shit.*

I tilt my nose down toward my armpit and can't smell anything yet, but who knows what alien noses can pick up? Just perfect. I'm sweaty, ripe, and out of breath for my first date with an alien.

The front of Parallax opens out to the walkway, allowing patrons to people-watch and view the luminescent synth gardens across the way. I scan the bar. It's not very crowded, just a few people chatting in groups and a handful grabbing drinks from the bartender. No sign of Craik—I must have beaten him here.

Rather than loiter awkwardly, I head inside. Should I order something to drink while I wait? Or will that look weird if I get something without him? I decide against ordering anything and sit down at an empty table near the walkway.

A few minutes pass. I check my comm to see if there are any messages. Nothing. A few more go by and my anxiety shifts to annoyance. All that rushing and he's late. I glance at my comm again. There's still no word from Craik, but Mezli messaged me. Probably to reassure me. I'm lucky to have a friend like her.

I open her message. There's nothing there but a photorealistic drawing of an enormous alien penis with glowing markings. God, now that's burned into my brain.

Of course, a server chooses this exact moment to approach me. I scramble to shut off my comm and look up at a turquoise ankite, just in time to watch their features shift to appear more human.

"Can I get you something?" Their nose and mouth look just like mine, and it's unnerving.

"No uh, unless—oh sorry, was I not supposed to sit here unless I'd purchased a drink?"

"You're fine. Just wanted to check on you. You've been sitting there for a while. That and I wanted to see a human up close. I've never met one in person!"

I can't stop the slight downturn of my lips. My novelty is wearing on me.

"Oh, I hope that isn't rude to say!" the ankite adds, mimicking my frown.

I fix my expression to a more neutral one. "It's fine. And yeah, I'm okay. Just waiting for someone."

"A gangly nexxit?"

"Yeah, how did you—"

"I noticed one walk up, stare at you for a moment, and then leave. It was while you were looking at your comm."

Oh god, he saw me and bailed?

"Oh. I see." Tears of embarrassment and frustration well up in my eyes.

"If it helps, you are *way* out of his league. Probably saw you in that gorgeous dress and realized you hopelessly outmatched him."

"That's kind of you to say." I will the water in my eyes to stay put.

"Let me get you a drink—on the house. It's the least you deserve for your wasted time." They give me a sympathetic smile.

I shake my head. The server is sweet, but I want to leave before I start crying. "Thank you. I think I'm just going to go."

"Sure thing. Don't let the idiots get you down, cutie." As soon as they head back to the bar, I leave.

Dammit. Why did I think this was a good idea? Hot tears roll down my cheeks and I search for a spot where I won't be a crying human spectacle.

Across the walkway, spindly glowing trees and incandescent blooms catch my eye. The synth gardens. Well, at least I can look at something pretty while I have my mental breakdown.

I slip in through the garden gate and head inside. The path winding through the foliage is empty, so I head further in. Once I'm out of view of the main walkway, I sink down into a crouch and let my tears flow.

Self-shaming thoughts bubble to the surface of my mind—I'm not attractive enough, I shouldn't be crying over a guy I've never met, I don't have what it takes to find someone.

My comm buzzes and I see a message notification from the Syzygy app.

> Craik: Sorry, not going to make it. There was an emergency.

I scowl at the words. I'm hiding in a garden crying because some loser didn't find me attractive? Fuck this guy.

> Fina: Is that what you call ditching someone after you see them? You could've at least had the courtesy to tell me you weren't interested to my face.

I wipe away my tears and a smear of mascara comes off on the back of my hand.

Another message from Craik pops up.

> Craik: Screw you, ugly human whore.

He's writing out more, but I don't need to see anything else. I close the app and delete it. So much for my foray into dating. It's almost comical how bad tonight has been.

My indignant anger helps the tears subside. I stand back up and take a deep breath. There's a subtle floral aroma in the air from the synthetic plants, which oddly helps calm me further.

It's still early and I refuse to go home defeated by that jerk. I wander deeper into the gardens and approach an ankite and an aespian holding hands, admiring a lush bloom of golden flowers.

I sigh as I pass them. The hopeful romantic in me had pictured doing something similar with my date. That tonight would be the start of something special. Instead, I'm wandering around alone in dirt-speckled tights and tear-stained cheeks, like some unhinged weirdo.

The garden layout reminds me of a hedge maze, all looping

walkways and dead ends with benches for visitors to sit and enjoy the atmosphere. After a while, I relax enough to enjoy the strange and beautiful foliage. If they weren't synthetic, I'd swear that the flowers let off some sort of calming pollen.

That relaxation vanishes not too long after it sets in, when I realize that someone I passed a few turns back is following me. *Unbelievable.* First, I get stood up and now this creep. Is following someone while they're alone some kind of fun pastime for the aliens here? Wasn't Spire supposed to be more civilized than the Coalition?

I'm so deep into the gardens that there's no exit in sight. I reach into my purse as casually as I can and palm my "inhaler", just in case. Moving at a steady pace, I take an erratic path to make sure they really are following me. They are, and they're getting closer.

Fuck. Okay, I can handle this. I'll go around the next corner and get the inhaler ready. As soon as they round the bend, I'll spray them and run. If it works, I'm never judging my mom for her worries again. Heart racing, I make a sharp turn at the next intersection of paths.

A small, panicked shout escapes me when I almost collide with a tall, white-haired figure whose skin almost camouflages with the dark, glowing plants. I peer up at the seladin I've walked into and realize in surprise that I've met him before. What was his name? Meylon?

He glares down at me and a moment later, recognition crosses his face as well.

"Wait up, human. No need to hide from me," the creeper—a bulky shikzeth with flame red hair—calls out in an oily, unsettling voice.

Shit! Unable to use my "inhaler" in front of a witness, I do the only other thing that comes to mind.

"There you are!" I throw my arms around the seladin's neck, yanking him down into a tight-lipped kiss.

His whole body stiffens in shock, and he pushes away from me.

"What's this?" I hear my stalker mutter behind me.

I look up into bright, pupilless eyes, silently begging the familiar seladin to understand what I need. He glances at the person behind us and his eyes narrow momentarily before he drags me back up against his chest and presses our lips together.

This time, he's really selling it. A large hand slides down to grip my ass and when I gasp in surprise, his tongue slides into my mouth. I clutch at his chest and melt into the sensation of his long, slick tongue caressing mine.

The creeper lets out a frustrated curse, but I keep kissing until I hear their footsteps stomping away from us. When I'm certain they're gone, I reluctantly pull away from the intense kiss and give Maerlon—right, that was his name—an apologetic smile.

# 13

## ✦MAERLON✦

"Go home for the day." I'm barely through the threshold of my boss' office when the words come out of zir mouth.

I blink in confusion, searching zir face for some sign of what's going on. Rexlaina doesn't look upset—at least not any more than usual. As a shikzeth, zir harsh facial features take on a perpetual scowl that I've found has no bearing on zir actual mood.

"I'm sorry, what?" I ask as I set the datapad with my completed designs on zir desk.

Ze picks it up and sets it to the side without checking my work over. "You look like shredded *mslep*, Maerlon. You're no good exhausted. Don't come back until you've had at least a full day of rest."

I open my mouth to protest, but Rexlaina's flaming eyes narrow at me. "You're excused."

Stunned, I nod and head back to my office. *Fa-shar*, I can't believe ze just told me to go home. Do I really look that bad?

I catch my reflection in the darkened monitor on my desk as I bend over to pick up my satchel. Dark circles rim my barely glowing eyes. Shredded *mslep* was putting it kindly. I look awful.

I feel worse. The past few weeks have been brutal. CiaXera has had an influx of new clients, all of which need custom design work. I've doubled my output, coming in early to make sure I get everything done. That would be manageable if I wasn't also working late shifts at SimTech every night. By the time I'm done at SimTech, I only have time to crash back at my loft for a few hours before I'm heading back to CiaXera to start the cycle all over again.

It's exhausting. And pointless. It's not like I'm working at SimTech because I need the credits. The whole point of taking the job was to get free sim time. But I haven't had the time or energy to enjoy my own sim for weeks. Yet, I've worked every night shift. All because I'm foolishly hoping to see Fina again.

She hasn't come back. The chances of that happening feel slimmer with each passing night cycle. I don't even know what I'd do if she showed up. Probably act like an idiot and scare her away for good.

*Esh'et*, the whole point of taking the job at SimTech was to distract myself from heartache. Look how well that turned out. Instead of getting a mental break, I'm even more of a besotted mess now.

As I head out of the office and toward the transit station, a nagging voice in the back of my head chastises me. Telling me I'll lose my job if I keep this up. That I'm not valuable enough to the company. That I'm not enough for anyone.

It takes effort to push back those all too common thoughts. I'm not getting fired. It's normal practice at CiaXera to encourage a work/life balance. And even if they decide to fire me, I have enough credits saved up to help support my family. I'm not a failure. I just need to get my head together.

Something feels off when I return to my small loft in Sagittarius district. At first, I think it's just my foul mood. But when I approach the door, I notice the green light near the handle. It's unlocked.

Every muscle in my body tenses, and I freeze. *Esh'et*, someone broke in. I futilely dig through my hip pouch for something I can use as a weapon, but there's nothing remotely useful. I'm not a violent person. Never needed to be, with my frightening appearance.

I stand at my full height and roll my shoulders back, making my posture as intimidating as possible, and slam the door open. My vicious, feral snarl quickly flickers to a wince though, as my carefully tended kressi bloom that rests atop the table by my front door topples over and shatters. Soil and red petals spill everywhere.

"Maerlon, shit, you scared me!" shouts a voice from the kitchen. My ex's voice.

"*K'thress?* What are you doing in my loft?" I stomp past the broken planter and into the kitchen to see the familiar silvery-blue ankite standing there in shock. They're holding a sauce-covered ladle and wearing an apron—and nothing else.

Their features shift and sharpen, and they give me a cocky smile, ignoring my incredulous stare. "I'm making you an 'I'm sorry' meal, darling. I didn't think you'd be home for another hour. It's not ready yet. But I can think of a few ways to pass the time." K'thress licks the ladle suggestively to punctuate their words.

Heart still racing from preparing to scare away an intruder, I inhale through my nose and close my eyes for a moment, trying to calm down enough to process what they just said.

When my eyes open again, K'thress sets the ladle down and moves closer, one hand undoing the ties of their apron to let it fall to the ground. They run a manicured hand down the flat plane of their chest, looking me up and down. "Speechless, I see."

I watch their hand trail lower, my pulse pounding in my ears. My body reacts to the familiar sight of their lithe form, and a hint of yearning builds deep within me.

It would be easy to go to them now. To drown myself in them, ignoring the pain I've struggled with since they left. But when I take a step closer to kiss them, I realize their lips aren't the ones I want on mine. The memory of Fina's soft lips ghosting against mine through the holo interface shakes me out of K'thress' spell.

I tear my eyes away and place a hand over my face. "You broke up with me. I've heard nothing from you in weeks." I spit out the words like I'm trying to expel the poison of their actions.

"I know. Hence the apology meal. You know I don't cook. I even brought *hreski* pie for dessert—your favorite." Their tone sounds condescending, like they shouldn't have to explain this to me. That I'm going to accept the apology and act like nothing happened. A not insignificant portion of me wants to do just that.

K'thress moves closer and pulls my hand away from my face, bringing it to their shoulder. They lean in and lick a searing stripe along my neck. I shudder, need and rage warring within me.

"You need me, Maerlon," they whisper against my skin.

The casual confidence of their words burns me. I pull away with a snarl and pick their apron up, shoving it in their direction without looking at them. "You should go." The hurt and anger welling up is threatening to explode out of me, but I keep my voice calm.

K'thress shows no similar restraint. "Are you fucking serious?" Their voice drips with vitriol.

I clench my jaw and continue to hold the apron out. A moment passes before they curse again and snatch it out of my hands. "Unbelievable. You should be grateful I'm giving you a second chance!"

That's it. I've had enough.

I meet their gaze, the flames of my anger threatening to engulf me. "Give *me* a second chance? *You're* the one who left *me*! You're the one who ripped my heart out. Took our two-year relationship and decided that I wasn't good enough for you because your family is a bunch of *fa-shar* xenophobes."

K'thress' eyes narrow, and they tilt their chin up with cool disdain. "With the way you're acting, perhaps I should have listened sooner when they told me that Y'thir seladin are worthless scavenger scum."

I flinch, the cruelty of their insult piercing into my heart like a blade.

K'thress' expression shifts from anger to shock at their own words. "Fuck...I didn't mean that."

My whole body shakes and my nails cut into my palms as I clench my fists. "Yes, you did."

"Maerlon, I—"

"Just get out," I say through gritted teeth.

K'thress shakes their head and grabs a few things from the kitchen, slipping on a jacket as they head for the door.

I don't watch as they leave. If I do, I worry that some weak part of me will ask them to stay. As soon as I hear the door close, I lock it. Then, I sink down to my knees and begin scooping the soil scattered across the floor back into the fractured pot of my kressi bloom.

Tears blur my vision as I remember K'thress' sweet smile when they gave the plant to me after our first date.

I give myself a moment to wallow in the knowledge that both the plant and my relationship are unsalvageable. Then, with a shuddering exhale, I get up, toss the mess down the recycler chute, and set my comm to block K'thress.

A PING on my comm wakes me up from a fitful nap in which I spent more time thinking about my relationship with K'thress than sleeping. Even though I blocked them, I tense, thinking they messaged me.

With a groan, I roll out of bed and grab my comm. It's a message from my manager at SimTech.

> Breks, reminder that we're closed tonight for system updates and maintenance.

Right, forgot I had tonight off. I sigh and lie back down, but I'm too tense to fall asleep. I can't just sit in my loft and endlessly replay the events from earlier, either. It's too late to vid comm Dezlon and neither my mom nor my older sister, Ulena, would know what to say if I called them. I could try seeing if any of the coworkers I'm friendly with are free, but it's been ages since we've hung out outside of work.

What did I do before I started working nights? Oh right, I spent all my time with K'thress. I wander around my apartment, trying to remember how to deal with free time.

As I pass the window, I pause, looking down at the synth gardens below. Even though they're right outside my building, I've spent barely any time in them. I should check them out while I have time. Maybe I'll bring my sketchpad—it's been years since I've drawn anything that wasn't for work. I slip my jacket back on, grab my sketching tablet, and head out the door.

A pang of homesickness hits me as I enter the gardens. The glowing synthetic plants remind me of the bioluminescent flora my mom grows in her botanical lab. According to her, they're the last surviving cuttings from the groves on Sela before the planet became uninhabitable. The sight of them reproduced here fills me with an odd, bittersweet nostalgia that's appropriate for the day I've had.

Once I find a quiet corner of the gardens, I pull out my tablet and get started. I'll have to send my mom the sketches when they're done—though I know she'll critique me for not capturing their likeness with accuracy. She doesn't quite get the concept of artistic interpretation.

My skills are rusty, but it's good to draw again. I forgot how much it helps me calm my mind. The sweet scent infused in the plants wafts in the air, and I close my eyes for a moment, inhaling deeply. I let myself melt into the process and everything else fades away—until a new scent cuts through the floral aroma.

It's a mixture of something herbal and an underlying, unique musk. The strange scent entices me, and though I try to focus back on my sketch, I'm too distracted to continue.

Intrigued, I put my sketchpad back in my jacket and take a deep breath in, trying to determine the source. It's close. I hear hurried footsteps heading in my direction—perhaps they're the scent's source.

I peek around the hedge and almost run right into something. Or rather, someone. A short, purple-haired someone who smells incredible. *Fina.*

I blink down at her in surprise, unsure of what to do. Should I pretend like I don't remember her?

Her eyes grow large and a moment later she says, "there you are!" and grabs me. Before I can register what's happening, her lips mash against mine.

I pull away from her, confused. For a moment, I panic, thinking she knows that I'm Breks. But then I see an unsavory-looking shikzeth approaching. They appear upset she's pressed against me, so I glance back down into her eyes.

She's terrified. Not of me, but of the person behind her.

I'm overwhelmed by the urge to protect her and show the shikzeth she's mine. A little voice in my head protests that she most definitely isn't mine, but baser instincts win out. I pull Fina back to me and press my lips to hers.

She gasps and I push the kiss further, letting the taste of her lips, her delicious scent, and the feel of her soft body in my arms consume all rational thought. This may be the only chance I'll have to kiss her with my own lips. I have to make it count.

# 14

## ✦MAERLON✦

When our lips finally part, Fina looks breathless. I know I'm staring down at her like a fool. That kiss...*vash-ka*. I wish it had never ended. That nothing else in the galaxy mattered except the feel of her lips against mine.

Her face is flushed a bright red, though I can't tell if it's in a good way or not. Stars, I hope it's in a good way—that she felt even a fraction of the desire that's coursing through me.

She shakes her head, as if trying to break out of a trance, and then gives me an apologetic smile. "I'm so sorry about that. Maerlon, right? Thank you so much for helping me."

She remembers my name even though we only met briefly. Either I made a bad enough impression to be memorable or she's just good with names. "It's fine. You're...Fee-la?" I say, pretending that her name isn't constantly on my mind.

She giggles. "Close! Fina."

"Ah. Fina." I nod and take a step back because she's still so close and her scent is making it hard for me to focus. I pray my jacket hides the telltale bulge in my tight pants from view.

Now that Fina's not pressed against me, I drink in the sight of her as surreptitiously as I can. She's wearing a shimmering silver dress that hugs her curves, and she's pinned up her hair, showing off her delicate neck. A strand has fallen out of her tight bun and I yearn to tuck it behind her ear like I did on the beach. Then pull her close again and kiss her until everything melts away, and she's making those soft little sighs of pleasure that make me desperate for her.

I shake the thought away and try to focus. Fina's smiling at me, but her eyes are puffy and ringed with smudged makeup. Has she been crying? My arousal vanishes, replaced with concern. Her hands are trembling, and I feel like a fool for only now realizing how terrified and upset she is.

"Are you alright?" I reach out to take her hand in mine, but she flinches at the gesture, so I pull back. She doesn't want me to touch her. Why would she? She probably had no desire to kiss me, either. I was just her only way out of a dangerous situation. I scowl at what might have happened if she hadn't run into me.

"I-I'm okay," Fina says with a nod, but her lip quivers when she tries to smile.

"No, you aren't. Stay here—I'll find that shikzeth and take care of them." My words come out in a low snarl and they surprise me as I say them. I have no clue how I'll deal with them—I've never been in a fight and am not a violent person. But I'm burning with anger at the idea of someone hurting my precious Fina.

*Esh'et*, she's not mine. What's going on with me? Do humans give off some kind of pheromone that's causing my brain to revert to a primal, possessive state? That might explain why she smells so maddeningly *perfect*.

Her forehead wrinkles, and she shakes her head in a firm no. "They're gone now. Besides, I can take care of myself."

I raise my brow at her. Fina's body looks designed for all kinds of intriguing activities, but self-defense doesn't seem like one of them.

Her lips downturn, noting my skepticism. "I may not be tall and imposing like you, but I have something to protect me."

"Of course. My apologies for doubting you." I repress a smirk at her indignant tone. I'm curious about what this "something" is, but don't want to press her or make her more upset.

Fina must see the curiosity on my face. She sighs. "I get it. My appearance practically screams, 'come harass me, I'm vulnerable'. Plus, I'm sure this ridiculous dress doesn't help."

I glance down at her dress, confused and disturbed by her insinuation. "That person was a predator. How you dress yourself or the way your body looks is never an excuse or an invitation for someone to bother or hurt you." That she thinks otherwise makes me worry about human culture.

"You're right, I just feel like..." She trails off and I wait for her to explain, but she shakes her head slightly and looks away. When she makes a sniffling sound, I realize she's crying and doesn't want me to see.

"I'm not afraid of tears." I touch her shoulder in reassurance, and she startles but doesn't flinch away this time.

"W-what?" Fina tilts her chin up toward me, but still isn't meeting my eyes as she wipes at the moisture on her cheeks.

I give her shoulder a light squeeze. "You're upset and you're crying. It's a very reasonable reaction to what you just experienced."

"Oh. I guess. Though crying makes most people uncomfortable, in my experience." She continues to wipe the tears from her face, like if she swipes at them enough they'll stop.

"Why? Emotions are meant to be felt and expressed, both the good ones and the bad."

Fina sniffs and finally meets my gaze, her eyes shining. Stars, I forgot what a mesmerizing shade they are. Her lips curl into a hint of a smile. "Shit, where were you when I needed a therapist?"

"Probably too busy crying myself." I smile at her in return.

Her eyebrows raise as she looks at my mouth with concern. *Esh'et*, I shouldn't flash my fangs at her. I close my mouth quickly.

She shakes her head, and her expression softens. "No, no, you can smile! It just surprised me. I didn't feel those at all. When we kissed, that is."

I let myself smile again, but keep it small this time, so my sharp teeth aren't as prominent. "I've had practice kissing a softer, non-seladin mouth, so I learned how to keep them out of the way." I have to suppress a frown as I remember how K'thress complained about my fangs after our first kiss.

"You have an alien partner?" She claps a hand over her mouth, her expression mortified. "Now I feel even more like a jerk for kissing you. You're not even single!"

"What? No. It's fine. I did, but they broke up with me a few weeks back." I rub a hand along the shaved side of my head, uncomfortable talking about my ex with the woman I'm secretly infatuated with.

"God, I'm so sorry! I should just be quiet and leave you alone. I keep sticking my foot in my mouth."

My lip quirks at the strange human idiom. "I don't know about your foot, but my tongue definitely was in there."

Her skin flushes the color of kressi blooms, but a moment later she laughs. "It sure was. That was a very convincing fake kiss."

That's because nothing about it was fake to me. Not that I can tell her that. "It wasn't too much, was it? I may have gotten too immersed in the role of possessive boyfriend."

"N-no, it was perfect."

I'd love to think that she means it was a perfect kiss. It was perfect for me. But it's much more likely she means it was a perfect ruse.

"Since I've already taken on the role, is there anything else you need from your fake partner?"

For some reason, this makes her turn an even deeper shade of red. I catch her giving me a quick look up and down before she looks away. Did I embarrass her?

We're both quiet for a moment and a million things run through my head.

*Offer to walk her somewhere safer.*

*Show her around the gardens.*

*Ask her to kiss you again.*

"Do you live around here?" she says, breaking the silence.

The question catches me off guard. "Yes, my loft is in a building right next to these gardens. Why do you ask?"

"I...well..." She stops, takes a deep breath, and mutters something to herself that sounds like "brave babe" and then looks at me with fierce determination. "Can we go back to your place?"

I rub my ear, thinking my translator malfunctioned. There's no way she just asked if I'd invite her up. Am I dreaming?

"For tea! Or whatever the seladin equivalent is. It's just...I'm having a difficult time making any friends since I moved here and you've been so kind and I know Mezli likes you and—you know what, forget I asked!" The words spill out of her with barely any space for her to breathe.

Hopeless affection flutters in my chest. Stars, she's adorable.

"Yes. I would like that." It stings to confirm that she's only interested in friendship, but I'll gladly accept it.

Fina's eyes light up. "Really? Thank you, Maerlon!"

I smile back, basking in the glow of her excitement. "One condition, though. No more surprise kisses."

She laughs, and the sound fills me with heartaching warmth. "You've got a deal."

# 15

## ✦FINA✦

Brave, badass babes put themselves out there and make friends. Brave, badass babes don't let fear keep them from living. Brave, badass babes invite themselves to a sexy alien's apartment. I repeat my ridiculous affirmations in my mind to keep from freaking out.

It's not helping—what the hell am I doing?

God, please don't let him be a murderer. I don't think Mezli would be friends with a murderer, but she has questionable tastes sometimes so...

No, calm down. He's not a murderer. He helped protect you and has been nothing but kind. A little gruff, but that could be his normal tone of voice. That deep, rough growl of a voice that makes me shiver.

"This is my place." Maerlon's raspy voice cuts through my thoughts.

I startle and realize that I've walked past where he's stopped. I turn around and scurry back to him, hoping he didn't notice how distracted I am. He scans a keycard, pushes a door open, and gestures for me to enter.

This would be the perfect time for him to attack. While my back is turned and he's blocking my exit. I hesitate and he looks perplexed, but goes in ahead of me. I let out the breath I'm holding and follow him inside.

Maerlon's apartment is not at all what I was expecting. For someone who I've only seen dressed in black and whose appearance exudes dark, intense energy, it's *vibrant*. Exotic, colorful plants and abstract paintings decorate much of the open loft. Large windows overlook the synthetic gardens below. Everything is clean and orderly, but his decor infuses the space with life. It puts my bland, messy apartment to shame.

He closes the door and locks it behind us.

"Now I'm trapped with you," I say, joking. At least I hope I'm joking.

He scoffs at me, his breath coming out in a huff. "If anyone should be worried, it's me. You're the one that attacked me with a kiss and then invited yourself up. For all I know, you're some serial killer who preys on the kindness of gullible aliens."

"Shit, am I that obvious?" The tight coil of nerves in the pit of my stomach eases somewhat.

He laughs, the sound of it low and rumbling. "I'll just have to keep an eye on you." He flashes a sharp-toothed smile that gives me goosebumps, then gestures toward a sitting area, where there's a curved, armless sofa and a small faux fireplace set into the wall. "Make yourself comfortable. I'll get us some tea."

I nod. "Thanks!" I take a seat on the couch as he heads into the kitchen and I hear him punching a code into his food synthesizer.

What seems like an eternity passes as he makes the tea. In an attempt to appear casual, I open up my comm and decide to send Mezli a message to let her know where I am. Just in case my potential murder needs to be avenged.

I bring up our chat and the photorealistic drawing of an enormous, erect penis with glowing markings pops up. *Oh god.*

There's a choked sound behind me, followed by a hiss of pain. I whip around to see Maerlon standing there with hot tea soaking into his shirt. I scramble to close the chat and hide the image, but he *definitely* saw it. "It's not what it looks like! Are you okay?"

"I'm fine." He pulls the wet fabric away from his chest with a wince, then raises his dotted brow at me as he hands me my cup. "Dare I ask?"

My entire face feels like it's on fire. First, I assault him with a kiss. Then, I invite myself back to his place. And now he finds me looking at an image of a seladin dick. God, I must seem like some deranged human pervert. "I was going to message Mezli to let her know my date was a bust and that I'd run into you. I forgot she'd sent me *that.*"

"Right." Maerlon's glowing eyes narrow.

"I swear I'm not a pervert! I didn't believe her when she mentioned seladin were so uh, well-endowed." I take a sip from my cup and glance away, wanting to die from embarrassment.

"Is that considered large to a human?"

I almost choke on my tea. He gives me an inquisitive stare with his strange, lamp-like eyes and I flounder, unable to formulate a response. A moment later, his lips curve and I realize he's teasing me. "That sounds like Mezli," he says with a wry smirk. "Go ahead and send your message. I need to change this." He gestures down to the tea soaking into the front of his shirt.

"Oh gosh, of course." I wait for him to walk away before opening my comm back up. I quickly hide the image, then write out a message to Mezli.

"You said something about a bad date?" Maerlon calls out. I glance up just in time to see him stripping off his wet shirt on the other side of the loft. He's facing away, allowing me to drink in the sight.

He is *beautiful*.

Dim glowing marks dot down each side of his spine and along the back of his arms, contrasting against his deep slate-gray skin. His lean, muscled torso is longer and more tapered at the waist and hips than a human, giving him an angular appearance. He bends over to pull a shirt out of a dresser, and I admire the tight curve of his ass.

When I realize I'm blatantly ogling him, I yank my eyes away and back to the teacup in my hands. I wanted to befriend him, not perv on him.

"Yeah, Mezli had me sign up for that dating app, Syzygy. Against my better judgment, I agreed to meet with a guy, but he bailed as soon as he saw me. Guess the reality of me didn't match up with my profile." I keep my tone light, but it hurts to admit to this handsome alien how undesirable I am.

"*Vash-ka*, what an idiot. Dating apps are horrible. I was lucky to avoid them for so long," Maerlon says as he joins me again, sitting on the other end of the sofa.

"Right, you mentioned you had a partner until recently. If you don't mind me asking, how long were you together?"

He tenses, the fingers resting on his legs digging in slightly.

Shit, what's wrong with me? That's way too personal of a question to ask someone I barely know.

He runs a hand across the shaved side of his head, looking away. "Two years." The sharp, talon-like nails on his other hand dig even further into the fabric of his pants.

"I'm so sorry," I say, unsure of how else to respond. It's obviously painful for him to talk about.

"It's funny. I was just getting over them, but then they showed up here earlier today and told me we were getting back together. They barely apologized for leaving me. Acted like I'd be okay pretending that nothing ever happened. I told them no, and in response, they called me Y'thir trash."

He pauses to take in a shuddering breath, the wound from the insult still fresh. He continues, his voice softer now. "I don't want to be with them, but it still hurts knowing that I cared for someone who never even respected me."

My chest aches at his pain and the vulnerability he just shared with me. "Shit, I'm sitting here complaining about being rejected by someone I've never met, and you're dealing with real heartbreak. I don't know what that insult means, but no one deserves cruelty. Especially not from someone who supposedly cares about them." I reach a hand over and place it on his, realizing that he's shaking slightly when I touch his warm skin.

He stares down at my hand for a second, looking startled. I worry that I've made some cultural faux pas by touching him, but he doesn't move his hand away.

Maerlon huffs out a heavy breath before speaking. "Y'thir is part of my name. Or you could call it a designation. Seladin surnames reflect our role in society. As the second child, I'm Y'thir—the designation for those who leave the colony ships and Sela II to learn from other cultures and provide for their families. Y'thir who don't have a skilled trade often end up as scavengers or even pirates, so some species think the designation denotes a lack of societal value."

I squeeze his hand. "Thank you for explaining. I'm sorry for being so ignorant. Excuse me for saying this, but it sounds like your ex was the trash, not you."

He snorts, looking back up at me as amusement creeps onto his face. "I suppose you're right." He turns his hand over and clasps mine gently. "Thank you, Fina." His voice is gentle, reminding me of someone else.

Before I can think of who, both of our comms ping. We quickly release our hands like we were caught doing something naughty and I check my comm.

> Mezli: You're with Maerlon?! Ask him to show you the goods, he'll back me up!!

Maerlon lets out a small amused sound next to me, then looks up from reading his comm. "Mezli message you too?"

"Yeah, nothing important though." My face heats thinking about what she told me to do.

His brow scrunches and his eyes glow brighter. "She didn't tell you to examine me more thoroughly?"

"N-no! Why, what did she tell you?" I blink back at him, trying to keep my cool. I can imagine what Mezli messaged him.

"Hmm. Her message told me to show you my cock. I thought it was a strange request, but I don't want to be rude if this is a human custom." His voice pitches low, sending a surge of excitement through me.

"It's not—I'm sure it's very nice, but I don't...is it hot in here?"

"You should see your face." He grins at me, and this time I'm not as alarmed by the sight of his sharp fangs.

"Ugh, you're almost as bad as Mezli!" I cross my arms and shake my head at him, wishing that I had something cool to drink instead of the hot tea. I'm so overheated, I might combust.

"I think you like it." His luminous eyes shine with amusement and a hint of something else I can't quite place.

My whole body tingles as he looks at me. I think I more than like it.

# 16

## ✦ MAERLON ✦

When Fina leaves, I'm tempted to pull her into my arms and kiss her. Obviously, that's not something a new friend does, so I wave goodbye instead and close the door to keep from staring as she walks away. I offered to escort her back to the transit station, but she insisted that she'd be fine, so I didn't press her on it.

Sitting next to her on the couch, close enough to touch and breathe in her scent, was an exquisite form of torture. Fina up close was even better than in the sim. The way her eyes sparkle in amusement at a joke. The expressive little wrinkles on her brow when I said something surprising. Stars, the little groan of pleasure she made when she bit into a slice of *hreski* pie, her pink tongue darting out to lick a crumb from her lips.

*Vash-ka*, everything about her entrances me. Especially the tiny pigmented dots on her pale creamy skin that don't just adorn her face, but scatter across her chest and arms as well. I wanted to peel off her dress to reveal what other parts of her they decorate. By the end of our conversation, I could barely focus, distracted by each tiny new detail I'd discovered.

Of course, Fina was friendly, and in no way indicated that she felt the same attraction. At least she didn't seem too frightened of my appearance by the time she left. That's better than nothing, I suppose.

I sink back onto the couch and her scent hits me again, pulling a groan from me as my relentlessly hard cock twitches, begging for some kind of relief. Closing my eyes and letting her scent take over my senses, I pull it out, sighing as it's freed from the confines of my pants.

I wonder what Fina would've done if I'd been serious about my offer to show this to her. Would her plump pink lips have parted in shock seeing me so ready for her? Would she turn that lovely red shade of embarrassment and arousal as she watched me take my cock in hand?

A bead of moisture leaks from the tip and I slick it down my shaft, imagining Fina watching me as I do it, licking her lips at the sight. I give my cock a hard squeeze and moan as I imagine locking eyes with her, stroking myself leisurely and reveling in her reactions. She'd squirm under my gaze and the overpowering scent of her arousal would flood my senses, letting me know she's just as turned on as I am.

I imagine sliding a hand up under her dress and the shuddering gasp she'd make as I touch her. My movements speed up, until I'm pumping my cock in quick, brutal strokes, twisting as I get to the head. In my fantasy, Fina cries out as I caress her hot, slick cunt over and over until she grabs my wrist and moans my name as she comes.

My orgasm slams into me and thick jets of my seed splatter across my stomach. I shudder with the force of it and there's another spasm as I think about how Fina would react to the sight.

*Fa-shar*, it'd probably disgust her. Just like it'd disgust her that I jerked off thinking about her. Shame creeps up my spine.

I want to spend more time with Fina, but I can barely have one conversation with her before I'm about to come in my pants. It's not fair to her to pretend like I'm okay with just friendship and then fantasize about what she looks like naked. How will I become her friend if I can't control these desires?

I should distance myself now rather than let a friendship develop further. She's already had enough lecherous aliens behaving atrociously toward her. I don't need to add myself to that list.

My heart sinks at the thought of hurting her feelings, though. I can tell she's lonely, despite the positive front she puts up. I've been where she is—alone and surrounded by unfamiliar species. It's overwhelming. Surely I can learn how to control my cock and be the friend I would've wanted.

No more of this. I chastise myself as I grimace at the sticky mess coating my abdomen.

## ✦FINA✦

By the time I return to my apartment, I'm dragging. I kick off my boots and strip off my dress, wrinkling my nose as I lift my arms and get a whiff of myself.

Oh jeez, did I smell that bad when I was hanging out with Maerlon? Now that I think about it, he flared his nostrils a few times, but I thought it was just part of his facial expressions. Shit, that's mortifying. I hope seladin don't have an enhanced sense of smell.

Part of me wants to message him and apologize for my stench. But that might make things even more awkward.

Other than unfortunate odors, tonight turned out surprisingly okay, even after the date ditcher and my brush with that plant pervert. Something was looking out for me when it put Maerlon in my path. Otherwise, I would have ended up in jail for using a banned chem in self-defense. Instead, I made a friend. Or at least I think I did. I worry that if I think about it too much, I'll ruin the friendship before it goes anywhere.

Maerlon is not at all what I imagined after our brief first meeting. Sure, he's still stiff in his mannerisms. But he has a surprising sense of humor beneath that dark, brooding exterior.

Not that I mind his exterior at all. The more I see his angular face and glowing eyes, the more intrigued I am. Even his fangs are kind of charming when he allows himself to smile. They also make me think about what it would feel like for him to run them against my neck. Or along my inner thigh.

Definitely not a thought I should have about a new friend. Still, there's a squeeze of arousal deep inside me when I remember how his long, nimble tongue tangled with mine. He claimed my mouth with fierce possessiveness and heat. If it had lasted longer, I would have melted into a puddle on the spot.

No one's ever kissed me like that before. Well, no one but Breks, but that wasn't real, was it? Damn, neither was the kiss with Maerlon. It was just to protect me from that weird shikzeth.

I peel off my tights and groan at how slick I am between my

thighs. Just thinking about those kisses turns me on. I'm a mess—horny for unavailable, uninterested aliens.

When I slip off the rest of my clothes, a crumb from the incredible, tart fruit pie Maerlon offered me tumbles out of my bra. I should have asked him for the recipe. That'd be a good excuse to talk to him again. Better than asking him for a repeat performance of his scorching kiss.

I let my hair down and get into the shower for the second time today. Warm water pours over me and I massage my scalp. It's sore and tight from having my hair pinned up all evening. I frown, thinking about how I wore it up for the idiot who bailed on our date. So much for nexxit liking necks. I guess my neck wasn't sexy enough. My hand runs across my neck and I laugh at the absurdity of caring what an alien thinks about my neck.

I'm attractive enough by human standards, though some might think I'm too fat or too pale. But, I've always liked the way I look. Plenty of humans have no problem with chubby, ghostly pale women like me. But aliens? For all I know, I'm a pasty, fleshy abomination to them. I've tried to keep the policy of "ignorance is bliss" when considering the nuances of different species' beauty standards. It's impossible to be appealing to everyone.

Now that I've experienced an attraction to certain aliens, though, I wonder if I'm repulsive in their eyes. Or ears. Or noses. I cringe again, imagining Maerlon smelling my sweat the whole time we were sitting together and needing to fight off the urge to gag. Poor guy is probably running the air purifiers in his loft at full blast after me stinking up the place.

I scrub at my skin, continuing to consider myself. With each pass of my hands along my body, I wonder what other species would think about it. Are my breasts too large and prominent for the lithe, slender ankites? Am I too soft and short for a massive, muscular vuloi? Is my pale skin sickly looking to a dusky seladin? Does my lack of horns and plating make me appear weak to a shikzeth?

The list of differences and questions goes on and on. I have to shake myself out of that unhelpful thought spiral. I can't be everyone's cup of tea.

Why do I care so much about this? I didn't come to Spire to screw around with aliens. Well, at least that's not the *only* reason I came here. I'd be lying if part of the new life I imagined didn't involve romance. That fantasy is becoming more and more appealing now that I've met Breks and Maerlon.

At least with Maerlon, I could research seladin culture to see if there's any chance he'd find me attractive. His stony gaze makes that seem unlikely, but some of the things we talked about tonight made me wonder.

Breks, however...I don't even know what kind of alien he is. Though, it's clear he felt some attraction toward me. I could try to figure out what species he is by looking into which of my features appeal to aliens. That might be more productive and less harmful to my self-esteem than stressing about what parts of me aren't desirable.

Or, I could stop obsessing over aliens like a sex-starved maniac and go to bed before I pass out from exhaustion in the shower.

I drag myself out of the shower and get ready for bed, but when I lie down, my brain won't shut off. My mind won't let me rest—it just keeps spiraling with thoughts of alien attractions.

I rub my tired eyes and pull out my datapad. Guess I'm not getting any sleep tonight.

# 17

## ✦ FINA ✦

My food synthesizer pours an enormous, extra-caffeinated coffee as I frown down at my datapad. Crumbs from my decimated batch of cookies lay scattered across the table. After staying awake through the early hours of the day cycle, feverishly researching alien aesthetics, I have a haphazard list of my appealing features.

Part way into my "research", I focused on Breks. Thinking about what aliens might find me attractive was better than seeing how disappointing my appearance would be to others. Such as a seladin like Maerlon. Who I still shouldn't even factor in since he's my friend and I'm only setting myself up for disappointment by crushing on someone so far out of my league.

Even narrowing things down, I didn't come up with much. I'd

already eliminated ankite and seladin from my list of species that Breks might be. He'd mentioned that his homeworld had twin suns, but I couldn't find any homeworlds from the remaining Xi Consortium races that are in dual star systems. Either that fact was a fabrication or I misheard him.

So—hours later—all I have to work with is that my fuller figure might be attractive to vuloi, delicate facial features and large eyes are appealing to aespians, and nexxit appreciate the pitch and resonance of human voices. None of my physical features seem like something a shikzeth would appreciate, but they base a lot on scent. That rules them out for Breks, since I doubt holos have olfactory input.

I impatiently take a sip of my hot coffee, desperate for the caffeine, and wince as it burns my tongue. Even with this whole cup, I won't be up to doing much today. Damn my ridiculous crush and my brain for hyper-focusing on this absurd sleuthing with no regard for sleep.

My comm buzzes multiple times, and of course, it's Mezli. Shit, I forgot to message her after I got home last night.

> Mezli: I'm assuming you didn't message me because you saw that alien dick and couldn't resist hopping on it. And not that you're dead. Oh goddess, please don't be dead.

> Mezli: If Fina is dead and this is being read by her family, I'm sorry about all the dick jokes.

> Mezli: If this is her killer, I WILL FIND YOU AND MAKE YOU PAY.

I almost snort my coffee up my nose. God, I love her. Better send a reply before she starts her vengeance plot in full.

> Fina: Sorry, I was so tired when I got home and I forgot to message. Not because I saw or did anything with an alien dick! I think I might be friends with Maerlon now, I'm not sure.
>
> Fina: You know him, would he lie about that just to be polite? Also, do seladin care about smells a lot?
>
> Fina: I'm rambling, didn't get much sleep. Again NOT because of alien dick. But not dead. Unless I'm a ghost and am trapped here waiting for you to avenge my murder...

A minute goes by and then I receive a vid comm notification from Mezli. I open it up and an image of her expands in the air. She's got her hair up in a towel and is wearing a silky white robe. In the background, there's an olive green vuloi in her kitchen, cooking something and whistling to himself.

"Hey Fina! Glad you're alive." Mezli gives me her usual cheery grin and then peers at her vid screen as if she's examining my surroundings. "Damn, I was hoping you were lying, and I'd catch you in Maerlon's loft."

"Looks like you got enough action for the both of us." I gesture to the hulking dude making breakfast behind her.

She lets out a delighted giggle. "Right, because vuloi have two dicks!"

"I didn't mean it literally!" I say, sputtering. "Wait, are you serious?" I glance back at the behemoth holding a spatula.

"I can ask Grespran to show you."

"I'm good, thanks."

"In all seriousness, he's a sweetie. We didn't actually do anything but cuddle." Mezli looks back at Grespran with a dreamy smile.

"Oh, well, that sounds nice." And damn, it really does. I've been touch starved since arriving on Spire, so I'm more jealous of her getting lots of cuddling than I would be about getting laid.

Mezli leans toward the vid screen. "So what's this about you and Maerlon being friends? And seladin smelling things?"

"Oh, right. He was very nice and said he'd like to be friends, but he's kinda hard to read. Also, I forgot to put deodorant on last night and I'm worried I was ripe and grossed him out."

Mezli's lip curves in amusement. "If he didn't want to hang out with you, he wouldn't. Maerlon is blunt and doesn't care much about offending people if he doesn't like them. So if he talked to you and said he wanted to be friends, he does! That's one of the reasons I like him. As for your stinky ass, seladin have heightened senses of smell compared to you or me. But even if you smelled bad, I don't think he'd be rude about it. He may have tried to help freshen things up subtly if the scent was offensive. Did he light any candles or blow a fan toward you away from him?"

"No. Okay, good. That's a relief." Nice to know that I wasn't repulsive when trying to make my first new friend on Spire.

Grespran calls out something in a rumbling voice and Mezli blows him a kiss. "Looks like breakfast is ready! I'll talk to you later. Let's grab dinner tonight."

A LONG NAP and a few more jumbo cups of coffee later, I'm sitting in the space station equivalent of a mess hall while Mezli flits from vendor to vendor, choosing an array of alien dishes for me to sample. Conversations bounce off the walls of the food hall, creating a constant roar of noise that batters my sleep-deprived senses. At least it's not a nightclub for a change—I'm thankful I didn't have to squeeze myself into a skimpy outfit again.

Mezli weaves her way to the spot I claimed at a long, narrow table, precariously balancing an overloaded tray of food in each hand. She plops the trays down and then collapses onto the stool across from me, wiping her brow.

"Wow, you must be hungry," I say, looking down at enough food to feed at least four people.

"Not particularly."

"Then why so much food? There's no way I can eat even half of that."

"It's not just for you." Her tone is dismissive as she slides me a toxic-green carbonated drink.

My brow scrunches in confusion at her. If it's not all for me and Mezli, then—

"Jezrit! Maerlon!" Mezli bounces off of her stool and waves to something behind me with all four hands. "Perfect timing! I just got back with the food."

Looks like she invited more people to dinner. Great. She could have at least warned me.

I turn over my shoulder and come face-to-face with Maerlon. Or rather, face-to-crotch, since I'm still sitting. I rip my eyes away so I'm not staring and he slides in to sit on the stool next to me.

When I compose myself enough to look at him, he nods at me. "Fina." Just the sound of my name in his deep, gravelly voice makes my face tingle with warmth.

Across the table, Mezli sits back down and a lanky aespian with a minty green carapace and gigantic eyes takes the stool beside her. Their small antennae twitch as they stare at me. "Mezli didn't mention that we'd be dining with a human. How novel," they say in an oscillating vocal tone most aespians have.

"I didn't? Well, Jezrit, this is my best friend, Fina. Try not to let her human beauty dazzle you too much." She gives them a wink.

"Fina, this is Jezrit. He works at CiaXera, in the design department with Maerlon."

"Is that a concern? Can humans blind others through visual stimuli?" Jezrit's eyes grow even wider and he leans forward toward me, almost knocking over a steaming bowl of soup in front of him. Maerlon makes a low grunt of amusement, and Mezli lets out a peal of laughter.

"Uh, not that I'm aware of. Nice to meet you, Jezrit," I say, trying not to shy away from his intense stare.

"Nah, I just meant that she's gorgeous and you shouldn't forget about me just because she's here." Mezli places a hand on Jezrit's shoulder and sticks her tongue out.

The answer seems to satisfy him, and he leans back. His eyes flutter between Mezli's hand and her face in mild confusion, but she keeps her hand on him and gives him a flirty smile.

"What about pheromones?" Maerlon asks. He looks at me, then at Mezli.

"What about them?" Mezli's eyes light up and she grins that evil way she does when she's about to tease me mercilessly.

I glare daggers at her, worried about where this conversation is heading.

"Humans don't have visual hypnosis capabilities, but do they emit mind-altering pheromones?" Maerlon asks again. His eyes bore into me and his nostrils flare.

Oh god, is he referring to my sweaty smell last night?

"Excellent question! Do they?" Jezrit sniffs in my direction.

"N-no! I don't have any form of mind control. Please stop sniffing me." This is by far the weirdest conversation I've had with aliens.

"A pity. That would be useful." Jezrit gives me an apologetic look, though I think that has more to do with my lack of psychic influences and less with the weird questions and sniffing.

In an attempt to appear unfazed by this bizarre discussion, I grab something from the smorgasbord of unfamiliar food and take a bite of a beige dish that looks like potatoes. My mouth instantly feels like it's on fire and I choke it down, barely able to keep from spitting it out. Sweat beads on my brow and I chug the strange carbonated goo to fight off the flames engulfing my face.

"I've never seen anyone but a shikzeth eat *skrllpt* on its own. It is very hot," Jezrit says.

Mezli giggles and looks at me with sympathy. "Ouch, yeah. Maybe let me explain what something is before chowing down."

Maerlon taps my arm and slides a slimy dough ball over to me. "This should help. Chew it slowly though, it's made by those of us who have sharper teeth," he says in a murmur that makes it feel like I'm alone with him instead of in a crowded cafeteria. He flashes his fangs in a sharp smile to punctuate his suggestion.

My stomach flutters at the sight. If he's trying to cool me down, that isn't helping.

I gingerly put the dough ball in my mouth. It has an odd consistency and wants to stick to my teeth. But the flavor is sweet and slightly earthy and it soothes my poor burned tongue as I chew. He watches my mouth intently, which is glued shut by the dough, so I give him a thankful nod instead of saying anything.

After my initial disastrous foray into alien cuisine and my dining companions' curiosity about humans, the meal becomes more enjoyable. Mezli flirts with Jezrit, who seems oblivious to her advances, taking her words literally despite them dripping with innuendo. I wonder if that's an aespian thing or a Jezrit thing.

Maerlon is quiet, apart from laughing occasionally at Mezli's jokes or steering my food choices. Despite our physical differences, seladin and humans must have similar palettes. Every time I show enjoyment of a dish he suggests, he gives the slightest hint of a smile, just the edge of his lip curling up. It's so charming that I play up my reactions just to see it again. But when I involuntarily moan as I bite into a delicious spiced pastry, his nose flares and he looks away. After that, I get no more recommendations. Guess he's not a fan of hearing me make that kind of sound.

When we finish the meal, Mezli suggests we go bar-hopping. Maerlon mutters something about already having plans and leaves with a stiff "goodbye". I wish he could have stayed.

The rest of us wander through Sagittarius district's walkways for over an hour until Mezli decides what bar to visit. She's obviously interested in Jezrit and spends most of that time chatting with him. Not wanting to be a third wheel, I make an excuse about being tired and let them go off without me.

It's getting late into the night cycle already and I should go home, but all the caffeine I had earlier has kicked in. I'm so wired I'll bounce off the walls of my apartment and spiral back into obsessive scrolling on my datapad.

My mind goes to Breks and the "research" I did last night. That damn mysterious alien occupies my thoughts far too much. I should go to SimTech tonight. He asked if I'd come back and trying to push him out of my mind didn't work. I could see if he's working and...

And what? Try to seduce him? Beg him to show me his true self? I already know how he'll respond to that—words haven't convinced him I won't go screaming in terror.

Despite those thoughts, my feet carry me past glowing neon holo-ads and tipsy club-goers as I head toward SimTech. By the time I get there, I know what to do.

If Breks won't believe my words, what if I *show* him I'm attracted to aliens other than ankites?

# 18

## ✦MAERLON✦

"Your simulation time has expired. You need to authorize the credits to extend your session, or dress and leave." I can barely keep my exasperation out of my voice. A nude vuloi scowls toward the source of the room's audio comms, her thick arms crossed against her muscular chest. It's times like this that I'm glad I don't have to interact with customers in person.

"I'm not done yet! I was just getting started!". She bares her sharp teeth.

"As I said, I'll be happy to extend your session if you provide the needed credits."

The entrance motion sensor beeps. *Esh'et*, this isn't the time to deal with a truculent customer. I flip over to the holo-receptionist's visual feed to see the line of customers waiting to check in has increased.

"I already gave you too many credits. Get me your manager!" the vuloi screams, pulling my attention back to her.

"I *am* the manager. I've filed your complaint," I lie. She doesn't need to know SimTech is too cheap to hire more than one tech for late night cycle shifts. I flag the customer in our system, banning her from using our services in the future.

The vuloi shouts something my translator doesn't pick up and kicks the blank wall of the suite.

Enough of this nonsense. "Any damage to the suite will get automatically charged to your credit tab. Would you like me to call station security to escort you out?"

She grumbles a string of profanities, but dresses and storms out of the suite. Who knew that interrupting a vuloi mid-meditation sim would be such a volatile situation? I almost feel bad. She seems like she needs the practice.

As cleaning and repair bots reset that suite, I'm finally able to address the line. It's busy tonight, though I haven't figured out why suddenly everyone needs a late-night sim. Maybe SimTech is running some new holo-ads.

I pop into the holo-receptionist and apologize to the customers. A pair of ankites book a suite together, then turn to have a brief conversation with the people in line behind them—a nexxit and a customer I can't see from the holo-receptionist's spot at the desk. I overhear something about "looking for a third" and I'm surprised when the nexxit agrees and says, "I have four hands, so I should put them to use." It's way too much information, but I've seen far weirder—the late night cycle attracts a certain crowd.

I check them into their simulation, set it to run, and then go back to the holo-receptionist as quickly as possible, praying that the line hasn't grown again.

"Busy night?" asks a familiar voice. My gorgeous human obsession stands in front of the desk, her hands clasped together behind her back.

"Fina?" I startle and blink a few times to make sure my visual input isn't deceiving me.

"Good, you're Breks! I was worried it wouldn't be you."

"Oh? Did you miss me?" I attempt to wink like I've seen Mezli do when she's being playful.

She laughs and shifts her weight onto one leg, placing a hand on her hip. The stance accentuates the beautiful curves of her body. "It's been a while, hasn't it? Took me a bit to decide if I wanted to come back." She worries her lower lip with her teeth.

I lean forward and the holo-receptionist follows my movement. "I'm certainly glad that you did," I say, giving her what I hope is a seductive smile. It's easier to do as the holo-receptionist, who doesn't have a mouth full of sharp fangs. Excitement fills me when I see that adorable red tinge rise in her cheeks at my words. "Come on back."

The path to an empty suite illuminates on the floor, but she doesn't move. "Aren't you forgetting something?"

"You need more warming up before I get you alone?" I'm feeling bold tonight and can't help pushing the flirting further.

She laughs and shakes her head, then reaches into a hip pouch and pulls out her credit tab.

Right, she has to pay. I should pay *her* for the pleasure of interacting with her like this. I scan the tab and charge her for the cheapest sim type we have—I have hours of unused comped simulations I get for working here that can cover the rest of her sim.

Fina heads back to her suite, and doesn't startle this time as the door closes behind her. I check on the other running sims, then switch my audio over to her suite.

"So, what kind of simulation would you like tonight?"

"I have an idea, but may I ask you a question first?"

"Of course, anything."

"Anything?" Fina perks up at my reply.

"I didn't say I would answer."

She rolls her eyes at my stupid joke. "Can your holo-interface appear like anything other than that ankite?"

I'm intrigued by her question, though I hope she won't ask me to appear as myself again. She's seen the real me and is not interested. "I should be able to shift the interface to most of the pre-programmed holos we have in our sims. The physical differences between myself and the holo might cause some weirdness, but it should work. Why? Do you not like my normal look?" If she doesn't like the handsome ankite, there's zero chance she'd like me as I truly am.

"No, that's not it! I just want to try something new. If you're free to join me."

I shouldn't. But all suites are booked for the evening and those simulations are running smoothly. They won't miss me hovering over them. I can always pop out of Fina's sim if there's an issue. "I'm intrigued. Yes, I can join you."

Fina looks somewhat surprised. "Right, okay. I wasn't expecting you to agree without asking what I want to do."

"What do you want to do, Fina?" My voice comes out huskier than I intended.

She thinks for a moment, looking down at her hands. "Hmm. Are there any hot springs simulations?"

Immediately I imagine her floating in steamy water, completely naked, and my mouth goes dry. "Wanting to make things...steamier?"

She chuckles and nods. "You could say that."

I find the code for a hot springs sim that doesn't have any other holo interactions, so the program won't interrupt us by trying to seduce her. That's *my* job.

*Vash-ka*, is this really happening? I set the program to run and then activate my holo in her suite. When I appear, she's looking around at the new environment with amazement. I'll admit, it's a stunning view. And not just because she's there. There's a large natural pool of steaming, purple-pink water set in a cave that looks like it's made from pure crystal.

Fina walks toward the edge of the pool and dips a toe in. "Wow! This is better than I could have imagined. Is this from your homeworld too?"

I shouldn't have mentioned that last time. "No, I'm not sure where this is. If it isn't just a complete fabrication."

I move to join her at the water's edge, but she shakes her head at me. "I'd like you to be something else."

"Ah, right. Any preference other than 'not an ankite'?" I still don't understand why she wants me to switch to something else. What if she asks me to be a seladin? Then it'd be impossible to conceal my identity from her.

Not that I want to. I'd love for her to see that I'm Maerlon and pull me into another passionate kiss like the other night. But she won't say seladin. She's not attracted to me when I look like myself.

"Hmm, I'm not sure...guess I should do this alphabetically?" she mumbles. "Let's go with an aespian." Fina shrugs, as if she's uncertain in her decision.

Now I'm even more confused. An aespian?

I miss seeing her getting into the water as I search for an

aespian holo I can use. Probably for the best. I'm already too aroused at even the thought of her naked.

My holo shimmers as it shifts to a lanky, dusky purple aespian with iridescent wings and prominent antennae. I won't be able to do anything to control the wings, but I think they're vestigial, anyway. The aespian is already nude—it's from a pleasure sim and they didn't bother to program any clothing for it. I bring my hands down to cover my groin and realize that there's nothing exposed, so I shift my hands to my hips instead.

Fina blinks up curiously at my new form and I slide into the water before I get too nervous about her staring at me. She continues to study me, then gives me a shy smile. "Sorry, just adjusting. You look...nice."

I glance down at my carapace and shrug. "Thanks?"

She wades closer to me. I swallow hard, seeing more of her body through the water, the top of her full breasts peeking above the surface. I reach down to adjust my hardening cock in my pants and realize with curiosity that the holo's penis is sliding out of the protective plating at its groin.

Fina presses a hand against the rigid chest of my holo, her body just a few inches from mine. "I think this could work," she says, gazing into the holo's eyes.

My mind flashes back to dinner and her interactions with Jezrit. Is she using this to explore a burgeoning attraction to him? The thought makes me want to tear his inquisitive, oblivious throat out. But then Fina presses her body against mine and all thoughts of Jezrit vanish. If this is how she wants me, I'll make it work. Better here with me than with Jezrit.

I return her heated gaze and press her closer. "So, now what?"

# 19

## ✦FINA✦

Hearing Brek's raspy voice coming from the aespian looking at me is off-putting, but the familiar way he holds himself reassures me. He wraps his arms around me and my breasts press more firmly against his wet skin—or rather, his carapace. It's an odd sensation, but not unpleasant. Not the best type of alien for cuddling, but I could get used to it.

As he holds me tight, I realize that the hands resting on my back have only three fingers. I gaze into the holo's huge, dark eyes and before I can psych myself out, I press my lips against his lipless mouth.

He groans and parts his mouth, eagerly allowing my tongue to dart inside. His tongue is much thinner and pebbled in this form and I startle a bit when it plunges in to claim my mouth in return. It's odd. But not odd enough to stop, because I know Breks is the one kissing me.

His hands grasp me, fingertips digging into my hips as if he's desperate to keep me anchored against him. I rub against his smooth body under the water and he slides a leg between mine. I grind against it without thinking, letting out a small moan. It's a little embarrassing that I just tried to ride his leg and I pull back, but he makes a low sound in his throat and holds me in place. He moves his mouth to nip at my throat and runs his textured tongue along my sensitive skin. I rock against his leg again, my whole body tensing with need.

"Breks, I..." I whisper as he trails his mouth down to kiss the top of my breast.

"*Fina,*" he rumbles against my skin, sounding just as needy as I am.

I pull him back up into a rough kiss and he slides one hand down to grab my ass and the other to cup my breast. He caresses me, sliding a thumb against my nipple until it stiffens and I gasp.

Our lips part and we gaze at each other, both breathless. He keeps playing with my nipple, making me want to rub myself against him again.

He looks down at me reverently. "Stars, you are so beautiful. I wish I could truly feel how soft you are in my hands."

*You could,* I want to insist. *I want you here.* But I don't, because I know how well that turned out last time. "Me too."

A long moment passes and I worry that even saying that ruined the moment. But then he speaks again. "I want to touch you, even like this."

"Isn't that what you're already doing?"

He shakes his head and then spins me around in the water, pressing my back up against his chest. "No, Fina. I want to *touch* you."

Breks slides his hand further under the water until it rests between my legs. My breath catches as he brings his mouth down to kiss my neck, but he doesn't move the hand. He just waits there until my hips rock forward, desperate for more.

"Do you want me to touch you, Fina?" he whispers, his breath on my neck sending tingles down my spine.

I rock my hips again. "God, yes. Please."

He slips a thick finger against my pussy, his touch slow and teasing. His other hand comes to my breast and caresses me in tandem with the one between my thighs. I squirm against his touch with a feeble moan, my arousal building.

Breks continues to tease me, running his finger along my entrance and then swiping over my clit with the lightest of touches. He leisurely explores me until I'm grinding my hips against him and letting out little sounds of need that should embarrass me, but I'm too turned on to care.

After a while, he removes his hand from my breast and guides my hand between my legs gently to rest on top of his. "Show me what you need."

Oh. Of course. I shouldn't assume he'd know how to touch me. Everything else has seemed so natural. My cheeks warm and my arousal wanes at the realization about how different I might be from whatever species he is. Am I too weird and different for him to like this?

When I hesitate, Breks kisses my neck and runs a soothing hand along my arm. "You're perfect, Fina. I want to please you. I *need* to. Show me how."

The tension and longing in his voice makes my pussy clench. I push back my nerves and guide his finger to my clit, rubbing around it in small circles. I moan in relief. "Keep touching me like this."

I move my hand away and he follows my instructions, stroking my clit like I showed him. Desire builds inside me as he touches me, and after a few minutes, my hips are moving to meet his touch.

When I grind back against him, he groans and shifts his hips. Heat flares up in me as his hard length presses up against my ass. I'm curious to see what it looks like, but he keeps me pinned against his chest as he fervently strokes my pussy. His breath fans out over my neck in heavy sighs as we move together.

It's incredible, but I need more. I draw a hand up to my breast and knead it roughly. Breks notices and grabs my other breast with his free hand. When he pinches my nipple and nips at my ear, I cry out and rock back against him again.

"Don't stop," I gasp. My release builds as he continues, his touch and the heat of the water making me overwhelmed. I still need something more.

He rocks himself against my ass, and I realize what I need. I reach back behind me and grasp his cock. His hips stutter. "Fina, you don't have to." The way his voice shakes with need says otherwise.

"I know you can't feel it much, but I need to touch you." I stroke him firmly, hoping he's getting at least a bit of sensation from it. His cock is longer and thinner than a human's, the head more flared. I think about what it might feel like inside me and my pussy clenches.

Breks groans and wraps his hand around mine and pumps my fist up and down his straining cock in rough, hard strokes.

"I'm so close." My orgasm is just out of reach.

He moans and bites at my throat again. "Does stroking my cock make you ache for me? Are you thinking about how it would feel if I spread your legs and sunk into your tight heat?" His words are filthy, but they're just what I need.

"Yes, you would feel so good...yes, oh!" My orgasm slams into me in crashing waves, and I cry out. Breks pumps my hand over his cock frantically until he tenses behind me and moans my name. Another wave of pleasure courses through me, knowing he came as hard as I did.

I turn around and almost startle—I'd forgotten what he currently looks like. He gives me a dazed smile and affection erases that small moment of apprehension. I reach up and pull him down into a languid kiss.

When our mouths part, he looks down at me with wonder. "You're incredible."

"You're not so bad yourself."

He laughs. "Given that I'm not working with a body I'm used to, I'll take it." He gestures down at his aespian form with a grin.

"So you're not an aespian, then?" I know I'm moving into dangerous territory, but this alien just fingered the life out of me, so I'm feeling more daring than usual.

Breks' smile falters, and he shakes his head. "No. Does that disappoint you?"

"Not really." Inside, I'm a bit relieved. That was incredibly hot, but it would take some time to fully adjust to a lover with a carapace. But what just happened makes me more certain it doesn't matter what sort of alien he is. As long as he's Breks, I want him.

He looks at me quizzically. "Then why did you ask for me to be an aespian?"

There's no point in being coy about my intentions. "I want you to know that I'm interested in you. Whatever the real you is."

His eyes widen in surprise, but a moment later his expression closes off. "You're kind to say that, Fina. But the real me will only disappoint you."

I want to grab him and shake some sense into him. Instead, I lean forward and kiss him again. As we part, I pause with my face still next to his. "I'll just have to prove to you that isn't true."

# 20

## ✦MAERLON✦

Despite my recent release, arousal spears through me again when Fina whispers about proving her interest in me. I press my hand against my cock and will it to go down.

*Vash-ka.* I just jerked off at work. The harsh reality of the situation pulls me out of the moment. "I should make sure the other sims are running smoothly," I say, pulling away from Fina's embrace.

She looks disappointed, but nods. "Of course." A moment later, I hear her continue in a much quieter voice. "I'm sorry to distract you." Her arms cross over her chest and she looks away.

Now I've upset her, *esh'et*. I place a hand on her flushed cheek and she turns back to me, eyes watery. "I would let you distract me for hours."

I run my thumb across the edge of her full lips. Fina's mouth parts slightly and her breath hitches. I want to see what she'd do if I slid my thumb in her mouth, but I'm worried that'll break my resolve to get back to work.

"Y-you should go before we—I don't want you to get fired," she says, echoing my thoughts.

Reluctantly, I take my hand away from her face and force my senses back to my body. I groan when I see the mess I've made of my hands and the splatter of my spend across the desk. Shame pricks at me as I wipe it away and spray it with a sanitizer. Thankfully, SimTech doesn't monitor its technicians. Otherwise, I'd surely get fired for this transgression. I don't need this job, but if I lost it, then I'd lose the chance to be with Fina.

The thought makes my chest ache. I've plunged even further into my infatuation with her. Even when I try to distance myself, she's impossible to resist.

I clean myself off and my cock twitches when I remember the way she gripped me while desperately grinding her hips against my hand. Stars, that image and the needy way she said my name will keep me up at night. I tuck my length back into my pants before I let the thought carry me away.

The other sims appear to be running smoothly. There's an hour left in my shift and I doubt we'll get any more customers this late, so I can go back and spend the time with Fina. Still, I should avoid getting so wrapped up in her, just in case. I check the occupied suites again and then send myself back to Fina.

I return just in time to see her stepping out of the hot spring. Beads of water slide down her body as she emerges from the pool, the liquid glittering against her pale skin like the crystals lining the cavern. I freeze at the sight, wishing I could capture this vision of her for eternity.

Her abundant curves make all rational thought flee until I'm filled only with *need*. Need to caress, to taste, to hold her in my arms and sink deep inside her. My gaze slides down as I think about being between her thick thighs and I notice the patch of hair there is a dark brown rather than purple, like the hair on her head. Fascinating.

She wraps an arm across her breasts and brings the other hand down to cover herself where I'm staring. There's the telltale flush of her embarrassment at my intense gaze.

"Sorry, I just…" I trail off, unable to put into words what seeing her does to me.

"I know I'm not at all what you're used to. That I-I'm…a lot." Her voice shakes a bit as she speaks.

In all my worrying about how she'd react to the real me, I never stopped to consider that Fina might be just as concerned that I wouldn't find her attractive. Her beauty was irrefutable from the moment I saw her. It seems so strange that she might doubt that. After seeing her vulnerability right now, I realize how brave she's been with me. I wish I had her strength. The courage to expose myself to someone despite insecurities and fears.

"I'm honored that I get to see you." The words feel trite as soon as they come out of my mouth. I should've told her I think she's perfect. That she charms me more each time we meet. That she's gorgeous.

Fina's eyebrows raise. "Honored in an 'explorer seeing a spatial anomaly' kind of way?"

"If you're asking if I would like to explore your body further, the answer is very much yes."

She peers up at me through her dark lashes, but her posture

relaxes somewhat. I close the distance between us and run a finger along the arm she's using to cover her breasts. Pinprick dots rise on her skin at my touch, and she shivers.

"I'd be honored to see you too," she says, her voice barely more than a whisper. I go to reply, but she furrows her brow and speaks again. "I know you can't. It's okay." She rises onto her toes to press a tender kiss to my cheek. When she begins to move away, I bring a hand to her hair and lower my mouth to meet hers. I keep the kiss light to stop myself from diving back into the heady desire that's threatening to overwhelm me again.

Fina sighs softly as our lips part. As I peer down into her sparkling eyes, I resolve to be brave. To show her my true self. I just need to figure out how to do that without scaring her away.

What a complicated mess I've made. And it's growing more complicated each time I see her as Maerlon. I have to worry about both her reaction to my appearance—which hasn't been good so far—and her reaction to her new friend secretly being her sim suite hookup. We've passed the point where I could bring it up and still be able to laugh off the coincidence of meeting both in and out of SimTech. Sure, I didn't actively seek her out as my real self. But there's no scenario I can imagine where she won't be upset that I didn't tell her right away.

The more I think about it, the worse I feel. My cowardice and how much of a mess I've made of things shames me.

Fina must sense the shift in my mood, because she takes my hand in hers and gives me a reassuring smile. "It's okay. I'm not giving up, but I'll give you as much time as you need to feel safe with me."

I attempt to return the smile, but worry more time will only make things worse.

# 21

## ✦MAERLON✦

"So, how are you holding up?" my sister asks with a hint of hesitation, as if she already knows my answer will be negative.

"Not too bad. Things have been a bit weird. But interesting," I say, a smile creeping onto my face. It's been a few days since I saw Fina, but she's been on my mind almost non-stop.

Dezlon narrows her eyes at me in disbelief. "Not too bad? I thought you were still struggling with what happened with K'thress."

Oh right. We haven't had a chance to vid chat in a few weeks. She's been too busy with supply runs and visiting trade outposts across the Consortium. My sister is H'spith, part of the seladin merchant class. She's never been one to stay in one place for too long, so it suits her, but I wish it didn't limit our opportunities to catch up.

"A lot has happened since we last talked." I fill her in on how K'thress tried to get back together with me.

Her head shakes in disbelief, and she calls out to someone off vid. "He actually stood up for himself. Can you believe it?"

"No shit? Proud of you, Maerlon. K'thress was an asshole," a high-pitched, melodic voice calls back. A few seconds later, Dezlon's wife, Rhysti, appears next to her. She wraps two of her dark pink arms around my sister's waist and leans against her. Dezlon looks down at her adoringly and I'm left waiting for them to break their love-filled gaze.

I've always been jealous of what they have. When I met K'thress, I romanticized the idea of being with a different species because of what Dezlon has with Rhysti. I foolishly thought that because my sister found love with an alien, it was a sign that I would also have a soul bond with one. Obviously, that's not what happened with my ex.

"If you both hated them so much, why didn't you tell me? Would have saved me two years and a lot of tears."

They peer at me and then exchange an amused glance. "You think you would have listened?" asks Dezlon.

Probably not. No, I definitely would have just gotten pissed and hurt. "...Fine. Anyway, you don't need to worry about me anymore."

"Why do I get the sense that you're not telling me something? Even if you stood your ground, shouldn't you be mopier? Shouldn't he be brooding?" Dezlon's eyes narrow until I can barely see their glow, the markings on her brow ridge drawing closer together.

Rhysti nods in agreement. "You're right. He seems...no, that can't be right. He looks...*happy?*"

"You both are ridiculous. Just because I'm not staring out my window wistfully or glowering at everything doesn't mean I'm hiding something."

"Did you see how his eyes flared when he said that? You *do* have a secret!" Dezlon points an accusatory finger at her vid screen, and I know that if she were here in person, it would have been a sharp poke in my shoulder.

"Spit it out, Maerlon. Otherwise I'll have to spend the next few cycles listening to your sister's theories on what's going on," says Rhysti, smirking at Dezlon's accusations.

Should I tell them about Fina? What would I even say? "It's complicated."

The two exchange a knowing glance and then turn back to me. "You've met someone," says Dezlon, full of confidence.

There's no point in denying it. "Yes. Kind of. Like I said, it's complicated."

"Complicated how? Are they unavailable? Are they another entitled rich *fa-shar* prick?" It's clear that Dezlon won't let this go.

"No, she's available. And the loveliest person I've ever met."

"Oh Maerlon, you've got it *bad*. You sound like me when I first met your sister." Rhysti smiles gently at me. Dezlon grins and leans down to kiss her cheek.

"So what's the problem?" Before I open my mouth, Dezlon holds a hand up. "Tell me the condensed version—I know how you like to overcomplicate things."

"It's bad..." I hesitate to tell them, but it would be good to talk to someone about it. My own thoughts haven't gotten me anywhere. They might be able to help.

They both stare at me with crossed arms and wait for me to continue.

"You know how I took that job at SimTech after the breakup? Well, I met someone who came in and we hit it off. But I was using an ankite holo, so she doesn't know what I look like. She's new to Spire, and I didn't want to scare her."

"Why would she be scared of you? Sure, you're the uglier sibling but still handsome enough."

"Sounds like you're making a big deal out of nothing. Just let her see you and one way or another you'll know if she's into you," says Rhysti.

I frown. If only it were that simple. "I'm not finished. After we met at SimTech, I ran into her out in the station at a bar. It turns out she's friends with Mezli, my coworker at CiaXera. I gave her the name Breks at SimTech, but Mezli introduced me as Maerlon. She—Fina—practically fell over in fear at the sight of me. So I didn't tell her I'm Breks. And now...I've spent more time with her as both Maerlon and Breks and it's too late to tell her we're the same person."

A long silence stretches out while they process what I just said.

Rhysti speaks first, her voice gentle. "Fina's a pretty name. Unusual. What species is she?"

"When you say you spent time with her, what do you mean?" Dezlon butts in, giving me an accusatory glare.

"She's a human."

Both of their eyes widen in surprise.

"I tried to just be friendly. I didn't think I'd see her again as Maerlon, but we ran into each other and she wants to be friends since she's new to the station. With Breks, she's come back twice and each time it's been more...intimate. She's asked me to show her my actual appearance and promised that I won't scare her, but I've seen how she looks at me."

"*Es'het*, that's a mess." Dezlon shakes her head at me and Rhysti elbows her in the side with a frown. "What? It is!"

"You must really like her." Rhysti's voice is kind, and she smiles at me in sympathy.

I'm enthralled by her. All I think about is her. "Yes, she's wonderful."

"Stars, look at his face! There's your answer right there. Quit being an idiot and tell her." Dezlon grins at me, like it's the simplest thing in the world.

"He doesn't want to lose her. I understand his hesitation," says Rhysti, touching Dezlon's arm. "You're certain that she's not attracted to you as Maerlon? It took your sister almost a year to realize that I was flirting with her and not just being friendly. Expressions can vary between species."

"Hah, true. Take her at her word—if she says she won't be scared, you need to believe her."

"That doesn't factor in that I've been deceiving her!" A stab of shame pierces me as I admit it out loud.

"You can't change what you've already done. You can only decide how to go forward. Either face the consequences of telling her or end things. It's not right to lead her on, Maerlon." I can always count on Dezlon's blunt honesty, even when it hurts to hear.

Now I *am* in the bad mood she expected. My chest aches with guilt and I'm at a loss for what to do.

"I know it's easier for us to tell you what to do than to do it ourselves. You'll make the right decision. Both of us know you will," says Rhysti, her voice a soothing contrast to the bite in Dezlon's tone.

She sounds so confident, but I have no clue what the right decision is. All options seem like they lead to me hurting Fina and losing the woman I care about.

# 22

## ✦FINA✦

After a week of obsessing over my crush on Breks—and touching myself every night thinking about him—I'm eager to visit SimTech again. When I'm not frantically rubbing one out to the memory of his hands on me, I'm researching and testing cookie recipes that are safe for all Consortium races to eat. My coworkers love the sudden influx of treats that I'm bringing into the office for them to taste. Little do they know that all my baking isn't for their benefit. It's for Breks.

I want to bring him something special the next time I visit him. Unfortunately, seeing him will have to wait. Tonight, Mezli wants to have what she called a "friendship celebration", which translates to a night of dancing with her friends. Almost every day at work, she's insisted that we meet up for a caffeine break with Maerlon and Jezrit. At first I thought it was because she was determined to help me befriend Maerlon, but now it's clear that she's crushing hard on Jezrit. I don't get it at all—and neither does Jezrit, who's either ignoring her obvious signals or is oblivious to her advances.

Throughout these gatherings, Maerlon's been polite but reserved. I can't shake the sense that I make him uncomfortable or that I've somehow offended him. The only time he looks relaxed around me is when he's taste-testing my cookies. I've tried to research if I made a seladin cultural faux pas, but found nothing. Maybe he thinks that Mezli's trying to turn our meetings into a double date and he's put off by the thought.

Shit, I hope that isn't what tonight is. I wouldn't put it past Mezli to try to set me up with Maerlon.

My apartment door chimes, letting me know that Mezli's here to help me get ready to go out. I told her I could pick something out on my own, but she loves playing dress up with me like I'm her human doll. I open the door and she bursts in, her arms full of bags.

"Are you moving in?" I ask, looking at the ridiculous array she's brought with her.

She laughs and pushes past me, heading into my bedroom and dumping her bags onto the bed.

That's not an answer.

An hour of fussing over my appearance later, I'm standing at the entrance to Epiphany in an iridescent white outfit that resembles a strappy harness more than an actual dress. It reveals slices of bare skin across my breasts and hips and I feel a bit like a mummy that's unraveling. But Mezli squealed in delight when she saw it on me and refused to let me wear anything else. So here I am with far too much of my body on display, my arms wrapped around my waist in a feeble attempt to cover myself.

A few people glance my way as they enter the club. At least I'm getting used to the attention now that I've explored Spire more. There's always initial surprise or intrigue at seeing a human, but then their eyes slide off me and they move on.

I check my comm as Mezli chats amicably with the bouncer. There's a light tap on my shoulder from behind and a low greeting. I turn around to see Maerlon and Jezrit there, and my self-consciousness about my skimpy dress intensifies as Maerlon looks at me with narrowed eyes. He's obviously unimpressed.

"Hi Maerlon, hey Jezrit!" I say their names loudly, hoping Mezli will hear me and stop talking to the bouncer so I can get a reprieve from Maerlon's withering gaze.

She spins around and skips over, blowing a kiss over her shoulder back to the bouncer. Mezli gives Maerlon an enormous hug, which he stiffly accepts. Then she reaches out and touches the sleeve of Jezrit's jacket. "You both clean up nice!" she says with delight and leans in to give Jezrit a kiss on the cheek.

He looks confused for a moment, but doesn't seem bothered by the gesture of affection. Though he doesn't appear excited about it either.

"I did bathe before coming here," Jezrit says matter-of-factly, and Mezli giggles. No doubt she's picturing that bath, by the way her eyes roam over him.

"Don't they look good, Fina?" Mezli prompts, nudging me.

My forehead crinkles at being put on the spot. Jezrit looks fine. He has on a sleek metallic gray suit that compliments the shade of his carapace. Maerlon, on the other hand, looks far too sexy for me to form a coherent comment on his appearance. He's wearing a fitted, semi-transparent shirt under a vest and I can see the glowing markings running down his arms and chest through the material. His pants are tight, hugging his slim hips and long legs.

His lip quirks when he notices me looking at him.

"Yep! Very nice." I squeak out, embarrassed that he caught me checking him out.

Mezli nods and does a twirl in place, looking at them expectantly.

"That dress fits you well, Mezli," says Jezrit and she grins at him. "Yours looks like it is missing some of the fabric, Fina. But it's still adequate."

"High praise," I mutter to myself, and Maerlon chuckles under his breath. Damn, he has good hearing.

I hug my arms around my waist as Maerlon's eyes flick over my body, feeling hot and far too exposed as I brace myself for his assessment.

"It has the right amount of fabric," he says to Jezrit, his gaze still focused on my body.

Is that a compliment? The way my whole body tingles under his scrutiny makes it hard for me to tell.

"You both are terrible at compliments! Ugh, let's just go inside," says Mezli with a dramatic sigh. She grabs Jezrit's hand and tugs him behind her, leaving me and Maerlon to trail after them. The bouncer nods and lets us pass.

Maerlon opens one of the large metal doors into the club and gestures for me to go through. "You look very nice too," he says as I step past him. I almost don't hear it over the thumping music that blasts out from the club.

I glance back at him in surprise, but his expression is as closed off as usual. Did I mishear him?

We follow Mezli as she weaves through the dance floor to the bar. She waves and yells something to the ankite bartender she befriended that first night we went out together. They smile and point further into the club, where a balcony overlooks the dance floor.

She gestures for us to follow and leads us over to a muscular shikzeth standing near an illuminated floor panel. Mezli says something to them that I can't hear over the thudding bass and gestures over toward the bar. The shikzeth nods and points at the panel. Mezli and Jezrit step onto it, then Maerlon. I'm confused but follow their example.

A moment later, the floor rises into the air, and I wobble on my heels in surprise. Maerlon's hand grabs my hip to steady me and my face flames at the touch. Mostly in embarrassment, but also because his palm rests against a strip of my bare skin.

The platform stops at the balcony and we step off, Maerlon keeping his firm grip on me until I'm secure on the balcony. I give him a feeble smile, but I'm unable to meet his eyes, not wanting to see the judgment that's undoubtedly there.

From what I can tell, we're in a VIP area of some sort. Groups of vividly dressed aliens sit at tables along the edge of the balcony and gather around a gleaming chrome bar. A few glamorous ankites gyrate on a technicolor dance floor, and I can't help getting caught up for a moment as I watch their sensuous movements. When I realize I've trailed behind, I hurry to follow our group over to a pair of curved fluorescent couches that shift colors along with the beat of the music.

Mezli flops down and claps her hands together in delight. "Isn't this perfect? Only the finest for our friendship celebration!" She gestures around the balcony. Before anyone can answer her, she leaps up and scurries over to the bar.

This is way too fancy for me, but Mezli's in her element. I glance over at Maerlon, who peers down toward the crowded dance floor below us. He doesn't look comfortable either. Jezrit scans the balcony with interest and seems happy to observe others and not make small talk.

Mezli returns with a tray of tall, thin glasses filled with neon pink liquid. I take mine, knowing by now that if it's something Mezli ordered, I need to sip it slowly. She can drink and have only a slight buzz from something that will knock me on my ass.

Jezrit sniffs his drink and then pokes out a long, slender tongue into the glass to sample it. He waits a moment and then unceremoniously downs the whole thing.

"Yeah, let's get this party started!" shouts Mezli, clapping him on the shoulder.

I wince as her voice pierces through the music, causing others on the balcony to glance our way. Already making a scene and we've been here less than five minutes. I love Mezli, but sometimes my anxious self wishes she could be a bit more subdued. Especially when I'm already out of place surrounded by a bunch of stylish, attractive aliens.

Jezrit chatters about the drinks and the club's atmosphere while Mezli hangs onto his every word. After a few minutes, I'm certain she used this get-together as an excuse to go on a date with him.

"So, what do you think the odds are that Jezrit will pick up on her flirting?" Maerlon leans close to me so only I can hear him, and my skin prickles as his breath caresses my neck.

"Not good. Do you know if he'd be interested if he did?"

"Hmm. Now that you mention it, in the time I've known him, he's never mentioned a partner or dating. But I don't know. He's hard to read."

He's not the only one who's hard to read. The glow of Maerlon's pupilless eyes makes it hard to tell what he's thinking. "Speaking of partners, are you doing okay? I'd be a wreck after what happened with your ex the other night."

Maerlon's eyes narrow at my question and I mentally kick myself for diving headfirst into such a personal question.

"I'm alright." A long silence passes and I think he's done with the subject, but then he smiles. "I met someone else, actually."

"Oh?" There's a brief stab of jealousy, but I shake it off. I have no reason to feel jealous. Maerlon's been clear that he's only interested in my friendship. "What are they like?"

"Intelligent, charming, gorgeous, and captivating." His smile widens, revealing more of his sharp teeth.

Of course they are. He's very attractive and smart, so it makes sense he'd find someone so perfect. I return his smile. "I'm happy for you. You deserve someone special."

His prolonged, intense stare following my words makes my stomach flip. When I say nothing else, he looks somewhat disappointed but nods. "Thank you."

What was that about? Did I say something wrong again?

"Don't look now, but someone's got their eye on you, Fina," says Mezli, snapping my attention back to our group.

I glance over my shoulder in confusion, following her eyeline. At first, I'm unsure what she's talking about. There's just a bunch of aliens hanging out and talking. But then an ankite in a sparkling dress shifts and I see them.

At a table near the balcony's edge, sits a seladin with cropped white hair and a black and gold jumpsuit open down to the waist in the front. And they're looking right at me. One of their eyes has the normal glow, but the other is a pinprick of green light, and I realize it's a cybernetic implant. A sharp smile crosses their face when they see me looking their way and they move toward our group.

"Shit, they're coming over here!"

Mezli shrugs her shoulders at me. "I told you not to look."

"I have to go to the bathroom!" I say in a panic and stand. Maerlon and Jezrit seem bemused, but Mezli just continues to laugh.

I get a few steps from our table when a husky, warm voice calls out to me. "Forgive me for staring. I didn't mean to scare you away."

I turn to find the seladin standing next me, a hand on one hip and a cocky, fanged grin on their lips.

"You didn't—I just, um…" Up close, they're very attractive. Not as good-looking as Maerlon, but striking.

"I came over to say that it's a pity such a gorgeous person isn't out on the dance floor," the seladin says, giving me an appreciative once-over.

I blush at their compliment. "You haven't seen me dance."

"Care to rectify that?" They hold a hand out to me in invitation.

I glance back over at my friends. Mezli nods furiously, Jezrit's not paying any attention to me, and Maerlon looks tense. Probably worried that I'll try to fake kiss him again to get out of this.

Fuck it, I'm here and this hot alien wants to dance with me. Brave, badass Fina dances with sexy strangers. I smile at the seladin and place my hand in theirs. "Alright, but don't say I didn't warn you."

They laugh and place a hand on my lower back, leading me to the dance floor.

# 23

## ✦ MAERLON ✦

When Mezli points out the seladin looking at us, I assume I'm the one that drew their focus. My people aren't as prevalent on Spire as other species, and because of that, we often know each other. But I don't recognize them at all. I'm not feeling friendly tonight, but I should introduce myself if they've already noticed me.

Fina draws my attention away from them when she exclaims she needs to use the restroom. Is that something humans normally inform others of? It's strange. She looks flustered and I have no idea why.

A sickening sense of dread creeps through me. Did she realize I was talking about her when I said I'd met someone new? I didn't think I was too obvious, but part of me hoped she'd make the connection between me and Breks in that moment. Now I wonder if she did, and the thought upset her so much that she had to get away from me.

I grab the glass sitting in front of me and take a heavy swig, grimacing at the liquor's saccharine taste.

"Looks like Fina's after some seladin action after all," says Mezli.

I glance back up from my glass with a frown and follow the nexxit's excited gaze across the dance floor. The glass almost slips from my hand when I see the seladin pulling Fina against them. Turns out I wasn't the one they were interested in after all.

Fina's face is flushed and her dress sparkles as she stands awash in the multicolored lights swirling over the dance floor. She giggles and puts a hand in the seladin's, who takes it and redirects it to rest on their waist.

Hot, possessive jealousy ignites within me as they move together. I should be the one touching Fina. The one gripping her plush hips as they sway enticingly to the music.

I slam my drink down on the table and stand, ready to go over and wrest Fina from the stranger's arms. Both Jezrit and Mezli startle at my sudden movement and my senses return to me. I can't just storm over there and grab her or tell her to stop. I have no claim to her. Still, the thought of someone else touching Fina makes me seethe with envy. I have to do *something*.

"I'll be back."

Mezli gives me a puzzled nod before going back to her conversation with Jezrit. With a friendly expression plastered on my face, I stride over to the dance floor with purpose. Fina's in front of the seladin now, their hands playing along her sides as they move together. Their fingers linger every time they slip against her bare skin. They lean down over her shoulder and whisper something in her ear, causing her skin to redden even further.

I restrain the growl rising within my throat as I watch their cocky smile at her reaction. Unable to stand them touching Fina any longer, I approach them and wave. "Hey! Usra, is that you?"

Fina steps away from her dance partner with a perplexed furrow of her brow. The seladin smiles cautiously, fangs revealed but not threatening. When they reply, their tone is warm but cautious. "I'm afraid not. But it's always good to see another Y'thir."

"My mistake, you look just like a friend of mine," I say, keeping my tone genial despite my desire to grab Fina away from them.

Their cybernetic eye slides over my face and then scans up and down my body. "I could be your friend if you'd like," they say in a flirtatious purr.

Now that I'm closer, I can see they're quite good-looking, at least by seladin standards. Their cropped white hair is silky, their nose is less hooked than mine, but still prominent, and their markings dot their skin in a way that makes their face appear angular and proud. Even the prosthetic eye adds to their rakish appeal. I might've found them attractive in the past, but seeing them with Fina takes away any of their appeal.

I place a hand on Fina's shoulder and her eyes meet mine, startled that I've touched her. I hold her gaze, and a moment later, she flushes and looks away. The seladin's nostrils flare and their brow lifts.

"Ah, I see." The seladin glances to where my hand rests on her shoulder, and my grip tightens. I've made my claim on her as clear to them as possible without alerting Fina to it. Fina's eyes dart back and forth between me and the other seladin, confusion written on her face.

"My apologies. I should see what my companions are up to. If you'll excuse me." They give us a slight bow before leaving the dance floor.

"Guess my dancing really *was* that bad," Fina mutters. She puts a hand on her hip and frowns, watching them leave.

I'm ashamed that chasing them off made her feel rejected. But not ashamed enough to not be relieved they're gone. I reluctantly let go of her shoulder. "I think I was the issue. I'm sorry, Fina."

"It's fine. I was in over my head, anyway." Her shoulders sag and I can't tell if it's in disappointment or relief.

"You looked great." Her eyes widen a bit at the compliment. "No crushed toes in sight," I add, making my words less forward.

"Hah, just give me a few more minutes!"

I would give her all the time in the galaxy if it meant getting to be close to her. "Alright."

"Alright, what?" She crosses her arms and scans my face, trying to determine if I'm making a joke of some sort. My eyes dart down to the delicious swell of her breasts as they're pressed together, but I quickly focus back on her face.

"I'll give you a few more minutes." I grin at her, letting the tips of my fangs show.

"Wait, you want to dance with me?"

My smile grows and I shrug, then hold my hand out to her. Inside, I'm dying to have a reason to touch her. "It's only fair after I chased away your dance partner."

She hesitates and my heart sinks. I go to pull my hand back, but she tentatively places her small hand in mine and smiles up at me shyly. Even this small touch fills me with a sense of warmth and rightness. I belong with her.

I lead her further onto the fluorescent dance floor, weaving between other dancers until we're hidden within the small crowd. I don't want to put her on display for the entire room like that seladin, especially if she's nervous about her dancing ability. She's not some shiny novelty to show off—she's someone to cherish and discover intimately.

Fina sways to the thudding beat, doing her best to not bump against me despite the press of the bodies surrounding us. I match her minuscule movements, letting her acclimate to my closeness. A small smile creeps onto her face as she relaxes, her movements becoming less restrained.

For all her protesting, by the time a new song starts, her movements are fluid and sensual. One hand comes up to lift her wavy purple hair away from her neck as she closes her eyes to feel the music. I swallow hard as she slides her other hand up her side, along the curve of her soft hips and waist, then ghosts it across the side of her breast. She basks in the pleasure of her own movements, taking my breath away.

Another dancer bumps into Fina, pulling her out of her moment of abandon. Her eyes flutter back open and she retreats to her smaller, inhibited movements.

I growl under my breath in frustration. Determined to help her continue enjoying herself, I take Fina's hand and spin her around.

She giggles, stumbling slightly and catching herself with a hand against my chest. "Sorry!" She looks up at me apologetically and bites her full bottom lip.

I wonder if she can sense how fast my heart beats for her as our eyes lock together. She's so close, and the intoxicating scent of her washes over me. It would take nothing to lean down and claim her soft lips, kissing her apologies away. Instead, my brow furrows in mock frustration.

"Careful." My voice comes out in a low rumble that I worry will betray my arousal. I bring my hands down to rest lightly on her waist, keeping her steady as we move with the music together.

Her hips sway in time with the beat, and I suppress a groan as I touch the exposed parts of her skin. Is she not wearing any undergarments? I want to slide my hands beneath the strips of fabric and find out. My cock stiffens just imagining it. I adjust my distance from her, keeping enough space between our bodies so that it doesn't accidentally rub against her. She keeps her eyes on my chest and I can tell she's nervous.

"My eyes are up here," I say.

She snorts in startled laughter and looks up into my face. Under the oscillating club lights, her pale skin and dress shift in color. Her oceanic eyes glitter in amusement, and I give her a gentle squeeze of encouragement.

I lean in so she can hear me over the music. "That's better."

She flushes and bites her lip again. A small bead of sweat rolls down her temple. I want to lick it off. I'm hard and aching for her now, thankful that the lights aren't bright enough to illuminate the evidence of my arousal. My eyes fall closed, savoring the feeling of her swaying beneath my hands, the sweet, musky scent of her that deepens as I focus on it, and the vibrations of the music pulsing through my body.

Before I can luxuriate in this perfect moment for long, a sharp stab of pain on the top of my foot snaps me back to reality.

"Shit, sorry!" Fina winces as she stumbles, trying to remove her heel from the top of my foot. She loses her balance and I reflexively pull her against me to keep her upright. She apologizes again, grabbing onto my arms.

Her body presses against mine, and my hips become flush with her stomach. She shoots me a startled look and I freeze—there's no way that she doesn't feel my erection. We stand there, our bodies molded together as dancers move around us. I can't hear the beat over the rushing roar of panic filling my ears. Fina blinks up at me rapidly, like she's prey caught in my grasp.

Is this the moment I confess my feelings to her? Should I stop hiding and come clean? My mind races and time slows to a crawl.

"It doesn't mean anything," I blurt out and pull away. As soon as I say those words, I want to scream at my cowardice.

"Oh. I understand." Fina can't even look at me. It's clear I've embarrassed her with my unsolicited arousal. Once again, I've made a mess of things.

# 24

## ✦FINA✦

My face burns as Maerlon moves away from me. One moment we're dancing and the next I'm accidentally rubbing up against his crotch. Where there was a very hard, large bulge. God, now I'm thinking about that picture Mezli sent me a while back. What little I know about seladin physiology suggests that it means he's aroused. I feel a thrill at the thought. But that's dashed when he exclaims it means nothing. For all I know, seladin get hard randomly. Or it happened because he was imagining dancing with the person he gushed about earlier, instead of me.

Before the situation can spiral into more awkwardness and ruin our tentative friendship, I decide to lean into our previous joking. "I didn't realize you were into pain. That explains why you agreed to risk your feet dancing with me."

My words have their desired effect. He scrunches his dotted brow together in momentary confusion, then lets out a loud laugh, his tense posture releasing. "You caught me. It's so hot, especially when your heel threatens to pierce all the way through my foot." He grimaces when he shifts his weight onto the aforementioned foot and then mimics a gasp of pleasure.

"Whoa, slow down there. Let's go check in on Mezli and Jezrit before you get too excited." I tilt my head over toward our table. He chuckles and nods. "If you're good, I'll step on you again later," I say, giving him my best over-the-top impression of a domme.

He tenses again. Whoops, I took the joke too far.

We head back over to the couches to find Mezli chatting with the seladin who abandoned me on the dance floor. Great, like things weren't already awkward enough right now. The seladin leans in close to her and whispers something, sliding a hand onto her thigh. Mezli giggles in delight and runs a hand through their hair. She looks up as we approach.

"Oh, there you are! I was wondering if you ditched me, too. I got so lonely that I had to make a new friend," says Mezli, gesturing to the seladin still gripping her thigh. "Fina, Maerlon, this is Hadrell."

Ah, so that's their name. We didn't even get that far.

Hadrell gives us a lazy, fanged grin. "I'm not coming between something you have again, am I?" they ask, raising their brow at Maerlon.

Wait, did Hadrell leave because they thought Maerlon was my partner? It gives a new potential meaning to the tight grip he'd had on my shoulder. God, he must have thought that I needed saving from another alien creep. I should talk to him about not needing him to always be my fake boyfriend.

"What, me and Maerlon? Gross, no. That's not a thing at *all*," says Mezli before Maerlon can reply.

He snorts at her visceral reaction to the idea, and I can't help but laugh as well. "What happened to Jezrit? Did you scare him off?" asks Maerlon, and she scowls at him in return.

"Goddess, it's hopeless. I asked if he wanted to get out of here and he said yes. And then he left!" Mezli puts a palm to her forehead in defeat but Hadrell peels it off and brings it to their mouth to kiss her wrist.

"Anyone who doesn't want to be around you is a fool," they say in a purr. The two of them get lost in a heated gaze.

"It uh...it looks like you're having a good time with your new friend, so I think I'll call it a night." I avert my eyes from where one of Mezli's hands is rubbing Hadrell's upper thigh. She nods, only half-listening as Hadrell brings their lips to the shell of her ear.

"I'll walk you out," says Maerlon, shaking his head as Mezli slides onto Hadrell's lap.

We head back down to the main floor and toward the entrance. I pause as a song I actually know starts to play. Who knew they listen to human music here?

Maerlon cocks a dotted brow at my sudden halt.

"Sorry, it's just nice to hear something that reminds me of home." I turn to weave my way to the exit, but he grabs my wrist to stop me. I peer at the long, powerful fingers wrapped around my comparatively tiny, fragile wrist and then at Maerlon, confused.

"Let's stay for one more dance." He looks at me intently and his lip curves slightly, revealing just a sliver of sharp fangs beneath.

My heart flutters at the idea. I nod.

He tugs me gently so that we're standing closer together, and we begin to move to the music. He's graceful for such a broody, stiff alien. The strobing lights on the dance floor illuminate flashes of his muscled arms and torso through his semi-transparent shirt. The markings on his skin glow every time it grows darker, like little pinpricks of light shining through from beneath his dark gray skin. He sways to the music and the curtain of white hair he has on one side falls back. I notice for the first time that his flat, pointed ear has multiple piercings as they glint under another flash of light.

Everything about him is so alien and yet...I'm mesmerized by him.

I stumble in my reverie, and he chuckles, taking hold of my hand to steady me. Damn these stupid heels. "I told you I'd step on you again."

His eyes glow brighter and he laughs, then moves in closer, leaving barely any space between us. My stomach tightens with nerves and excitement as he slides a hand onto my waist.

We start to dance again, our bodies brushing against each other occasionally. His fingers ghost over the bare strips of skin along the side of my dress, and I gasp slightly as a talon-like nail scrapes against me, sending shivers down my spine.

I look up into his face to find him staring at me with startling intensity. Excitement thrums through me and I wobble a bit. My foot bumps up against the toe of his boot as I right myself and his fingers dig into my hip.

"Sorry," I mutter, my cheeks heating. I stare down at my feet, as if they're to blame for my clumsiness, and not the thrill of being close to him.

Maerlon lifts a hand from one of my hips and I think he's ready to stop dancing. But then his elongated fingers cup my chin and gently turn my head back to him. His thumb presses against the corner of my mouth and the fervent expression on his face makes my heart skip a beat.

"Fina...I have to tell you something." His eyes bore into me.

Is this really happening? I'm close to combusting. I want to part my lips and let him slip his thumb into my mouth. My eyes dart to his lips as I recall the sparks that danced through me when we fake kissed.

The song ends and as the next one comes on, someone on the dance floor gives an excited whoop. Maerlon stiffens and his jaw tenses, looking like he's been shaken out of a dream. He drops his hand from my chin. "Just wanted to say that you can step on me as much as you'd like. The song's over though, so we should head out." He clears his throat, looking away.

That doesn't seem like what he was planning on saying. His behavior is giving me whiplash. Am I reading things into it that aren't there? The way he looked at me felt charged, but I've never been good at telling when someone's interested in me. Add in that he's another species and I'm completely lost.

Oh well. I probably shouldn't make out with my only new friend, anyway.

# 25

## ✦FINA✦

I'm so busy with work over the next few weeks that I don't have time to overthink that night at Epiphany. Maerlon and I continue to see each other at the office for occasional caffeine and cookie breaks, and whatever I sensed when we danced is absent in our interactions. At first I felt disappointed, but at least there's no weird tension. I must have misinterpreted his behavior that night. Like I said, I'm terrible at knowing when someone's flirting.

I'm settling into a routine, and each day on Spire feels less overwhelming than the one before. The station would take years to fully explore, but parts are becoming more familiar. I've stumbled on some cute thrift shops in Perseus district and am finally getting around to making my apartment a home. Refurbishing old furniture and repurposing decor has always interested me, so it's nice to have a space of my own where I can finally explore that. Even if it means a few jammed fingers and strained muscles.

I'm still wary when I go out on my own at night, but I have to admit that the stun spray/"inhaler" that my mom sent me helps. Fortunately, there haven't been any more incidents with alien stalkers.

When I'm not working, exploring with Mezli, or making my place cozier, my thoughts drift to Breks more often than not. Though I want to see him again, I'm wary about developing things further without truly meeting him first. I don't want a holo facsimile of him. I want him actually holding me, touching me. He features in my dreams a lot, but they end up being just as frustrating as reality. Each time he shows up, he's a nebulous figure that I can't quite see or touch, and just when he's about to show me his true self, I wake up.

It's on a weekend when I wake from one of those annoying dreams that I find the solution to my problem. Well, "solution" may not be quite the right word. A work-around. Something that will let me be with him until I can prove to him he won't frighten me away.

Anticipation and nerves flutter in my chest all day as I think about seeing him tonight and telling him my idea. I'll need to wait until right before SimTech closes—I don't want to distract him from his job again. Hopefully, he'll be there and agree to try this.

After baking a fresh batch of shikzeth spice cookies—the unanimous winner of office taste-testing—I fret over what to wear, how to do my hair, and my makeup. When I've tossed all of my outfits on my bed in frustration and realize I only own high-waisted, giant panties, I impulsively order a bunch of things to be delivered today from a shop Mezli's mentioned.

Hours later, I've finally found something to wear. A tight, low-cut black dress hugs my body in a way I hope is flattering. It's not as flashy as what Mezli usually insists I wear out, but it's more my style.

Underneath is a different story. After far too much consideration, I've settled on a crimson lingerie set, complete with garter belt and sheer stockings. It's all incredibly impractical, but will hopefully be suitable. Anxiety bubbles up in me as I think about Breks seeing me in it. It's silly—he's seen me naked. But this lingerie somehow feels more revealing.

Late in the night cycle, I package up the cookies in a neat parcel, put a dark coat on over my dress, and head to SimTech. By the time I'm at the entrance, my palms are sweaty and my chest feels tight.

My footsteps echo through the empty lobby, and the familiar holo receptionist appears behind the welcome desk. Its generic smile turns into a shocked expression when it sees me and I release a shaky breath. That reaction must mean it's Breks. I approach the desk as the holo watches me intently.

"Sorry miss, we're about to close," he says with an apologetic look. For a moment I worry that he's serious, but then his face breaks into a lopsided grin.

I school my expression, looking disappointed. "Oh no! Is there any way I could convince you to stay open late? For me?" I lean forward to rest my hands on the desk, suppressing a giggle as the holo's brow raises.

"I think you could persuade me. What do you have in mind?" The holo-receptionist leans closer and eyes me up and down.

"Well, I brought you a special treat. I'll be happy to give it to you. Just wanted to wait until you're closed for the night. I don't want to get you into trouble or be too much of a *distraction*." I linger on the last word.

"Hah, so that's why you're here so late. I'm intrigued. And thrilled to see you again, Fina. I wasn't sure if I would."

Now I feel bad it took me so long to work up the courage to see him again. I didn't realize he'd been missing me as much as I missed him. "Sorry! I wanted to come back. I've thought about you a lot." An embarrassing amount, but I don't say that out loud.

His lips twist into a smile that makes my knees weak. "No apologies necessary. I'm just happy you're here now. Go ahead into the room and I'll be with you soon. I've got one customer in a sim that's about to end, so once they're gone, I'll lock up and join you."

The floor path illuminates and I follow it once more to a nondescript white chamber. The bag of cookies crinkles as I clutch it and I grimace when I realize I'm probably crushing the delicate cookies with my nervous grip. I set the bag down and pace around the room while I wait, fidgeting with the neckline of my dress, then adjusting my stockings. Whose dumb idea was it to wear such absurd underwear? I don't take off my coat yet—I won't until after he agrees to my plan.

I startle slightly when Breks' holo pops up in the room with me a few minutes later. "Everything is closed up, and I'm ready to give you my undivided attention. If I'd known you were stopping by so late, I would have had some caffeine." Breks fakes a yawn to punctuate his words. At least I hope it's fake.

"I'm hopeful I'll be able to keep you awake." My voice wavers as I speak, betraying my nerves. It's hard to flirt while anxiety roils inside me.

"Of that I have no doubt." His voice is a low purr, and I squeeze my thighs together at the sound. It's embarrassing how turned on I am already. "Should I be another holo, or is this one okay?" He gestures down at the ankite holo he's using.

Alright, the moment of truth. Either he's willing to go along with my idea or my hope gets crushed. I inhale deeply and force away the internal voice that's yelling at me to stop so I can avoid the risk of rejection.

"Neither, actually. I have an idea. It's alright if you say no, but I was thinking—I know you don't want me to see you. That you don't believe you won't scare me away. But I don't want a simulated version of you. I want to actually feel your touch. I want to be with *you*. So I was thinking...what if we do something like the first time I was here?"

Breks' holo stills and lifts his brow. "The first time you were here? I thought you had a terrible time."

Ugh, he's going to make me say it. My cheeks burn and I fight to maintain eye contact. "It was just because I wasn't expecting it. I wouldn't mind now, if it were with you. It doesn't have to be a whole kinky thing if you don't want that. I was thinking more about the blindfold. So that I can't see you."

He considers for what seems like an eternity. My heart threatens to thump out of my chest and the room feels way too bright. Too exposed.

Finally, he nods, then gives me an assessing glance. "How could I possibly say no? You, letting me do all the things I've longed to do to you? It's more than I could have dreamed of. And trust me, you've been in my dreams a lot." He moves closer to me and runs a finger across my lips, making me shiver.

"You're okay with this?" I whisper, not convinced that he won't change his mind.

"More than okay, Fina. Just remember—your safeword is 'aquamarine'." His holo winks at me and then disappears.

# 26

## ✦ MAERLON ✦

*Esh'et. Vash-ka.*

    I rip off the holo controls, my heart threatening to burst out of my chest. I rest my face in my palms with a groan, begging my logical mind to come on board and help me out.

Fina is here, ready and willing to be with me. More than willing. The thrill of that overrode any sense within me. Including the part of my brain that knows that without the modulation the holo interface applies, she'll recognize me by my voice.

*Esh'et.* I curse again. She's waiting for me and I can only delay for so long. I frantically poke around in the simulation interface, searching for a way to alter my voice while I'm in the sim. With some warning, I could've figured it out. With my panicked, racing thoughts, there's no hope. I'll just have to speak as differently from my normal voice as possible. And not speak much.

*Or you could confess who you are,* argues an internal voice that sounds a lot like Dezlon. I meant to tell Fina that night at Epiphany. If I couldn't do it then, when everything seemed like it was building to my confession, how am I supposed to tell her now?

I load the simulation into her suite, removing any pre-programmed scenarios and holos, then connect back to the holo in her suite, appearing beside her.

"Does this look okay to you?" My voice wavers. I need to get myself together, fast.

The room is lit by low candlelight, with a bed, a set of plush chairs, and a wall of bondage equipment. Fina's eyes go big, a mixture of nerves and arousal. Stars, she'd look so perfect tied up.

She goes over to the wall on shaky legs and picks up a black blindfold. "Y-yeah, it's great. I'll put on the blindfold now..." Fina sits down in a chair and ties the fabric across her eyes, testing it out by waving a hand in front of her face. "Wow, yeah. You're safe. I can't see anything. Hopefully, I won't end up accidentally smacking you in my blindness." A tiny, nervous giggle follows her words, and she clasps her hands in her lap, fingers fidgeting against each other.

"How do you know that's not my kink?" I ask, then tense when I realize that's too similar to a joke we made in the club. Fina giggles again, showing no recognition or sign of alarm beyond her nerves.

I'm overthinking this. She won't know it's me. I just need to be more careful.

"I'm heading there now, last chance to flee."

"I won't run from you, Breks." The tenderness in her voice catches me off guard. This means more to her than she's letting on.

"Fina, I—if I do anything you don't like, promise you'll tell me? Your pleasure is all I desire."

She inhales sharply and a tinge of pink rises to her cheeks. "Of course. I want the same from you. If you need to stop at any point, we can. I don't want to push you."

My stomach clenches at her concern for me, a confusing blend of affection for her and guilt over my deception. "You aren't. I want this with every part of my being. I just—I can't shake the fear that if you knew who I truly am, you wouldn't want this. The last thing I want to do is abuse your trust."

Fina exhales softly and worries at her lower lip with her teeth, taking a moment to consider. "That you're concerned lets me trust you, Breks. Would I rather do this knowing everything about who you are? Yes. Of course, I would. But I can't stop thinking about you. And if I have to choose between being with you like this or not at all...I choose this. Unless you're secretly my boss or my ex from the Coalition fleet, I'm good."

"What if I were your friend or a coworker?" I ask before I can think, kicking myself at the question's obvious implication.

"Mezli, is that you?" Fina laughs and whips her head around, pretending to look around the room despite the blindfold. "I had no idea you'd go to such lengths to seduce me!"

Her laughter eases some of my worry. "No, I'm not whoever Mezli is. Hope you're not too disappointed."

She sighs dramatically. "Damn. It's probably for the best, though. Our love could never be—she's too much of a handful for me."

"I hope I'm not too much for you to take either." I didn't intend to be suggestive, but her cheeks flush even more and her lips part.

"I can take it," she whispers and squeezes her legs together, squirming in the chair.

I groan, feeling myself harden. So much for trying to do the right thing. If she says this is okay, I can't resist her anymore.

"Stay right there. I'm coming over."

## ✦FINA✦

As I sit waiting breathlessly for Breks, I realize I never took my coat off. I stand and rip it off, tossing it out of the way. Or at least I hope it's out of the way—I can't see shit with this blindfold. I slide back down into the chair and tug at the hem of my dress. For a woman that's about to have sex with someone she's never actually met, I'm awfully concerned about how much leg I'm showing.

*Calm down, Fina.* I inhale shakily as the usual litany of worried thoughts cycle through my mind while I wait. What if I look different in person and he doesn't like it? Am I too alien for him to do this? What if I'm too nervous to relax and enjoy myself? What if—

The hiss of the door to the suite sliding open yanks my attention back to the room, and my heart rises in my throat. "Breks?" A wild part of my mind worries that it's not him.

"Fina, it's me." His voice sounds different. A low, gravelly rumble that sends a shiver skittering across my exposed skin. It's so familiar, but I can't place why. Must be that his cadence is the same even without the holo's voice filter.

Oh god, he's here now. What should I do? Shit, I forgot about the cookies! I stand slowly, trying not to wobble on my heels. The sound of rustling fabric and footsteps rings out in the quiet room as he approaches.

I startle slightly when a hand rests on my arm, warm and heavy.

*Wow*, that's a big hand. His other hand brushes along the side of my face, and my skin tingles at the touch.

"You're exquisite, Fina." Breks slides his hand down from my arm to grasp my waist. His deep, seductive rasp startles me again, but I hold still, willing my body not to tremble. I'm so goddamned nervous and turned on.

"I wasn't sure what to wear. I hope it's okay," I murmur, light-headed knowing he's here with me in the flesh.

The hand on my face trails down my neck to rest above the swell of my breasts and my nipples stiffen in anticipation. "It's perfect. You're perfect." He pauses. "Though I wouldn't mind looking at what's underneath." Long fingers toy with the neckline of my dress, and I feel the light scrape of a sharp nail against my skin.

God, his voice sounds so familiar. I reach in my mind to remember who but it's tough to focus while he's touching me.

"I brought you something. A present of sorts." My voice comes out shaky and high, unable to stop myself from filling the silence with nervous words.

"Mmm, I can see that. Should I unwrap it?" He circles around behind me, dragging his hands across my body as he moves. Hot breath caresses the nape of my neck as he leans down to kiss my shoulder, the soft brush of his lips against my skin pulling a small gasp from me.

"They're cookies!" I blurt.

His fingers stop where they're working at the neck of my dress. "Cookies?"

"I baked them for you. They're over in the corner. As a present—I already said that part, didn't I?"

A low, throaty chuckle fills the air. "Fina, I'm touched you'd bring me something you've made. I know you're a wonderful baker."

"You know I'm a wonderful baker?" My senses sizzle at his closeness, but I can't help thinking it's out of character for him to flatter me without knowing if I'm actually good at something.

He tenses behind me. "I meant that I'm sure you're a wonderful baker. Why? Should I be worried that you're trying to poison me?"

"Hah, no! Not unless tonight goes a lot worse than expected." We both laugh and it helps diffuse some of my anxiety.

"Is it okay if I sample the cookies later? There's something else I'd like to taste right now." He punctuates his words with a kiss on my neck and suddenly I'm filled with fluttery nerves and anticipation again.

I nod, and his fingers go to the nape of my neck. He unzips my dress, the cool air prickling against my bare skin as it opens. Big, warm hands grasp the shoulders of my dress and push it down until it slides off my body and pools by my ankles.

Breks inhales sharply when he sees my lingerie, and he lets out a groan. "You're going to kill me, Fina," he rumbles, grasping onto my hips and kneading into my thick curves in appreciation.

"Please don't die yet. I'd like to at least kiss you for real first."

Breks chuckles low in his throat and turns me around, pulling me flush against his body.

Oh wow, he's big. My breasts press against the smooth, hard plane of his bare chest, nipples straining under the thin fabric of my bra.

His hips press forward as I rub against him and oh wow, he's *really big*. Something long and thick and hard presses against my belly. A thrill of arousal rolls over me.

A hand under my chin tilts my head up, and then his lips are against mine. The kiss starts gentle, almost hesitant, but his soft, full lips pressed against mine sparks a fire within me. When I moan, he makes a throaty sound and his kiss becomes hungry and desperate. A slick, textured tongue presses against the seam of my lips and I let it slide into my mouth to dance with mine. The power of the kiss threatens to make me lose my balance and I grip tightly onto his arms.

God, it's good. And so fucking familiar, like kissing déjà vu. Though I guess that makes sense. We've kissed before, just not in person.

Brek's lips trail down my neck, sucking and nipping at my skin. All my senses are on fire and I gasp as he cups my breasts. I'm much more than a handful for humans, but they fit perfectly in his hands. His fingers brush over the delicate fabric of my bra and he lets out a satisfied hum as he brings his face down to kiss my breasts. I moan when he licks my nipple through the lace and press myself against his mouth.

He reaches behind me and his large fingers struggle to undo the clasp of my bra. His nail snags in the fabric and he mutters a curse, then growls to himself and tears through the fabric. I gasp, shocked by his strength.

"Sorry. I'll buy you a new one." He murmurs the apology against my skin as he pushes the straps off of my shoulders and lets the bra fall to the ground. Before I can complain about him ruining my fancy lingerie, his mouth is on my nipple, sucking and teasing it while pinching the other with his fingers. A shuddering breath escapes my lips, the flame of my arousal flaring bright within me, already threatening to burn out of control.

I whimper when he moves his mouth lower, kissing down my stomach. He grips my waist and squeezes, and it's accompanied by a frustrating twinge of self-consciousness and uncertainty about my size. I tense, and Breks notices.

"Stars, you feel so good in my hands. So soft, I could touch you for hours." His voice sounds thick as he continues to run his hands down my stomach, then around to squeeze my ass. His mouth trails down further until he's at the top of my panties. I squirm thinking about his face so close to where I desperately need it.

I whine as his lips pull away, and he chuckles at my reaction. His hands are on my hips again, guiding me back to sit in the chair. I almost trip over the dress around my ankles and he whispers an apology, then disentangles it from my feet.

"Spread your legs for me," he commands, pressing his hands to my knees to guide me. My cheeks burn but I obey, letting my legs fall open. Breks inhales deeply, and he releases a shuddering moan. "*Esh'et*, I can smell how turned on you are."

Oh god. My legs snap shut and my face flames with embarrassment.

"You smell intoxicating—it's driving me crazy. Let me taste you, Fina." He strokes along the insides of my thighs, coaxing me to spread my legs again.

"Really?" My previous partners weren't as enthusiastic about going down on me, so it's hard to believe.

He presses a nipping kiss against my inner thigh. "*Yes.*"

"O-okay, if you insist."

I gasp as a large finger pulls the fabric of my panties to the side and runs along my folds.

"You're so wet. This is good for humans, right?"

I can't stop my choked giggle. "Yes, wet is good. Very good."

He removes his hand and I want to grab it and push it back between my legs, but then I hear him moan. "You taste incredible," he murmurs, and I realize he must have licked the finger he'd just touched me with.

I'd find it embarrassing if it didn't turn me on so much. "Please," I whisper, not entirely sure what I'm asking for.

"I can't wait to taste your release on my tongue." His voice is full of gravelly resonance, and then his mouth is between my legs.

"Oh!" I cry out as his textured tongue swipes along my entrance and then catches my clit with a flick.

"Ah yes, I remember…this is the spot you like." He flicks his tongue against my clit a few times and then circles it slowly, making me gasp. He devours me, pushing me closer and closer to release faster than I thought possible.

A thick finger slides to my entrance and pushes inside me. We both moan at the sensation and he begins to pump his finger in and out of me while his tongue continues its relentless circles around my clit.

I'm shaking, so close to release as he adds a second finger. I reach out blindly, looking for something to hold on to. My hands land on his head and I feel long silky hair beneath one hand and smooth skin under the other. I rock my hips up to meet the thrust of his fingers and he groans against my pussy, sucking and licking me with feverish devotion.

"Oh god, I'm going to—oh fuck, Breks!" I gasp as my release crashes over me and I tighten my hand in his hair, grinding against his face as I clench around the fingers inside of me. He continues to lick me until the waves of my orgasm dissipate and I release my tight hold on his head.

"*Fina.*" He groans as he rests his head against my leg, sounding just as dazed as I feel. Languid pleasure consumes me as I come down from my release. "Thank you," he whispers.

I suppress the urge to laugh. I should be the one thanking him for the best orgasm of my life. I do my best to pull his face up to meet mine and kiss him, my lips landing on his chin until he readjusts and then my mouth is on his. I can taste myself on his tongue. While I've never thought it was a particularly good or bad taste, I tingle again, thinking about how much he liked it. And how I want to know what he tastes like.

"Now I want to taste you," I say when our lips part.

Breks groans softly, as if the thought is too much to bear. "You don't...it's not necess—"

"Please. Let me," I interrupt, echoing his earlier words.

# 27

## ✦MAERLON✦

Fina sits before me, legs spread and cunt glistening with her release. Her taste is still on my lips, heady and intoxicating. I want to bury my face back against her folds and hear the throaty gasps she makes when my tongue circles that one fascinating, sensitive spot.

When she offers to take me in her mouth, I hesitate. The idea makes my cock twitch in anticipation, but it feels like I'm taking advantage of her. Would she really want to do that to me if she knew who I was?

*Vash-ka*, I'm weak. When she insists, I can't say no. I stand up from my kneeling position between her legs, and the sight as I look down on her makes me groan.

Candlelight dances against her skin and her ample breasts rise and fall with her excited breaths. Her lips are parted and she tilts her head, trying to track my movement despite the blindfold covering her eyes.

I shift to stand between her legs, and find that her seated position lines her face up perfectly with my straining erection. I can't resist reaching down to cup her face. She's so lovely, all creamy skin and softness. Fina is nothing like anyone I've been with before and learning her body feels like an honor I don't deserve. But one I'll take, nonetheless.

Her hands reach out and land on my thighs, then feel their way up slowly. When she brushes against my stiff length, her breath hitches. One hand traces over the outline of my cock and I have to hold myself back from rocking against her touch.

"Wow...this is—you're huge," Fina says in surprise as she squeezes me through the fabric.

A choked sound escapes me, and I almost come at that small touch. She's a lot smaller than me. I hadn't considered our size difference as a potential issue until I felt how tight she was against just two of my fingers. I'll need to go slow and be very careful—the last thing I want to do is cause her pain or distress. Stars, just the thought of sliding into her wet heat threatens to overwhelm me.

"Can you take me, Fina?" My voice is a tight mixture of concern and arousal.

Her breath quickens, and she brings her hands up to the fastener of my pants, deftly undoing it with her delicate fingers. "Yes," she whispers, then slips her fingers into the waistband. She pulls, tugging both my pants and my underwear down, and my cock springs out eagerly, almost hitting her in the face.

This is really happening. It feels like I'm watching from outside my body as her hand reaches out and finds purchase on my cock. Slender, short fingers wrap around me, but they don't come close to meeting. My cock pulses as she gives it a tentative stroke and a bead of lubricant leaks from the tip.

"It's—you're textured." She gasps softly as she brushes against the bumps near the head and then traces the ridges along the top and underside.

"Is that a problem?" I choke out as her thumb swirls across the head, smearing my lubricant along with it.

"N-no! Just that humans are smooth. I almost forgot for a moment I'm here with an unknown alien." She lets out a nervous laugh and my cock softens slightly. Would she prefer me to be human? Is this part of me not compatible with her desires?

She gathers up more of my slick as her fist passes over the sensitive head of my length. Her lips downturn as she tests the lubricant between her fingers.

"Oh...did you come?" she asks with gentle hesitance. Like she doesn't want to offend me.

"N-no, not yet. That's my slick—a kind of self-lubrication to make things...easier. I suppose that's another weird alien thing about me, isn't it?"

Her cheeks flush a bright pink. "Different, not weird!" She gives my length a reassuring stroke and some of my anxiety dissipates.

Her lips part and I bring a hand up to cup the back of her head. Her mouth is so close to my cock now that it twitches when her warm breath hits it. She uses her hand and my touch to guide herself to the tip, and her short, pink tongue gives it a testing lick.

She considers for a moment and then runs her tongue over me again, circling slowly around the head and tasting more of my slick.

"*Vash-ka*," I curse under my breath with a hiss as she opens her mouth wider and feeds the tip of my cock between her lips. My fingers delve into her silken hair, encouraging her. Looking down at her small, plump lips stretched around me almost makes me spill into her mouth.

"Stars, that's too good. You look amazing with your lips wrapped around my cock."

Fina moans against my cock and slides it further into her hot mouth until it reaches her throat. I hold back from thrusting along with her movements as she slides my cock in and out of her mouth, barely able to take a quarter of it. Her hand strokes along the base to cover what her lips can't reach, and the wet, sloppy sound as she sucks me eagerly is filthy.

I won't last. It's too good. I'll never recover from the sight of my cock between Fina's pretty pink lips.

"Fina—I...ahh!" My release barrels toward me and I try to pull back, but she takes me into her mouth as far as she can and her moan of encouragement vibrates against my cock. I erupt with a strangled cry, pumping my hips into her mouth as my seed pulses out of me in thick, hot jets. She swallows most of it, but as I reluctantly pull out of her mouth, a trickle of my spend escapes her lips.

"I'm sorry, I didn't mean to—"

"Fuck, that was hot." Fina interrupts me before I can finish my apology. Her tongue darts out to lick the escaped seed from the corner of her mouth. "You taste better than I expected. I could see myself getting addicted to it."

My cock starts to stiffen again at her words. A breathless moment passes between us as I gaze down at Fina. Hair still tangled in my hand, a thick blindfold over her eyes, and her lips wet and parted, she's a vision of pure debauchery.

"Mmm, I'm so hot and tingly. Please touch me," she moans, her hand reaching down to cup her breast and play with her nipple.

She doesn't need to tell me twice. I'm immediately down on my knees again, burying my face between her legs, desperate to get another taste of her.

"Yes!" She cries out, rocking her hips up to meet me. An image of her rubbing her pussy against my face as she sits astride it flashes in my mind. I reach my hands under her legs and scoop her up. She gasps at the sudden movement and clings to me as I carry her over to the bed, setting her down and crawling between her legs.

"Feels so good. Everything is glowing, my skin is buzzing." She lets out a shuddering moan as I lick her and let my tongue dip inside. She continues to mutter nonsensical things as I work her with my mouth and slide two fingers inside her. With a trembling gasp that shakes her whole body, she comes, but I keep licking her through her release, not wanting to stop. I can't get enough of her.

"Put it inside me, Breks. I'm burning. There are stars everywhere. I need it," she whispers, pulling my focus away from making her come again. *Vash-ka*, my need to be inside her like she begs is too strong to resist.

I remove my mouth from her cunt and look up at her from between her legs. A deep pink flush colors her face and chest as she breathes rapidly. A moment later, she writhes and gasps again even though I'm not touching her anymore.

"Fina, are you okay?" Something about this seems not quite right.

"I'm amazing. I can taste your scent. Tastes like moonlight and yearning. Need you inside me before I melt away." She brings a hand down between her legs and groans with need as she touches herself.

Something definitely isn't right. I reach a hand up and press it against her red cheeks. Her skin is burning up. *Fa-shar*. I pull her blindfold off, uncaring about the consequences of her seeing me.

Fina gazes up at me with an unfocused grin, her eyes glassy and her pupils so dilated they almost blot out her entire iris. "You glow. Everything is so bright and shiny—you're *beautiful*," she gasps, touching my cheek with no sign of recognition.

Panic slams into me. She's sick. I have to help her. She's hallucinating and feverish. Is it an allergic reaction?

"Hold on, Fina. Everything will be okay." I say it more to reassure myself than her.

She watches me with carefree delight, reaching out to play with my hair as I lean over her. I open my comm and send a frantic message to Mezli, praying that she's still awake at this hour.

> Maerlon: Something's wrong with Fina. I need your help. It's urgent.

A tense minute passes. Fina keeps rubbing herself and whispering about how shiny I am and how she wants to taste my markings. Finally, Mezli's reply pops up.

> Mezli: Why are you with Fina—WAIT, are you fucking????!!!

I ignore her question. There are more important things to do than explain our situation.

> Maerlon: She's babbling, and she keeps saying she's tingling. Her skin is flushed and hot. Please, I don't know what to do.

> Mezli: Fuck. It could be an allergic reaction. Is her breathing okay?

I press a hand to Fina's chest, and she moans, practically panting. "Touch me. I need you so bad," she pleads. I pull my hand away before she can bring it down between her legs. The sound of her begging for me would normally be a dream, but this is more like a nightmare.

> Maerlon: She's breathing heavily, but not wheezing.

> Mezli: Could still be allergies. Does she have a bag with her? Check for meds.

My eyes dart around the room frantically until they land on a small purse. I pour the contents out onto the bed next to a dazed Fina and sift through them.

> Maerlon: I found an inhaler. Should I use that?

> Mezli: It can't hurt. I'm heading there—are you at her place or yours?

> Maerlon: Neither. We're at SimTech.

> Mezli: What? Why? Never mind, I'm on my way.

Fina paws at my arm and brings my hand to her lips, darting her tongue out to lick my fingers and sigh.

"Fina, I'm going to give you your inhaler."

She giggles and shakes her head. "Shhh, that's a secret." Her words slur together somewhat, increasing my worry.

If this doesn't work, I need to take her to a hospital. Though I don't relish the thought of dragging an incoherent, undressed human through the walkways this time of night. No one would believe that a human would voluntarily be intimate with me, a Y'thir seladin. I know what they'd assume—that I drugged her and forced myself on her. But if she doesn't improve, none of that matters. I'll do anything to make sure she's okay.

*Vash-ka*, please let this help. I bring the inhaler to her lips and she licks at it, winking at me. I depress the pump and a mist of medicine hits her mouth. She coughs and then her eyes roll back in her head as she falls unconscious.

# 28

## ✦FINA✦

My throbbing head wakes me from sleep. It feels like a horrific hangover, but I didn't drink last night, did I? I wince as I open my eyes to a beam of light falling on my face from a crack in my bedroom door. Everything is too sharp and bright. I should go turn that light off, but getting up seems impossible. I shut my eyes and shove my face against the cool side of my pillow with a groan.

Sleep begins to take hold of me again, but I cling to precarious consciousness when I hear hushed voices coming from my living room.

Who would be in my apartment while I'm sleeping? I should be more concerned, but I'm so tired...

"I can't fucking believe you!" someone hisses. Sounds like Mezli.

I should go say hi, but my limbs feel like lead. I burrow further under the covers and yawn.

"You're not saying anything I haven't already told myself. But she agreed to it. I did everything I could," murmurs a deep, pained voice.

Huh...what is Breks doing here?

"Bullshit. Doing everything you could would have been telling her the truth before fucking her!"

"I know. *Vash-ka*, I never wanted to hurt her. I just wanted to—" Wait, that's not Breks...is it Maerlon? I wish I could get myself to focus, but my thoughts are sluggish and fuzzy.

"I don't give a fuck what you wanted, Maerlon. Get out before she wakes up. She doesn't need to deal with your garbage while she's recovering."

"Don't call him garbage...his ex said that," I say weakly. The image of someone with glowing eyes and dark skin dotted with luminous markings looking down at me with concern floats into my mind. Maerlon is so handsome—why does he look so worried? As I try to remember, my mind finally loses against the fatigue and sleep drags me into oblivion.

THE BUZZING of my comm from the living room wakes me up again. I sit up slowly, groaning at the stiffness in my muscles. My head feels clearer, though I still have a dull headache.

"Hey there, Mrs. Kress!" Mezli's voice calls out from my living room.

Why is she here? And why is she answering my comm for me?

"Mezli? Hi. Where's Fina?"

I push the covers off and stand, wobbling as I get my feet under me. I need to get in there before Mezli tells my mom about all the clubs we've gone to. Or starts hitting on her.

"Oh, she's just sleeping something off," Mezli says cheerily.

"Sleeping what off? Is she okay??" I can practically hear my mom's frown.

I open the door and Mezli turns away from the vid screen to give me an uncharacteristically apologetic smile. Oh god, what's wrong?

"Hey mom, I'm fine. Sorry for oversleeping." I nudge Mezli to make room for me in front of the vid comm.

"Christ, Fina! You look awful. Are you sick? Is she sick, Mezli?" My mom's eyes dart between us, worry creasing her features.

I open my mouth to make a joke about how dramatic she's being, but Mezli replies first. "Don't panic, Mrs. Kress. She...uh, ate something last night that caused an adverse reaction. We tried using her inhaler, thinking it was allergies. But that, mixed with whatever was going on, knocked her out. Her vitals are fine, I promise. I checked them three times."

All the color drains from my mom's face. "You used her inhaler?"

That explains the horrible headache and fuzzy sleep—I was stunned! But the allergic reaction...I don't remember eating anything weird yesterday.

"Yes, was that wrong?" Mezli looks surprised at my mom's reaction and she frowns.

"It's not for allergies. It's stun spray. My mom insisted I carry it," I say with a sigh, rubbing my head to ease the throbbing.

"Oh shit. That's badass, Mrs. Kress!" It's unsurprising Mezli's impressed by her sending me an illegal drug.

My mom shakes her head and places a hand over her eyes in frustration. "Fina, you have to be more careful about what you ingest! You can't just go eating things without checking that they're human-safe."

My cloudy brain finally clears enough for me to catch up with the conversation and I squeak in shocked embarrassment. I didn't eat anything last night. But I swallowed Breks'...oh god, I'm an idiot.

Mezli sees the understanding dawn on my face and snorts. "She'll be more careful about consuming alien substances from now on. Won't you, Fina?"

"Right." I glare at her, praying my mom doesn't pick up on her meaning.

"Good. Don't do anything today. You need to rest. I love you—please be more careful."

I can't help thinking that some of this is my mom's fault. After all, she sent me the stun spray and insisted I carry it. But I'm too weak and tired to bring that up right now. "I will. Love you, mom."

"Bye, Mrs. Kress!" Mezli blows a kiss at the vid screen and my mom rolls her eyes, ending the call.

"Well, you heard the woman. Back to bed with you!" Mezli clucks at me and points toward the bedroom.

"Mezli. What the fuck is going on?"

Her brow furrows, and she hesitates for a moment before speaking. "What do you remember from last night?"

My cheeks heat.

"Girl, don't give me that look. I know you were up to some freaky shit at SimTech. That's no big deal. Do you remember who was there with you?" Her tone sounds teasing, but her lips turn down into a concerned frown.

"A guy who works there. His name is Breks. We've been...seeing each other. He thought his appearance would scare me, so I don't know what he looks like. God, that sounds fucking weird, doesn't it? I have a massive thing for an alien I don't even really know."

"I wouldn't say that," replies Mezli with a snort.

"Not everyone is as adventurous as you, Mez! It's weird for me."

"That's not what I was laughing about. Shit, why is it on me to tell you this?" Mezli scowls in frustration.

I don't understand why she's upset. "Are you mad at me?"

"Goddess, no! I'm mad at that coward, Maerlon."

"Maerlon? What did he—"

Everything clicks into place at once, and my knees almost give out under me. I stagger over to the couch and collapse down on it. The voice that sounded so strangely familiar. The hazy, dark face with glowing eyes staring down at me in concern. The things Maerlon said at Epiphany.

Fuck, how did I not know?

"You were blinded by horniness," says Mezli, sitting down on the couch next to me with a sympathetic smile.

Whoops, must have said that last part out loud.

She rests a reassuring hand on my shoulder. "You don't need to feel bad. You did nothing wrong. That lying jerk did."

"I don't understand. Why wouldn't he just tell me? I told him over and over that I didn't care what he looked like...was he doing it just to mess with me?"

The thought stabs me like a knife to the gut. Did I fall for a guy who just wanted to play a fucked up game with me? Could he really be that cruel?

My comm pings with a message from the person in question.

> Maerlon: I'm so sorry, Fina. I've hurt you and betrayed your trust. All I wanted to do was please you and instead I ruined everything. I'm a coward.

Mezli scowls at the message over my shoulder. "You don't have to respond to him. You don't owe him anything, Fina."

My chest tightens, a mixture of pain at being lied to and concern for the man I opened my heart to.

> Fina: You could have told me.

A few moments pass before he replies.

> Maerlon: I've seen how you flinch when you look at me. I was a fool who wanted to cling to the illusion that you could care for me. It blinded me.

What the hell is he talking about? I thought he was attractive from the moment we met. But then again, I thought he was looking at me with disdain and he's been into me this whole time. My head aches again. I need to lie down.

> Fina: We've both been blind.

> Fina: I need to rest now.

I close the comm before I can see his reply and get sucked back into the conversation. I'm so tired and overwhelmed—all I want is to crawl into bed and never leave.

Mezli wraps her arms around me, and unexpected tears run down my cheeks. For once, she doesn't make a quip or witty remark. She just holds me tight, letting me know that I'm not alone.

# 29

## ✦ MAERLON ✦

A million replies to Fina's message race through my mind. But bothering her again would be selfish. I'm sure she doesn't want to hear anything from me right now.

Or ever again.

She said we've both been blind. How was she blind? Does she mean she should have seen through my deception? I kept her in the dark, afraid for her to see who I truly am, and it exploded in my face.

I should have listened to Dezlon and Rhysti. Now it's too late and I've irreparably hurt the woman I care for. I had so many chances to tell her, so why couldn't I? What's wrong with me?

It hurts to acknowledge I'm the reason a relationship ended before it could start, especially after my breakup with K'thress. Was

I so desperate for affection and validation after they left me that I clung to my attraction to Fina even though I knew it wouldn't work?

Every time my comm pings, my stomach flips, hoping that it's a message from Fina and dreading what she's said if it is her. The night cycle comes and goes, but I hear nothing.

I'm itching to message her and say the things I've imagined telling her while I've waited. Sleep-deprived and jittery, I cave and send a message to Mezli to at least see if Fina is okay. I get a curt "yes, she's fine" back, but nothing else.

Of course she didn't say more. Mezli was furious with me when she showed up at SimTech to find an unconscious, undressed Fina. I explained the situation, and she made it abundantly clear how little she thought of me and my cowardice. I wish Fina would scream at me like Mezli did. Then at least I'd know where we stand and could ignore the foolish hope of somehow salvaging things.

Hours pass, morning fading to late afternoon. I'm curled up in my bed, fruitlessly trying to make up for my sleepless night when my comm dings. Panic shoots through me and I'm instantly filled with adrenaline and dread. Heart racing, I check the message.

> Fina: It turns out that getting stun sprayed is no joke. I only woke up a few hours ago.

> Fina: Meet me for dinner? We need to talk and I'd rather do it face-to-face. I've had enough talking through the barrier of technology to last a lifetime.

I wince at her words. If that reference to my deception is any indication, it won't be a pleasant conversation. But I need to hear what she has to say. I owe her that and so much more.

> Maerlon: Are you sure you're up to it? I'll gladly meet and hear everything you want to say. But please don't feel pressured to do that if you're still unwell.

A painful minute passes as I wait for her reply.

> Fina: I don't want to wait.

She sends me the name of a restaurant in Orion district and a time to meet. Now, I just have to figure out how to stay sane until then.

✦

I ARRIVE AT DINNER EARLY, unable to stand pacing around my loft any longer. I considered getting flowers or some kind of token to supplement my apology, but decided against it—I don't want Fina to think I'm trying to buy her forgiveness. With a deep breath, I brace myself and head inside.

The restaurant is an intimate bistro tucked away from the main walkways, with small candlelit tables and soft music wafting through the air. I tug at the collar of my shirt. The too-tight neck chokes me, but I wanted to look nice for Fina. Seeing the assortment of well-dressed couples that fill the restaurant, I'm glad I wore it.

This looks like a date spot, but I don't let that encourage me too much. She could have chosen this place because she'd enjoyed it with another partner. I'm jealous at the thought, though I know I have no right to be.

I scan the space, looking for Fina's distinctive purple hair and I see her at the back of the narrow restaurant. She's looking down at

I so desperate for affection and validation after they left me that I clung to my attraction to Fina even though I knew it wouldn't work?

Every time my comm pings, my stomach flips, hoping that it's a message from Fina and dreading what she's said if it is her. The night cycle comes and goes, but I hear nothing.

I'm itching to message her and say the things I've imagined telling her while I've waited. Sleep-deprived and jittery, I cave and send a message to Mezli to at least see if Fina is okay. I get a curt "yes, she's fine" back, but nothing else.

Of course she didn't say more. Mezli was furious with me when she showed up at SimTech to find an unconscious, undressed Fina. I explained the situation, and she made it abundantly clear how little she thought of me and my cowardice. I wish Fina would scream at me like Mezli did. Then at least I'd know where we stand and could ignore the foolish hope of somehow salvaging things.

Hours pass, morning fading to late afternoon. I'm curled up in my bed, fruitlessly trying to make up for my sleepless night when my comm dings. Panic shoots through me and I'm instantly filled with adrenaline and dread. Heart racing, I check the message.

> Fina: It turns out that getting stun sprayed is no joke. I only woke up a few hours ago.

> Fina: Meet me for dinner? We need to talk and I'd rather do it face-to-face. I've had enough talking through the barrier of technology to last a lifetime.

I wince at her words. If that reference to my deception is any indication, it won't be a pleasant conversation. But I need to hear what she has to say. I owe her that and so much more.

> Maerlon: Are you sure you're up to it? I'll gladly meet and hear everything you want to say. But please don't feel pressured to do that if you're still unwell.

A painful minute passes as I wait for her reply.

> Fina: I don't want to wait.

She sends me the name of a restaurant in Orion district and a time to meet. Now, I just have to figure out how to stay sane until then.

I ARRIVE AT DINNER EARLY, unable to stand pacing around my loft any longer. I considered getting flowers or some kind of token to supplement my apology, but decided against it—I don't want Fina to think I'm trying to buy her forgiveness. With a deep breath, I brace myself and head inside.

The restaurant is an intimate bistro tucked away from the main walkways, with small candlelit tables and soft music wafting through the air. I tug at the collar of my shirt. The too-tight neck chokes me, but I wanted to look nice for Fina. Seeing the assortment of well-dressed couples that fill the restaurant, I'm glad I wore it.

This looks like a date spot, but I don't let that encourage me too much. She could have chosen this place because she'd enjoyed it with another partner. I'm jealous at the thought, though I know I have no right to be.

I scan the space, looking for Fina's distinctive purple hair and I see her at the back of the narrow restaurant. She's looking down at her comm, her posture stiff. As I approach, she looks up and a surge of emotion hits me when her blue-green eyes lock onto mine. She looks heart-achingly beautiful as she gives me a tight smile and a tentative wave.

If this is my last chance to spend time with her, I want to soak in every detail. From the dusting of pigmentation that sprinkles across her cheeks and chest to the soft roundness of her stomach in the tight, pale pink dress she's wearing.

"You're early!" She pops up out of her chair as I reach the table.

I freeze, brow tightening in concern. "Should I go wait outside for a bit? I'm sorry, I was anxious to see you."

Her lips curve into a slight smile. "No, it's fine. You can stay."

We both stand for a moment too long and my hands twitch, wanting to haul her into my arms and hold her there until she understands how sorry I am. I realize I'm still standing and staring at her when she clears her throat and sits down again.

Fina watches me for a moment as I sit across from her, and I dread what she's about to say. She looks just as tense as I am. When I can barely stand the silence any longer, she speaks.

"It's nice to meet you, Breks. I'm Fina."

I'm confused. Does she want me to admit that I'm Breks? She already knows that.

"Breks is a name I use for work. You can call me that if you'd like, but most people call me Maerlon."

She nods. "Which do you prefer?"

I don't care what she calls me as long as I get to talk to her. "Maerlon, I suppose."

"Right, well, like I said, it's good to meet you. How long have you been on Spire?"

My brow knits as I try to grasp why she's acting like we've never met. Is she still experiencing the residual effects of the stun spray and whatever caused the allergic reaction?

"Fina, we know each other."

She levels her gaze on me and her lips downturn. "Do we?"

Ah. I see. My face falls and I stare at my hands, unable to look her in the eyes as she reminds me of my shame.

After a moment, Fina sighs. "I'm sorry. I had the silly idea that we could start fresh—pretend that we're strangers and maybe that would make things easier. But I know we can't."

She's willing to give me a fresh start? I glance up to see that she's staring at me, chewing on her bottom lip.

"Fina, I—"

A nexxit waitress appears beside the table, interrupting me. She takes our orders in a chipper voice, babbling about the specials and her recommendations. I nod politely, silently begging her to stop talking and go away with my eyes.

When she finally leaves, I turn back to Fina. "So, what's it like being a human on Spire?"

She blinks a few times in confusion. "What?"

"Is that inappropriate to ask on a first date?"

A hint of a smile crosses her lips. "No, not at all. It's overwhelming, but fascinating. I get to meet all kinds of interesting people that I never would've if I'd stayed with the Coalition fleet. What about you? I haven't seen many seladin on the station."

I consider the question for a moment. "Being away from my people is eye-opening. And a bit terrifying, though most of the time other species act like I'm the one who is frightening. But more than anything, it's been a blessing because I met yo—uh, some very special people."

Fina's eyes soften. "Maerlon..."

Here it is—the moment when she tells me she can't forgive what I've done. That I've caused too much hurt.

I speak before she can continue. "Fina, I could keep pretending that we haven't already had this conversation. But you don't owe me another chance. I've been a coward and a fool, and I don't deserve it."

There. I've said it for her. Now she doesn't have to confront me about what I've done. I know how much she hates conflict.

Her eyes are watery, filling with tears. "Why didn't you tell me? Was it because you didn't want anything serious?" Her voice lowers to a whisper. "Am I not good enough to be more than someone you fuck in secret? Are you with someone else?"

She can't hold the tears back any longer and furiously wipes them away as they roll down her face. "Fuck, sorry. I didn't want to cry. I just...be honest with me, please. Even if you think it will hurt me. I can't stand being lied to anymore."

I want to reach across the table and pull her face to mine, to wipe away the tears and kiss her until she understands just how deeply I care for her. Show her how sorry I am for hurting her. How could she think I would want anyone but her? That I would be ashamed to be with her. If anything, she should be ashamed of being with me.

"I'm in love with you, Fina," I blurt out. *Esh'et*, why did I say that? I guess I can't hide from her any longer.

Her eyes widen and her mouth falls open slightly. "W-what?"

"I'm hopelessly in love with you. Since that night you hid from those ankites and talked with me for hours. I know I shouldn't be telling you this. I don't expect you to feel the same. But it's part of the answer to your question. I was too scared to tell you because I've seen how you react to me. You said you wouldn't care who Breks was, but then every time I was near you, you'd flinch or look away. I'm not saying this is your fault—not at all. I didn't tell you because I couldn't confront the reality of you not wanting me when you saw Breks' true face."

The waitress, with impeccably horrible timing, approaches the table with our drinks. I thank her but can't hear her reply over the roar of dread in my ears. I sip my drink to calm myself, but it sloshes over the side of the glass and onto my hand because I'm shaking.

Fina's hand darts out with her napkin, and she wipes at the spill. I turn my palm up so it's facing hers and hesitantly take hold of her hand through the napkin's fabric. She looks at me with shining eyes and I give her a reassuring smile.

"I deeply regret my cowardice and any hurt I caused you. But I can't regret any moments I shared with you. I'll cherish the brief time I held your affection for the rest of my days." My chest tightens and my eyes threaten to fill up with tears. I blink rapidly, trying to fight them off.

Fina pulls her hand from mine and I lose the battle, letting the hot, heavy tears slide down my cheeks.

The table wobbles and suddenly Fina's hands are on both sides of my face, pulling me forward until her lips crash against mine. Stunned, I let her kiss me for a moment before I groan with need and return it. She leans even closer and the glass in front of me tips over. Fina curses as the liquid pours onto my lap, but I couldn't care less. Nothing matters other than her mouth on mine.

Hope flutters desperately in my chest. Maybe I still have a chance to make things right.

# 30

## ✦FINA✦

"I'm so sorry!" I cringe as I back away from my disastrous kiss. It felt right at the moment, as my feelings for Maerlon burst forth. I didn't consider my wrecking ball boobs, and now I've made a mess.

"For kissing me?" Maerlon's dazed smile falls. "It's okay, Fina. I understand, you—"

"No! For spilling water all over you. Now your lap is soaked." I pass my napkin over, giving him a sheepish look.

He takes it and pats at his wet pants, keeping his eyes locked on mine with an earnest, hungry expression. If I wasn't so embarrassed about spilling his drink, it would be sexy.

The waitress bustles over in concern and asks if we need any help. Some patrons looked over during the commotion, but have returned to their meals.

"Apologies for my clumsiness! If you have a towel, I'm happy to clean up any mess I've made," Maerlon tells the waitress, dabbing at the spilled water on the table.

She softens at his apology and insists that she cleans things up, chatting with us the entire time about other incidents she's seen at the restaurant. Apparently, someone caught their sleeve on fire with the table candle and their date panicked and tried to put it out with an alcoholic drink.

As sweet as the waitress is, I'm thankful when she brings our food and leaves. Silence falls over our table as we both taste our meals. Neither one of us quite know how to continue.

"How's your food?" Maerlon finally asks, gesturing at my bright orange and green noodle dish.

I swallow my bite, almost choking in my hurry to respond. I cough and take a sip of my water, eliciting a concerned look from Maerlon. "It's great! I've been meaning to try more nexxit dishes, and Mezli said this place is the best authentic nexxit cuisine on Spire."

"It won't bother your allergies?"

My cheeks heat. Right, he doesn't know what caused that reaction I had. This is *awkward*.

"I'm pretty diligent about checking out what I can and can't eat ahead of time. My mom's a medic, so she drilled safe eating habits into me before I left the fleet. I, uh, didn't factor that into the consumption of other...substances. So that's what caused my weird reaction when we were..."

I trail off as Maerlon's brow raises, and he rubs the shaved patch on his head, drawing my attention to how the tip of his pointed ear has become darker than the rest of his skin. "You ate something other than...oh. *Oh. Esh'et,* I'm so sorry. I had no idea that would happen." He looks mortified.

"I don't think either of us knew that I'd have that kind of reaction. Honestly, it wasn't unpleasant for me—just unexpected. I know it was probably scary for you, though."

Maerlon frowns and shakes his head. "I endangered you by keeping you in the dark. You could have been seriously hurt. Is that why your inhaler didn't help?"

He looks so concerned and ashamed—I want to kiss him again to reassure him I'm okay. Yes, I'm still mad. Yes, we still have a lot to talk about. But I can finally see his genuine emotions and that makes me want to comfort him.

I lower my voice so that only he can hear. "Uh, well, that wasn't exactly a real inhaler. Do you remember when I said I had a way of defending myself? That's what it was—my mom made stun spray for me and insisted I carry it."

Understanding flashes across his face. "Your mother is right. I was an idiot and used something on you without knowing what it was. I should have taken you to a medic."

"God, I'm glad you didn't. I don't think I could have handled a doctor telling me I tripped balls from drinking your cum. And let's not forget that I had a banned substance on me."

Maerlon lets out a loud, sputtering laugh and looks up at me, eyes brightening in surprise at my colorful word choices. A few people at nearby tables glance over at us, no doubt wondering if I've spilled another drink on him.

"Perhaps a conversation for another time," I say, giggling at his reaction.

The conversation lulls for a few minutes as we eat our food. I watch him surreptitiously between bites, feeling oddly shy when our eyes meet. When his gray tongue darts out to lick sauce off of his lips, my stomach clenches as I recall what he did to me with that tongue. His nostrils flare a moment later and his eyes burn brighter. I dart my eyes away—god, he can't smell that I'm turned on, can he?

"Sorry, sometimes I'm not the most elegant when I eat. I know I can be off-putting." He gestures at his face, giving me a slight, fanged smile.

I've had enough of him acting like he is some kind of hideous monster. "Stop it, you know you're handsome."

Maerlon freezes and his brow creases with a deep furrow. "You don't need to soothe my ego, Fina. I know that's not true."

Who filled his head with such nonsense? I grab his hand and stare him dead in the eyes. "Maerlon. I mean this with all the sincerity I possess: There is no universe in which you are unattractive. I'm almost intimidated by how hot you are."

"But you—I've seen how you look at me..."

I release his hand and throw both my hands up in exasperation. "I didn't want you knowing how attracted I was to you, you big, sexy idiot!"

The women at the table next to ours glare over at me and I flush, poking at my noodles and pretending they're the most fascinating thing in the universe, so I don't have to acknowledge my outburst.

A foot nudges against mine under the table. Maerlon has a quizzical expression on his face as I look up. "Why didn't you want me to know?"

"I had no reason to believe that you found me attractive at all! Plus, you'd just gotten over your ex and I didn't want to jeopardize our new friendship."

"Me either. I still don't want to. If you only want friendship, I'll be glad to have you in my life at all. But if you'll allow me, I'll court you properly." He gives me an earnest, saddened look, as if he's waiting for my inevitable rejection.

My stomach flutters. It seems absurd to be "courted" at this point, but maybe that's what we need. "I think I'd like that."

The sheer relief and longing on his face in that moment almost has me knocking more drinks over just to kiss him again. The waitress arrives with the bill before I give into the urge. Maerlon insists on paying and leaves an overly generous tip to make up for our messiness. We leave the restaurant side-by-side, pausing once we're out on the walkway.

His eyes scan over me and he keeps his arms tightly at his sides, like he's trying to restrain himself. Taking the initiative, I step closer and loop my arms around his neck. He places his hands on my waist and looks down at me with such desire that I can't resist pulling him into a kiss. It's a soft, slow exploration that builds in intensity until we part, flushed and breathless.

Maerlon reluctantly releases his hold on my hips. "I should let you go."

"Right, yeah." I shake myself out of the spell of his embrace. I'm a little disappointed that he's saying goodnight, but if we keep kissing like that, I'm going to beg him to come back to my place.

"Thank you for giving me another chance, Fina. I know I don't deserve it."

I give him a mock stern look. "I expect to be wooed and seduced this time."

"Challenge gladly accepted," he says in a low rasp that sends shivers down my spine.

# 31

## ✦FINA✦

Luminescent flowers sitting on my desk greet me when I arrive at work the next day. It seems Maerlon is earnest about "courting" me right away. The gorgeous violet and black plant comes with a note explaining they're cuttings from his mother's botanical lab. She claims these flowers are some of the only remaining flora from Sela, the original seladin homeworld. If that's true, this plant is worth a fortune. It's incredibly touching, but I worry I'll accidentally kill it—I have the opposite of a green thumb.

The accompanying note also invites me to dinner at Maerlon's place tomorrow night. He could've just messaged me on my comm—we've been chatting almost non-stop since last night. But it's sweet that he wrote this out. Unsurprisingly, his handwriting is elegant and precise. I smile at the note and then blink at it in shock, realizing the significance of him writing this out. It's in Coalition Standard. A language I'm pretty sure he doesn't speak, let alone write. How long did it take him to copy the words over so perfectly?

Throughout the day, I pull the note out between meetings, touching the soft vellum with wonder. Mezli stops by my office to check on me and catches me thumbing it with a no doubt dreamy look on my face. I'm hesitant to tell her about my decision to give Maerlon a chance. She was pissed and worried about me and I don't want her to think less of me. But she takes one look at the flowers on my desk paired with my expression and lets out a wry laugh.

"So, things went well with Maerlon?" Mezli comes closer to inspect the blooms, raising a knowing eyebrow at me. "These are pretty, but he needs to do a lot more than give you flowers to make up for his shitty behavior."

I tuck the note back in my desk drawer. "I'm giving him a chance. There were a lot of mixed signals and misunderstandings. Now that I know where he stands, I want to try."

"I'm sorry—Did *you* pretend to be someone else for weeks and seduce him as your alter-ego? This was all on him. He better not have tried to convince you otherwise!" Her face twists into an angry grimace. I'm fortunate to have a friend who cares so much about me. Though I'm glad she didn't decide to take bloody revenge on Maerlon before I could make my own decision.

"He didn't! He took total responsibility and feels terrible. I'm not saying I'm going to trust everything he says blindly, but...I care about him a lot and he made it obvious how much he cares for me."

"You sure he isn't just a good actor? He had you fooled for weeks." Mezli's scowl softens, but she still doesn't seem convinced.

"No, I'm just oblivious," I say, rolling my eyes at her jab.

She chuckles and nods. "True. After all, you still haven't realized that I'm madly in love with you." She leans over my shoulder and turns my head with one of her hands until I'm looking into her huge, glittering eyes.

I know she's probably joking, but the look she's giving me is intense. "Uh, Mez?"

"Hah! Oblivious *and* gullible." She pinches my cheek and then sticks her tongue out at me.

"That's me." Damn, I really am easy to mess with.

"Seriously though, as mad as I am at Maerlon, he's my friend too. A friend who I'm pissed at, but a good guy at his core. If you want to forgive him, I will. I just want you to be happy."

I stand up and pull her into a hug, which she happily reciprocates. "You're the best friend I could ever ask for. Thank you."

I let go, but she squeezes me tighter, crushing me with her four arms. "You're my best friend. And if Maerlon hurts you again, I'm cutting off his balls." She releases me, a feral smile curling her lips.

I snort. "Deal."

The rest of the workday is painfully slow. With the big ad campaign we've been busting our asses on wrapped up, there's not much for me to do. I'm about to head home early and get a head start on freaking out about what to wear to dinner tomorrow when my boss, Zandra, pings me.

> Zandra: Fina, do you have time to meet with a new client before leaving today? I wouldn't have bothered you with this after all the extra time you've been putting in, but they say they know you.

Someone that knows me? I wrack my brain, trying to figure out who I know that would need CiaXera's marketing services, but come up blank.

> Fina: Of course, I'm happy to.

> Zandra: Great, they're headed to your office now.

> Fina: Wait, who are they?

There's a rap on my open office door, and I glance up from the screen before I can see Zandra's answer.

"Pardon me, I was looking for Serafina Kress, but I think I have the wrong office. The Fina I know doesn't have purple hair." A familiar stocky, tan human man with short curly black hair and an amused slant on his mouth leans on the doorframe.

My brain stutters for a moment, not able to process the sight before me. Out of all the people in the galaxy, I was not expecting my *ex* to show up at my office.

"Paul?! What are you doing here?" I leap out of my chair and rush over to him. He wraps me up in a powerful hug and a rush of emotion seizes my chest. I haven't seen Paul, or anyone from my old life, in what feels like ages. It doesn't seem real, but I smell his spicy aftershave and feel the familiar warmth of his arms. Tears prick my eyes, but when the hug ends, there's a huge smile on my lips.

"Surprise," he says with a roguish grin.

I lightly punch his shoulder, then wipe the water from my eyes. "You should have told me you were coming to Spire!"

"You know I can't resist a dramatic entrance. The look on your face was priceless." He steps back to give me a quick once over and his smile grows even broader. "Damn, Fina. Space station life looks good on you."

I grin despite my frustration at him keeping this a secret from me. "That's sweet, but enough flattery—tell me why you're here!"

He laughs at my impatience. "Alright, alright. The Coalition is finally establishing a Human embassy on Spire. The ambassadorial office is consulting with CiaXera to make sure it isn't a PR shitshow with the locals. So here I am, a representative coming to speak with their Human Cultural Consultant before this project gets started. I would've reached out ahead of time, but the deal was under NDA until today."

I stare at him, stunned. I thought it'd be decades, if not centuries, before the Coalition got off its ass and integrated more with the galactic community. This news is monumental—and it means I won't be one of the few humans on Spire for much longer.

"This is unbelievable, holy shit. I'm—wow, that's huge! Does that mean that you're staying here?" The thought of having another friend on the station is thrilling. Even if his friendship comes with a ton of baggage.

"Yeah, at least until things are settled. So, a few years minimum. Unless the Xi Consortium decides that we're just a bunch of uncultured troglodytes and kicks us out."

I beam at Paul and blink away the tears that've welled in my eyes again.

"Fina, babe, I didn't know you missed me so much." Paul takes my hands into his and rubs them reassuringly with his thumbs. In the past, the gesture might have sparked some heat inside me, but I don't feel it now.

"I didn't," I say, shaking my head at him. I've given barely any thought to him since I left. Post-breakup Fina wouldn't believe how true that is. How liberating it feels to not want him—at least not for anything beyond friendship—anymore.

"Ouch! So those are tears of sadness?" He releases my hands and brings his own to his heart, feigning insult. I catch a hint of true surprise in his eyes that he can't quite mask.

"No, sorry! I mean, I *have* missed you. But I've been so busy there was no time to think about home. Well, my old home. Seeing you here made it hit me all at once."

"Well, home has definitely missed you." He wraps his arms around me, and I hug him back, unable to resist grounding his presence here in reality. I feel his chuckle reverberate against my chest.

Paul rubs a soothing circle on my back. "You're so fucking brave, you know that, right? I only convinced myself to take this assignment because I knew I wouldn't be totally alone. That I'd get to see you again…I've missed you."

The intimacy of his tone surprises me, and I tense in his embrace. Paul was the one who ended our relationship a few years ago. I know now that it was the right choice, but at the time, it felt like he'd shredded my heart into pieces. He's never shown any regret about the decision, but his words feel weighted. Did he come here just for work? Or is he hoping for something else too?

Someone in the hallway clears their throat. "Sorry to interrupt, just wanted to stop by before I head out."

I let Paul go, and turn around to see Maerlon, his posture stiff. It's surreal to see the two of them next to each other, two completely different worlds colliding. I take a half-step toward him to embrace him, but stop, suddenly shy with Paul standing there watching.

I abort the hug and turn the motion into an awkward wave. "Maerlon! Hey."

He looks back and forth between me and Paul, trying to assess what he walked in on. His face remains neutral, not giving away any of his thoughts.

Paul gives me a questioning look and then a little nudge,

breaking me out of intent observation of Maerlon's reaction. "Oh right, Paul, this is my…"

I stumble, unsure of what to refer to him as. Friend? Lover? Something in between? "This is my…Maerlon." Maerlon's mouth quirks and I push forward, pretending I didn't just say something weird. "He works in the design department. Maerlon—Paul's an old friend from back when I worked with the Coalition ambassadorial office."

Shit, should I have said he was my ex? God, this is weird.

Paul nods in greeting at Maerlon, stepping closer to me. "A pleasure to meet you, Maerlon."

"Nice to meet you too, Paul. What brings another human to Spire? Are you here to save Fina from the scary aliens?" Maerlon punctuates his words with a sharp, fanged smile that has Paul flinching slightly.

I snort in amusement as Paul composes himself, schooling his face back to a relaxed expression. Maerlon looks fierce, there's a teasing flare in his eyes.

"I'm moving here for work. If anything, I'm sure Fina will be the one saving me—from any cultural stumbles and getting lost, that is," says Paul, his arm wrapping around my waist with obvious familiarity.

Maerlon's eyes narrow at the gesture. Paul squeezes me closer in response, no doubt in some macho attempt to stake his claim on me. A claim he doesn't have and hasn't had in years. I pull away and take a step back, grabbing my mug of tea from my desk to disguise my retreat from Paul's touch.

"I'm happy to show you around! It's kind of nice to think that someone else will be even more hopeless at navigating the transit system than I am." I take a swig from my half-empty, cold mug and pray for the tension to break.

"Can we start with a good place to grab dinner? I'd love to catch up if you're free tonight." Paul smiles at me with that pearly grin that used to make my stomach flutter.

I almost expect Maerlon to bristle at the invitation, but he just watches me and Paul with an even, neutral expression on his face.

Paul looks over at Maerlon with his signature charming smile. "You're welcome to come too, Maerlon." It's an empty offer, just him trying to appear polite.

Maerlon doesn't smile back. "Oh. Thank you, but don't let me intrude."

There's no way I'm going to dinner with just Paul. Not when he's acting so damn weird. But my brain fails to conjure an excuse to skip it, so I lean into inviting Maerlon, hoping he won't mind. "Dinner would be great. Maerlon, you should come!"

Paul's charming veneer flickers for a second and I catch a look of genuine shock on his face before he nods in agreement and his jovial smile returns. "Yes, please join us."

"Though you have to promise to not tell Maerlon embarrassing stories about me," I say, hoping to turn Paul's thoughts back to one of friendship instead of whatever weirdness is running through his head.

"Hah, I can't guarantee that!" says Paul, taking the bait.

"Should we invite Mezli and make it a night of teasing Fina?" Maerlon's hand brushes against my cheek, pushing a stray strand of hair behind my ear with one of his clawed fingers. I glance up at him and his eyes are shining down at me with amused affection. Paul's eyes track the movement with hawkish attention, but all I can focus on is how much I love even the smallest of Maerlon's touches.

"If you think she won't murder me on sight, I'd love to meet the infamous Mezli." Paul knows how much anger Mezli has toward him since he broke my heart. She sent him multiple threatening letters going into great detail about how she would destroy him if it wasn't for me holding her back. Now that I think about it, Maerlon's lucky she only cursed him out.

"Well, now she *has* to come!" Maerlon gives him a sharp grin. Paul flinches again at the sight of his fangs, but tries to play it off.

"You're both making me regret agreeing to this dinner," I protest, crossing my arms across my chest. Though having Mezli around would serve as a great deterrent to Paul's unexpected romantic intent toward me.

"You know you love it." Paul gives Maerlon a conspiratorial look. It holds his usual charm, but I know it's his way of telling Maerlon how well he knows me. Maerlon returns the look, then gives me a devilish smile.

I sigh and roll my eyes. "Okay, fine. I'll invite Mezli."

Maerlon squeezes my shoulder. "I need to head out. Message me the details?"

I nod. He dips his head at Paul and turns to leave. In a rush of affection, I grab Maerlon's hand and go up on my toes to give him a quick kiss. Even just that gentle brush of lips sends sparks through me, and the pleasantly surprised expression on his face makes it even more exciting. His luminous eyes brighten and he squeezes my hand before heading off.

Paul's mouth hangs open slightly as I wave goodbye to Maerlon. "He's..."

"Hot?" I finish dreamily.

"I was going to say scary, but honestly yeah, also sexy. Is he your...partner?"

I'm not sure how to answer the question, but I need to make it clear that I'm not interested in rekindling what I had with Paul.

"Why do you ask? Surely the most eligible bachelor from the ambassadorial office isn't jealous?"

He sputters, his cheeks darkening. "No, of course not!"

"Good. I love you, Paul. But we both know we're much better as friends. I don't want anything other than that." I give his arm a light pat. It feels so good to be brave enough to not circle around my feelings when I talk to him.

He senses the newfound confidence behind my words, judging by how he looks at me like he's seeing me for the first time. "Wow, you really have changed. In a good way! I liked the old Fina, don't get me wrong. But the directness is hot. Too bad we're just friends." Paul laughs, and this time, it lacks his normal bravado. A rare, genuine glimpse into his feelings.

"Hah, you'll forget about me once you realize you have a station filled with aliens looking to sate their curiosity about humans."

His eyes sparkle, considering the intriguing possibilities of dating on Spire. "True! I'll have to find my own hot alien to kiss."

"Oh boy, just wait until Mezli gets her hands on you. If she can get over her need to rip your balls off, she'll have you signed up for dating apps by the end of the night."

# 32

## ✦FINA✦

"Alright, let's get this over with, fucker!" Mezli's shout cuts through the din of conversation, echoing through the food hall. Dozens of aliens turn to watch her as she storms toward our table, radiating a menacing aura.

"Fuck, she really *is* going to kill me. I should go." Paul scrambles up from his stool.

"There's nowhere on Spire you can go where she can't hunt you down, so you're better off facing her now," says Maerlon with an amused snort. He doesn't seem to understand the severity of her protective anger, despite recently being on the receiving end of it.

My heart races as Mezli reaches our table and grabs onto Paul's arm before he can dodge out of the way. Another one of her hands darts out lightning-fast and cracks across his face. "That's for all the bullshit you put Fina through!"

"Oh god!" I gasp, echoed by the shocked bystanders around us watching this scene unfold. Holy shit, she really hit him.

Maerlon and I both stand, reaching out to tear her away before she can land another hit. But she's too fast. Mezli doesn't strike again, though. Instead, she uses her lower arms to pull Paul into a rib-crushing hug.

"And this is for your welcome to Spire," Mezli says, her voice filled with manic cheerfulness.

Paul gapes at us over her shoulder, a stunned look on his face to go along with the dark bloom of color from her slap. She lets him go and gives him a feral grin. "Don't fuck with Fina again. Let that be a warning to you too, Maerlon."

She pats Paul on the shoulder and then plops onto a stool across from me. Paul looks down at her as he brings a hand to his tender cheek, mouth still hanging open. "Well, don't just stand there. Come sit down, let's eat!" she says casually. Like she didn't just slap my ex in the face.

"R-right." Paul slides back into his seat next to her, watching Mezli warily. I don't blame him.

Maerlon bundles up some ice chips from his cup in a napkin and hands it to Paul. "*Fa-shar*, here, use this on your face." His dumbstruck expression matches Paul's, who takes the makeshift ice pack with a thankful nod.

"Are you okay, Paul?" I ask, scowling at Mezli. He nods, attempting to sink back into his cool demeanor. "No more violence, for the love of God, Mezli! I can't believe you hit him! One of these days, someone's going to call station security on you."

Mezli shrugs and grabs a bowl of noodles from the assortment set out on our table. "No court would blame me for seeking retribution for my best friend. But fine, I'll be good. I won't need to get angry again. Right, boys?" She levels her gaze at Paul and Maerlon, menace still simmering beneath the cheerful surface.

"I feel like I'm missing something. What did he do to deserve such ire?" Maerlon looks between me and Mezli, and I regret not introducing Paul as my ex earlier.

I sigh and speak before Mezli gets a chance to open her mouth. "We dated. For most of my time on the ambassadorial ship. He broke things off a few years ago. It was...painful."

Maerlon's dotted brow furrows, and he turns his glowing gaze to Paul. "Ah. He's the ex you told me about."

"He broke her heart. Left her with no warning and almost immediately hooked up with every available person on their ship," says Mezli with a humorless laugh.

"That's not—" Paul starts to defend himself, but Mezli's warning glare silences him.

"Enough! The past is over. Paul and I are friends, and he doesn't need you terrorizing him as he adjusts to life on the station."

"Fiiine." Mezli lets out an exaggerated sigh. "I'll just have to settle for giving Paul my regular Spire initiation." She winks at him, and a mix of confusion and relief washes over his face.

Our uneasy conversation settles into a more relaxed one once it becomes clear Mezli's going to play nice with Paul. At least for now. As we eat, he gets a lot of intrigued looks from the aliens around us. He startles every time he notices someone staring at him, and Mezli cackles in delight at how jumpy he is. Maerlon is more sympathetic. A few times, he even bares his sharp teeth to scare away gawkers before Paul notices them. Each time Maerlon does that, I squeeze his hand gently in thanks.

I was worried at first that Maerlon would be awkward or pull some sort of alpha male bullshit with Paul after finding out about our history. But besides the cool stares back at the office, he's been charming and relaxed. Maybe Mezli slapping Paul for his shitty behavior served as a deterrent for macho posturing.

Maerlon's behavior tonight reminds me of Breks. Which I mean, duh. He *is* Breks. But the Maerlon I've spent time with until now was pretending to be standoffish or extremely apologetic. I'm captivated by the twist of his lips as he makes a clever joke and the mischievous gleam in his eyes when he teases me.

I gaze at him for too long until Mezli gleefully stage-whispers to Paul about my obsession with the handsome seladin. She's doing it to provoke my ex, but she's not wrong—my mind keeps drifting away from the conversation to less dinner-appropriate thoughts. The way Maerlon keeps touching my leg under the table doesn't help. I told myself that I wanted to go slow and take time getting to know him, but my body obviously didn't receive the message.

Once we've finished the meal, Mezli demands that Paul go bar hopping with her. It should shock me when he agrees to go with her, but I know how Paul operates. Despite her violent greeting, I've caught him watching her with interest a few times. Mezli has been her usual flirtatious self, though with veiled threats and jabs at him sprinkled in. She would eat him alive and he knows it, but he's too reckless to care.

I really don't want to stay out late, but there's no way that I'm letting her go off with him alone. I don't trust her not to murder him in the back room of some club. Maerlon has things to get done tonight, so he declines the offer to join us. I consider begging him to come, but don't want to seem desperate.

We all walk to the transit station together, and I hesitate before parting ways with Maerlon. I feel weird giving him more than a soft kiss, especially when Mezli starts needling Paul about how bad it must feel for him to see me with someone else. Maerlon watches me with barely disguised hunger as I leave, which makes me regret caring that my friends were watching. I should have kissed him the way I wanted to. I'll just have to make it up to him at our dinner tomorrow.

We make it through two hours of whirlwind bar hopping, with Mezli using the night as a challenge to test Paul's alcohol tolerance. I stay sober, afraid of what will happen if I don't serve as a chaperone on this dangerous outing. They bicker like an old married couple after they get a few drinks into their systems, but at least Mezli seems less inclined to hit him again by the time we help him back to his hotel.

When I finally get back to my apartment, I drop my bag on the coffee table and flop down onto the couch with a tired groan. I've got to stop staying out so late, especially on a work night.

I glance over at the flowers Maerlon gifted me sitting on my kitchen counter. Their blooms have opened in the darkness, glowing with ethereal violet light. It's such a beautiful, special gift that my heart flutters.

I open my comm to message Maerlon and find that I've already received a few messages from him, each spaced a handful of minutes apart.

> Maerlon: Let me know when you get home.

> Maerlon: Sorry, you don't have to if you don't want to. I'm not trying to keep tabs on you.

> Maerlon: Just want to know that you're safe.

Wow, he worries about things almost as much as I do. I smile to myself and type back a message.

> Fina: Gosh, how dare you want to make sure I got home alright?

> Fina: But seriously, I'm home now. Hope tonight wasn't too much.

He replies almost immediately.

> Maerlon: Not at all. I had a great time. Plus, now I know to never cross Mezli. Is Paul still alive?

> Fina: Haha yes. I still can't believe she hit him. Other than her wild display, I hope it wasn't too weird to spend time with an ex of mine. I promise I don't have any romantic feelings toward him now.

> Maerlon: Not too weird at all. You don't need to convince me. I trust you.

> Maerlon: Though I admit, I had to suppress the urge to haul you against me and stake my claim when I met him.

The idea is primitive, but a part of me thrills at it.

> Fina: Really? And how exactly would you have claimed me?

> Maerlon: The usual way. Pressing you up against the wall, hiking up your skirt, and sinking deep inside you while I bite your neck to mark you as mine.

Oh wow, now I'm more than a little turned on.

> Maerlon: I wouldn't have stopped until you came over and over and my spend was running down your thighs.

I let out a choked sound as I read his filthy words. He certainly knows how to talk dirty. Me though? I'm terrible at dirty talk. I try to think of something sexy to write back but draw a blank.

> Fina: Probably for the best that you restrained yourself. Paul's head would have exploded, and we'd both get fired.

God, that's the least sexy response possible. Way to ruin the mood, Fina.

> Maerlon: Hah, very true.

> Maerlon: Did I take that too far? I don't want to do anything that makes you uncomfortable.

> Fina: No! Not at all. I liked it. A lot. Just couldn't think well enough to write a sexy reply, what with certain parts of me begging for my attention.

> Maerlon: Should I let you go so you can take care of that?

> Fina: Don't you dare!

> Maerlon: Why? Do you need my help? I can tell you what to do.

> Maerlon: Or I could come over and show you.

> Maerlon: If you're not ready for that, I understand. No pressure at all.

It's a very tempting offer. On one hand, I'm desperate to have him come over here, throw me on the bed, and fuck me until I can't walk. But on the other, I'm nervous about being with him. We've been intimate together, but as Fina and Breks, not Fina and Maerlon. I didn't realize how much the barrier of his previous anonymity helped with my own inhibitions. Being with Maerlon feels more significant. So much more *real*.

> Fina: You don't know how much I want to say yes. I'm just not there yet.

> Maerlon: I understand. We can wait as long as you need. If you're never ready, that's okay.

> Fina: Oh, I'll definitely get there.

> Maerlon: I'll follow your lead. Just tell me what you need. I'll do anything for you.

> Fina: Anything?

> Maerlon: Absolutely.

> Fina: What if I asked you to dress up like a chicken and do a sexy dance for me?

> Maerlon: Sure. I'll have to find out what a chicken is, so I can do it properly. Also, take some dance classes. You've seen how I move.

> Fina: Wow, such dedication!

> Maerlon: You're worth it.

Here come the tingly feelings again. He could be laying it on thick, but I sense his sincerity. I can picture him sitting in his loft, absorbed in our conversation with that intense look he gets where his eyes glow brighter.

> Fina: Fuck, that's remarkably hot. Not the chicken part, that you'd do it, no questions asked.

> Maerlon: I don't kink shame. You shouldn't be embarrassed about your chicken fetish.

I let out an undignified snort-laugh that I'm glad he's not around to hear.

> Fina: I don't have a chicken fetish! Okay, now I'm less turned on.

> Maerlon: That makes one of us.

> Fina: You're turned on?

> Maerlon: Just talking to you has that effect on me. I'm surprised you haven't noticed.

That mental image of him in his loft now involves him shirtless and lazily palming himself through tight pants while he messages me. I wish I could see that. Encouraged by his offer to do anything, I message back.

> Fina: Can you show me?

A few seconds pass and I kick myself for asking such a weird question. But then my comm pings with an incoming vid call from Maerlon.

Oh shit.

I accept the call, but leave my visual feed off so that I can scramble to sit up and fix my messy hair before he sees me.

I'm greeted by an image not too far from what I'd imagined—Maerlon's sitting on his couch, his legs spread wide in a relaxed position. He's shirtless and his skin markings glow a soft purple hue in the low light. He's gorgeous. I'm a mess in comparison.

"Are you psychic?"

He blinks in confusion, sitting up slightly. "Not that I'm aware of."

"While we were talking, in my mind you looked exactly like you do now. No shirt and all."

"That sounds more like you're the psychic one." Maerlon chuckles and the low rumble of it paired with the flash of his fangs makes heat pool in my stomach.

"It's unfair that you look that good even after a long day. I came home looking like a raccoon that had fallen into a dumpster." I walk into my bathroom to glance in the mirror and cringe at the accuracy of my description.

"I doubt that. Unless raccoons are beautiful. But you don't have to turn your vid feed on. As much as I'd love to see you, this isn't about what I want. It's about giving you what you asked for." He gestures down at himself, then laughs self-consciously.

I asked for this, didn't I? I hadn't considered what would happen next—I was just trying to be flirty. I figured he'd send me a dick pic or something. This is a lot more intimate. I'm flustered, but excited at the prospect of shamelessly looking at him without having to worry about my appearance. Now I understand why he enjoyed hiding behind the holo.

"Now what?" I ask.

"That's entirely up to you, Fina." One of his hands slides to rest on his upper thigh, just a few inches away from the obvious bulge in his pants, as if to punctuate his words.

"Will you...can you show me? You've seen me, but I haven't seen you."

"Can you be more specific? What am I showing you?" Maerlon gives me a wicked look and the hand on his leg moves closer to his cock.

Flames lick across my cheeks. My silly mantra runs through my head, urging me to be bold enough to ask for what I want. "Touch yourself for me. Tell me what you think about as you do it."

"With pleasure," he says, his voice low and husky. His teasing hand goes to the fastener on his pants, but he pauses. "Wait, this isn't just a scheme to get a video of me stroking my cock to blackmail me with, is it? Because if it is—well played. I deserve it."

I snort. "You caught me. But it's too late now. You said you'd do anything. Now whip that thing out and get to it."

"Such a devious woman."

My laughter falls away as I watch him stand, undo the clasp at his hips, and drag both his pants and underwear down. His cock springs free and then he's standing there in all his naked glory.

God, he's enormous. Enormous and *very* alien. I know I touched him, but seeing it emphasizes the differences between him and a human. The shaft is thick, with ridges along it on the top and bottom, the sides dotted with the same glowing markings that decorate the rest of his skin. The tip is bulbous and flushed a deeper gray and there's a ring of small bumps circling the head. His balls are full and heavy and he's hairless.

I'm thankful my camera isn't on, so he can't see the shocked way I'm staring at his penis.

He's so hard that it's almost flush with his abdomen. Maerlon gives himself a lazy stroke and translucent liquid beads at the tip. He slips his pants all the way off and then sits back down on the couch. His cock juts up proudly between his strong, angular legs. I get briefly distracted by the anatomy of his knees—I hadn't noticed before that they bend more sharply than a human's.

My attention snaps back to his face when he speaks. "Speechless? Or am I truly as terrifying as I was afraid of?"

A mean side of me wants to let him squirm a little longer, as payback for his deceptions. But worrying that his appearance would frighten me was the whole reason we got into that mess.

"Just wondering how that's going to fit inside me," I say, only half-joking. I had him in my mouth, but I'm realizing now that was probably little more than the tip.

His cock twitches at my words, and he groans slightly, wrapping a hand around it. "I'll make sure you're so wet and aching for me that I'll slide right into your tight cunt," he says huskily, pumping his shaft and squeezing when he reaches the tip.

I watch, mesmerized by the movement. With each pass over the head of his cock, his hand spreads the lubricant leaking from the tip.

I spread my legs and place a hand between them. My panties are already soaked, and I suck in a breath at the sensation of my fingers brushing against my pussy through the fabric.

"Do you like the sound of that? Are you touching yourself too, Fina?"

"Yes. God, I'm so wet just watching you. It's almost embarrassing." I push my panties to the side and glide two fingers along my pussy, then circle around my sensitive clit with a soft gasp.

His eyes close as he slows his strokes. "*Esh'et*, you make it hard for me to control myself and not just spill immediately."

I want to see him lose control. I keep touching myself, feeling my release building slowly. It won't happen before he comes, but it will be worth it to see Maerlon unleashed. "Don't hold back. I need to see you come."

Maerlon practically growls and pumps his shaft at a brutal pace, the sound of his slick hand sliding against his cock almost obscene. "*Vash-ka*...Fina. I want to taste you until you scream my name. Want your legs wrapped around me as I pump into that pretty, wet cunt."

My own touches are frantic, chasing a climax that is much

closer than I expected as he gets closer to the edge. I slip two fingers inside me with my other hand and gasp. They're not enough, but I need something inside me.

"I love watching you and thinking about how you'd fill me up completely," I say, willing myself to not stumble over my words. It's awkward saying the filthy thoughts that are coming to mind out loud. Dirty talk sounds so good coming from other people, but on my lips I worry it sounds silly. I'd never be able to do it if he could see how red I'm turning as I speak.

He shudders with need at my words, spurring me on despite the twinge of embarrassment.

"Do you want to fill me up? Would you come inside me?" The words fall out of my mouth before I can overthink them, and his fierce reaction sends a rush of excitement tingling through my body.

Maerlon grunts with need and strokes his cock furiously, his hips rising to meet his hands. *"Fina."* He shouts my name with a feral groan and I watch as he comes, his cum spilling out in thick ropes that coat his hands and stomach. He keeps coming, his cock throbbing with each new spurt of his release, and the sight pushes me over the edge.

I gasp as my pussy clenches against my fingers and a brutal climax surges through me, overwhelming my senses. Maerlon's hand finally stills and he releases his breath in a shuddering exhale. His eyes open, and he runs his clean hand through his hair, a sheepish expression crossing his face.

"Don't you dare think about apologizing!" I say, cutting him off.

He opens his mouth like he's going to protest, but pauses, shaking his head. A hint of sharp teeth flash as his lips curl up into a wry smile. "Was that enough for you? I can show you more in a moment, if you're...unsatisfied."

"I'm very satisfied. Surprisingly so." There's a slight throb between my legs as I come down from my orgasm.

"Mmm, good. I don't want to leave you in need."

My pulse quickens as I realize his cock is growing stiff again. "On second thought, I might need another demonstration."

# 33

## ✦ MAERLON ✦

The annoying chirp of my alarm comes far too soon. I glare at my comm, as if it's the reason I barely got any sleep last night. But no, that was my fault. Well, mine and Fina's...

We stayed up until the early hours of the morning, teasing each other over and over. I don't know if I've ever come that many times before. Something about her makes me constantly desperate for more. My cock stiffens just thinking about the little breathy sounds she made as she watched me. The filthy words she said to urge me toward my release. The throaty catch in her breath when she came.

*Esh'et*, now I'm aching for her again.

I ignore my erection and force myself out of bed. There's a lot to get done before work this morning to get ready for our dinner date.

Things I'd planned on doing yesterday after work. Not that I'm complaining about getting unexpected time with Fina.

After a quick, ice-cold shower and a mug of strong tea, I get to work. I tidy up anything out of place and set the auto-cleaners to run a deep cleaning cycle while I'm at the office. Then I find a recipe for a classic human dish and spend almost an hour fighting with my food synthesizer to input it into the programming. By the time that's finally set, it's time to go to work.

I groan at the list of my remaining to-dos. Hopefully, I'll be able to slip out early today and get everything else settled in time. I can feel the stress of all the last-minute prep raising my heart rate. Dezlon would tell me to take some deep breaths and chill out, but that's easy for her to say. She's always been the most laid back member of the family.

As I'm on the transit to Orion district, I send Fina a quick message to say good morning. She's just as tired as I am, so I stop into a cafe and grab her a strong caffeinated drink made from *xrulr* beans and a sweet pastry. The cafe worker assures me it's safe for human consumption, though they raise an eyebrow at me for asking something so obscure. I double-check on my comm that it's safe, then hurry to make sure I'm at the office at my usual time.

CiaXera says they don't monitor our arrival times, but I don't want to give them any reason to doubt my commitment to my job. I quit my gig at SimTech after the debacle the other night, so now it's even more important I keep my day job.

Fina's not in her office yet, so I drop the pastry and drink off at her desk. It's probably good that I don't see her again so soon—I don't want Fina to think I'm crowding her. I keep thinking of things I'd like to do for her, presents to give her, or what would make her smile. But I don't know if that's considered appropriate in human relationships.

When a seladin seeks to court someone—to create a soul bond with them—they dedicate themselves to showing their desired partner how much they appreciate them. Each gesture shows investment in the bond. My people don't believe in a destined mate and don't have a biological imperative that leads us toward mating bonds like some other species do. So when we choose to dedicate ourselves to another, it's a commitment we must consciously cultivate and tend to.

K'thress made me feel like that mentality was overkill. One of the many reasons we didn't work out. I don't want the same thing to happen with Fina.

I overthink whether I should've given Fina the drink and pastry as I head down one floor to my office. Jezrit waves to me as I pass his open door, but there's no time to stop in and chat today. Not if I want to get everything done in time to leave early.

I'm getting settled when a message from Fina pops up on my comm.

> Fina: Someone left a drink and a pastry on my desk. You wouldn't happen to know who, would you?

> Maerlon: Hmm, maybe an office ghost?

> Fina: A ghost? CiaXera is haunted?!

> Maerlon: Absolutely. But don't worry, they're all benevolent spirits.

> Fina: That's surprising! You'd think there'd be at least a few vengeful ghosts of past customers who didn't like our rates.

> Maerlon: It's shocking, I know.

> Fina: Well, I guess thank you to the mysterious spirit of caffeine and breakfast treats.
>
> Fina: They're very sweet and I really appreciate them.

> Maerlon: I'll pass your thanks on if I encounter them.

I'm filled with warm pleasure knowing that she liked my gesture. I'm overthinking things—I can get her breakfast without worrying that she's going to think I'm clingy. Fina isn't K'thress. Thank the stars for that.

✦

THE WORKDAY GOES by far too fast. I rush through my projects as quickly as possible, hearing my mother's voice lecturing me that if I do something, it should be perfect and precise. She told me this over and over while I was growing up and to this day, I can't shake the sense that she's watching over my shoulder, ready to give her unsolicited critique. Just one of the many way's her "expert parenting style"—her words, not mine—filled me with neuroses I'm working to unpack now that I have some distance from her.

I work through lunch, though I feel a twinge of guilt when Jezrit asks me to visit the office cantina with him. He says he's been trying to be more social lately, but really, I think he's afraid he'll run into Mezli alone. He thinks she's upset with him since he abruptly left her at Epiphany.

I should tell him she moved her flirtations on to someone else that same night, but I don't know if that would hurt his feelings. Aespians are tricky—they seem to interpret most things literally and don't lie, but there's a lot more complexity to it that's hard to fully understand if you're not raised in their culture.

I successfully manage to finish up an hour early and sneak out of the office before I can get roped into a friendly chat with my co-workers. The last hour of the day is their unofficial gossiping time. They're always trying to get me to join in, so if they see me away from my desk, they'll pounce.

On the way back to my loft, I stop at a salvage shop and a clothing boutique. Fina messages me to ask if she can bring anything to dinner while I'm scrambling to pick up everything I need for tonight. I inwardly curse that I haven't messaged her since this morning. Hopefully, she didn't think I'm being intentionally distant.

*Esh'et*, I really need to figure out the right amount of attention to give a human you're courting. I'm going to drive myself mad with all of this overthinking.

I'm tired and sweaty by the time I return to my loft, laden with packages. When I open the door, I gasp in horror. It looks like a drunk ryhslin beast rampaged through here—two lamps are knocked over, there's a huge puddle of sanitizing fluid on the kitchen floor, and a cleaning bot is tangled in a pile of my bedsheets on the floor. It beeps loudly with an error alert, like I couldn't tell from the mess that something malfunctioned.

Stupid *fa-shar* piece of garbage.

This is a nightmare. Fina will be here in less than an hour. Should I ask her to come later? No, that might be rude. I fight back the urge to kick the cleaning bot and curse as I scramble to fix the mess it made.

# 34

## ✦ FINA ✦

I'm bubbling with nerves and excitement all day, anticipating dinner with Maerlon tonight. I mentioned I was dragging this morning after our late night and he brought me the closest thing I've had to a latte since coming to Spire. My food synthesizer can't make a decent cup of coffee, let alone something with espresso. Paired with the flaky, sweet pastry similar to croissant, it felt like I was back home. The only thing that would've made it better is Maerlon sharing it with me.

Shit, I'm already falling for him. *Hard*. I know I should try to slow down, but he's so damn thoughtful. And so damn sexy...

Last night was the filthiest thing I've done with a partner. Though that's not saying much. It's not like I've had a wild sex life

—at least not until recently. I watched him come over and over, each time urging him on with my dirty thoughts. Thoughts I didn't know I even had in me. It was intoxicating; I couldn't help touching myself as I watched him. Guess I have to add voyeurism and dirty talk to my list of kinks.

Mezli would be so proud. I consider messaging her about it, but worry she'll think I'm moving too fast and forgiving Maerlon too soon. I'm trying to be cautious, but every time I think about him, I forget the reason I should be upset. Am I being foolish for opening my heart back up to him? Is it wrong to want to forget what happened and move forward?

It's times like these that I miss my therapist. That's a significant downside to living on a space station with few humans. There aren't any specialists in human psychology anywhere in Consortium space. So I have to sort out my messy emotions on my own.

My thoughts wander to Maerlon and my tangled feelings throughout the day. I resign myself to not getting much work done and end up taking a half day so I can stress bake something to bring to dinner. I figured out a recipe for the *hreski* pie he had the first night we hung out, so I bake that. Hopefully he likes it.

With my nerves calmed a bit, I freshen up for my visit. Just in case. Not that anything will happen tonight. We need to wait. I futilely tell myself that as I pick out impractical, lacy underwear that barely covers anything. I mutter it as I slip on a low-cut dress. And again, as I highlight the fullness of my lips with a dark red shade.

I check my reflection in the bathroom mirror before heading out the door. The practical side of me might be trying to convince me to wait, but the outfit I picked out screams "fuck me".

I should change. Wear something more casual. But then I'll be late. I want to pick something up for him on my way over. His version of courting involves gifts and thoughtful gestures, and I'd like to bring him something special in addition to the pie.

Oh well, guess I'll have to go looking like this. My body thrums with arousal, thinking about how he'll look at me in this outfit.

Shit. I'm losing my internal battle to protect my heart and take things slow.

GIFT SHOPPING PROVES to be more time-consuming than I expected. I message Maerlon with an apology, letting him know I'll be a bit late. He tells me to take my time, but I still can't help feeling bad. I hate being late.

When I arrive at his building, I'm sweaty from my frantic attempt to speed up my travel time. I take a second to catch my breath and blot the shine off of my forehead, eyeing a passing aespian warily. My track record for being in Sagittarius district alone isn't the best, so I shouldn't linger too long out here.

I go to buzz the comm for him to let me into the building, but the security sensor chimes at me as I approach and the entrance unlocks automatically. He must have input my station ID into a list of approved visitors. I should do the same for him. Or should I wait?

Ugh, I'm driving myself crazy with this waiting business. As I take the lift to Maerlon's floor, the fluttering anxiety from earlier returns. My adrenaline is pumping by the time I reach his door and the package in my hand almost slips out of my sweat-slicked palms.

This is ridiculous. I'm freaking out because I'm *not* scared of getting my heart broken. That I trust Maerlon despite what he's done. The alarm bells in my head that should tell me to protect myself are silent. Should I trust my gut or do the "reasonable" thing?

I wipe my hands on my dress and press the buzzer next to the door, inhaling and exhaling deeply to ground myself. The door slides open, but Maerlon isn't on the other side. I hesitate, unsure if I should enter.

"Sorry! My hands are full. Please come in!"

I step inside and am instantly hit by a delicious, familiar scent, though I can't quite place it. I'm struck again by how vibrant and well-decorated his loft is. Though, it looks a bit more lived in than the last time I visited. Now I don't feel as bad about the mess I left at my place.

Maerlon pops up from behind his kitchen island with an apologetic smile on his face. "Sorry about that! I'm running behind schedule and the food synth dinged right as you got here."

My mouth falls open, because *damn*, he looks mouth-watering. And not just because he's holding a tray with a bubbling, hot pizza on it. His hair is disheveled and his cheeks flushed a dark gray. There's only an apron covering his bare chest, and I'm almost disappointed to see he's wearing pants underneath when he moves to the side of the island.

Maerlon sets the pan down and wipes off his hands on a towel, then rushes over and pulls me into a hug. His embrace feels electric, like he's lit up from the inside from just holding me.

*What was I worried about again?*

He takes a step back and smiles down at me softly. "You look beautiful."

"You don't look so bad yourself. Though I wish you'd told me about the dress code of your restaurant," I say, touching the neck of his apron.

He glances down at his chest and then rubs the shorn side of his head. "*Esh'et*, I'm a mess tonight. Give me just a moment—I'll put a shirt on."

I want to tell him not to bother.

He takes a step toward the bedroom area of his loft, then stops. "I'm being a terrible host. Can I take your jacket and bag? Do you want anything to drink?"

He looks so uncharacteristically flustered. It's adorable. "You're not terrible at all." I hand him my coat and purse. His eyes fall to where my breasts are practically bursting out of my dress, and he swallows heavily before dragging his gaze back up to meet mine. "Did I mention how beautiful you look?"

I laugh and take a step closer. "You did. But I don't mind hearing it again."

"Good, because I'll probably say it many more times tonight." His face fills with longing, and I can't resist pulling him into a kiss. I keep it soft and light, but my insides still flutter at the sensation.

He inhales deeply as his face presses into my hair and an almost imperceptible groan vibrates against my chest. "You smell good, too," he murmurs against my lips.

*Take things slow. You need to go slow.* I chant to myself to keep from giving him another, much less gentle, kiss.

I try to diffuse the tension sizzling between us. "Thanks, I'm not as much of a stinky, sweaty mess as I was when I visited before."

"Your scent is always incredible. It was so strong that night, it made it hard to hide how much I liked it." He leans in and smells my neck, emphasizing his point.

"Wait, what?" My face heats. So much for my attempt to lower the sexual tension.

His lips twist into a wicked grin. "I'll go put on a shirt so we can eat before the piz-zah gets cold."

I use his brief absence to attempt to calm my overeager body down. He returns wearing an expensive-looking shirt that fits his lean torso perfectly. I go to follow him into the kitchen, but he shakes his head at me.

"Have a seat. I'll have everything ready in just a minute. What would you like to drink?"

I should pick something sexy, like shikzeth fire wine, but drinking will only loosen my remaining inhibitions. Plus, I'm not sure how well that would go with pizza.

I hold back a giggle. Of all the foods I was expecting for a romantic dinner date, pizza wasn't one of them.

"Water would be great, thanks. I brought something for dessert, where should I set it?" I ask, taking the carefully wrapped pie out of my bag.

"You baked for me?" His eyes widen and glow brighter when I unwrap the pie. "*Hreski* pie! Wow. Seladin are secretive about our baking—how did you get the recipe?"

"I may have bought a few from a bakery near my house and reverse engineered it. There was a lot of trial and error. It might not be exactly right, but it's pretty damn good."

"You did all of that? For me?" Maerlon steps closer, beaming down at me with surprised affection.

My legs go a bit wobbly under his gaze. "Of course. Baking is one of my favorite ways to show I care for someone."

"Thank you, Fina. I can't wait to try it." He leans down to kiss me and I barely resist the urge to linger too long. "Give me just a minute and I'll finish getting dinner set up."

"Are you sure I can't help?"

"No, just relax. It's my fault I wasn't ready when you arrived. Well, actually it's my *fa-shar* cleaning bot's fault."

"Your cleaning bot?"

"I had it programmed to do a deep clean while I was at the office and instead it malfunctioned and went on a destructive rampage through my loft." Maerlon lets out a rueful laugh as he bustles around, bringing things to a small dining table near the windows overlooking the synth gardens.

"Oh shit! I never would have known. Your place looks great."

Despite his request, I can't just sit still while he scurries around, so I get up and help him carry things. He looks surprised that I'm helping, and his eyes seem to glow brighter. I grab the present I set down absently when I took off my coat and bring it over to the table with me. Maerlon lights a tall, tapered candle and dims the lights in his loft, then pulls my chair out for me.

It's so cute and romantic. My heart squeezes with affection.

"Before we eat, I forgot. I brought you something else."

Maerlon's eyes grow even brighter in the dim light and his mouth falls open slightly. "Another gift? Fina, you shouldn't have, I...wow." His voice is filled with a mixture of disbelief and pleasure.

"It's nothing big. I just...you gave me those gorgeous flowers, and then the treats this morning."

He looks perplexed. "You didn't need to—I don't expect you to reciprocate."

My stomach lurches at his expression. Shit, did I make some kind of seladin cultural blunder?

"Also, a ghost got you those treats, not me," he adds with a straight face.

"Right, how could I forget? But seriously, I know I didn't have to. I wanted to. If tokens of affection are an important part of seladin dating—courting—then I want to give them to you too." My face and chest feel hot and my heartbeat speeds up with nervous anticipation, but I get the words out.

Maerlon's throat works and his eyes blink rapidly. He gives me the most aching, tender look I've ever seen. "Fina, you are too good to me."

"Hey now, wait until you see what I got you. It's not that exciting." I hand the package over to him. He takes it and stares at the ribbon-wrapped box in awe. "Just open it!"

God, I hope he doesn't hate it.

My urging breaks him out of his reverie and he chuckles, gently undoing the ribbon and opening the box. Inside, there's an assortment of paints, as well as a set of brushes. It was harder than expected to find a store that sold physical art supplies since most art is made digitally.

Maerlon stares down at the contents of the box in silence. I sip my water and wait for him to say something, but he just keeps staring.

"I told you it wasn't exciting..."

He finally looks up, his eyes watery. He blinks, letting a few tears escape. Happy ones, hopefully. "Thank you. This is a wonderful gift." His voice is thick with emotion. He wipes the water from his eyes and reaches across the table to squeeze my hand. After a moment, he clears his throat. "We should eat before it gets cold."

"Of course." I squeeze his hand back and reluctantly let go, so I can take a bite. It's a perfect slice of pizza. Better than anything I've been able to get my food synthesizer to make. "It tastes great!"

Maerlon takes a tentative bite and a bemused expression crosses his face. "It's odd..." He takes another considering bite. "I like it."

My lip quirks at his reaction. "I have to ask—why did you choose pizza for tonight?"

"Mezli said it's a traditional food eaten on romantic human dates," he says matter-of-factly.

"Oh, did she?" I choke back my laugh and take another bite.

"Is that wrong? *Vash-ka*, I knew I shouldn't have trusted her."

"No, no! It's perfect." I grin and take a big bite to show how happy I am about the pizza.

"I want to do things right. I tried to do some research on courting customs for humans—I found a datapad at a salvage shop, but the advice seemed...unwise."

"Well, now I have to know what it said!"

"It said that to woo a human woman, you should insult them and pretend they're not attractive. That they're drawn to a man who is dominant, and devaluing her will make her more willing to settle. It seems wrong and demeaning. Also, why is it just women being treated this way by men? If it works, wouldn't it be effective for any partner you're trying to court?"

He can't hide the disgust on his face. It's nice to confirm that he doesn't subscribe to that misogynistic bullshit from human history. I can't help trying to seem a little sad though, just to tease him.

A pained, apologetic look crosses his face. "I'm sorry if I'm insulting your culture. If this is what you want, I'll try to do it. I don't think I'll be convincing, but if you need it to feel properly courted, I will do my best."

I give him a serious nod, pinching my thigh to keep from laughing. "You'd do that for me?"

Maerlon nods solemnly. "Yes." He thinks for a moment, staring at me. "I don't like how radiant your skin looks in this low light. It looks too soft and touchable."

"That's not a very good insult," I say with an exaggerated pout. My serious expression breaks and I snort-laugh and then clap a hand over my mouth.

Maerlon shakes his head at me, but his eyes glitter with amusement. "You're a wicked woman, Fina."

"I know. I need to be punished." The suggestive words tumble out of my mouth before I can stop them.

Now there's only heat in Maerlon's gaze. "That can be arranged."

We watch each other and the tension rises with each passing breath, until I'm mentally begging him to swipe everything off the table and take me right there. I slow my breath in a feeble attempt to diminish the desire coursing through me before I get carried away.

# 35

## ✦MAERLON✦

Fina's eyes sparkle in the candlelight, her cheeks flushed an enticing pink. I hold my breath, desperate to scoop her up, toss her on my bed, and show her how good punishment can be. But I wait to see how she wants to proceed. I can tell she's aroused, but something holds her back.

That hesitation snaps me out of the fog of lust. What am I thinking? She needs more time. She needs proof that I'm trustworthy after what I've done. I take a long sip of my water to calm my overheated senses and try to think of how to steer us away from moving too fast.

"So, how did you know I paint?" I ask, gesturing at her gift. I'm trying not to read too much into it, but it seems like she understands at least some of the significance of a courting gift. When I saw what she'd given me, it stunned me even more. We've never talked about my art.

"Just a lucky guess. I know you're a designer and I remembered the beautiful pieces you have in your loft." Fina gestures to the paintings decorating my walls. "Did you paint them?"

Her praise of my art warms my chest. "Yes. Back when I lived on a colony ship, I used to paint all the time. If I wasn't Y'thir, I would undoubtedly become R'hbis—an artisan or steward of beauty for seladin culture. I haven't painted anything since I got here. Didn't feel the spark anymore."

"You have a gift, Maerlon. I imagine it was very difficult to leave that behind. Do you ever wish you didn't have to leave home? That you weren't second-born?"

What an odd question. I knew from a young age that it was my duty to be Y'thir. Everyone in seladin society has a place, and that's mine. "Not really. No one forced me to leave. I could have stayed and rejected that social designation. Plenty have done so, and no one bears them ill will. Being Y'thir is an honor for me—I get to support the people I love and experience the vast wonders that lie outside of seladin society. Wonders such as you."

Fina listens thoughtfully until my last few words, which make her scowl. "Are you calling me vast? Rude! I thought you wouldn't follow that horrible dating advice."

"That's not—I didn't mean—"

Her chest shakes, and for a panicked moment, I think she's crying. Then laughter bursts forth, amusement lighting up her entire face. The sound of it fills me with warmth and pleasure and I grin back at her like a lovesick fool.

"I'll stop teasing you." Fina eyes still sparkle with mischief. "You're so handsome when you smile, so it's hard to resist. I love being able to see all of you."

She's talking about how things were before I came clean about my identity, but my mind flashes to what we did last night. I quirk an eyebrow at her as she raises her glass to take a sip of water. "I'm well aware of how much you like to watch me."

She sputters and sets down her glass, and now it's my turn to laugh at her reaction.

The conversation flows throughout the rest of dinner. Talking to Fina feels natural, and the more she says, the more certain I am in my affection for her.

When I taste her homemade *hreski* pie, I'm transported back to my childhood name days, when my mother baked it as a special treat. It tastes like home. Being with Fina makes me as happy as I felt back then. Happier even.

Fina insists on helping me clean up after the meal, and the simple domesticity of the moment makes it hard to stop imagining our future together. What it would be like to live with this clever, caring person.

She catches me staring at her and leans over after loading the last dish into the auto-washer to kiss my cheek. "Thank you. This has been such a wonderful evening."

I set down the towel in my hands and close the space between us. I'll never tire of the way she fits in my arms or the way her breath hitches right before our mouths meet. Her lips eagerly part, and her tongue tangles with mine.

I grab her rounded bottom and lift her up, setting her on the counter so I don't have to lean over as much. She giggles and then kisses me with even more fervor, her legs locking around my hips to pull me in closer. At this height, our hips meet perfectly and she gasps when my hard length presses against her center.

"God, I want you so bad," she sighs between kisses. Her hips rock against me and it takes all of my control not to grind against her in earnest.

"I'm here, Fina. For whatever you need."

She pulls her face back to gaze at me and I see my longing reflected in her eyes. But there's also that same hesitation from earlier.

She brings a hand up to touch my cheek and sighs. "You're making it very hard for me to be logical. I know I should still be wary of you, but I'm not. I just ache for you. It's crazy—I should be more careful after what happened."

"It's not crazy. Your mind knows I hurt you, even if your heart doesn't. I can help you wait, if that's what you need." I ease myself off of her and take a few steps back. My body screams at me to stay close to Fina, and I miss her warmth already.

Fina sits on the counter for a few moments, eyes closed as she takes a deep breath. Her legs are still spread from where I stood between them. I bite back a groan when I see a hint of her lacy underwear and catch the heady scent of her arousal. I want to kneel down and nibble at her inner thigh, then delve my tongue inside her.

Her eyes open and she sighs. Her hips ease off the counter and she pulls the skirt of her dress down where it rode up. "Could we just sit and talk for a while longer?" She gives me a shy smile. "I'm having such a wonderful time with you and I'm not ready to go home yet. That is, if you're okay with me staying even though I'm not ready to..."

She thinks I would ask her to leave if we're not getting intimate? That I don't want her company if it doesn't lead to sex? The thought is absurd. All I want is to be around her, however she'll have me.

"Stay." It sounds a bit more like a command than I intended. "Please. I would very much like for you to stay longer."

She sighs, attempting to seem put out. "Well, fine. But only because you asked so nicely."

I take her hand and lead her into the sitting area. Unlike the first time she was here, Fina sits right next to me. She kicks off her heels and rubs at the arch of her foot with a slight wince. I watch her, entranced by how delicate her foot is. There are five toes to my three and each one looks impractically small and stubby. Is this why she stumbles sometimes?

I must stare too long because Fina gives me a chagrined look. "Sorry, I'm still not used to wearing heels. I should have asked if it was okay to take them off."

She goes to lower her foot, but I grab it and pull it up into my lap. She squeaks in surprise and then giggles, her foot twitching in my grasp as I run a thumb lightly against the sole.

Ah right, I forgot they're ticklish. I use a firmer stroke, pressing into where I saw her rubbing. Her eyes shutter and her head tips back against the cushion behind her.

"This okay?" I ask. Fina nods, sighing softly as I continue. My cock interprets the sound as an invitation to make its presence known. I ignore it and shift her foot further onto my leg so that the bulge in my pants doesn't make her uncomfortable.

"That feels incredible, thank you. I know it's silly to wear shoes that hurt my feet, but I like the way they look. Plus, the added height makes it easier for me to kiss you. You're ridiculously tall. Not that I'm complaining! I'm just a shrimpy human."

"I don't know what 'shrimpy' means, but I think you're the perfect height. When I look down at you, I always get an amazing view of your...assets." My gaze drops to her breasts.

She laughs and pokes me in the stomach with her toe. "Such a pervy alien."

"I can't help it. They're just so prominent. It's hard not to look."

Fina scoffs and tries to pull her foot out of my grasp. It brushes against my hard cock and I inhale sharply at the sensation. Her eyes widen and a wicked smile twists her lips before she rubs her foot across my length again.

"*Fina.*" I say her name in warning, my voice choked.

Humor and desire dance behind her eyes. "Sorry, I couldn't resist. I told you, I enjoy teasing you." She lifts her foot and lets me continue to rub it a safe distance away from my erection.

Her body becomes languid as we chat and I get far too much enjoyment from the small noises of pain-tinged pleasure she makes when I find a particularly sore spot.

Fina eventually sits up from her relaxed position and surprises me by asking if I'd like her to rub my feet. No one has ever offered to touch my feet before. It seems odd to make her handle my large, heavy feet, but she seems excited by the idea so I let her.

She exclaims over my "lack" of toes and the thick, rough padding on the soles. It's slightly uncomfortable at first, but then her nimble fingers find ways to dig into spots that feel very pleasurable. Almost too pleasurable, so I don't let her do it for very long.

It's so easy talking to her. I've had my guard up since I arrived on Spire, but she makes me feel safe to let it down. She also becomes more comfortable with me the longer we talk—there's much more teasing and sly looks and fewer embarrassed, unnecessary apologies. Though her cheeks still flush such a lovely pink when I say something suggestive. Which I find myself doing far too often. I can't help it. She's just so *enticing*.

She slides closer and closer to me until her legs drape over my lap. Her skirt has slid up, exposing the tops of her thick thighs, and I run my hands in small circles over the soft, bare skin. When I accidentally touch closer to the inside of her thigh, her breath hitches.

"Fuck it, I need this," she mutters and the next thing I know, she's crawling onto my lap. She straddles my legs and presses her mouth to mine in a heated kiss.

I groan against her lips, returning the kiss with equal fervor.

She writhes in my lap, grinding against my clothed cock with urgency. I grab her hips and pull her down onto me, meeting her movements. She bites my bottom lip and then slides her tongue against mine insistently. I absently remember that I'm supposed to be helping keep things slow, but that seems much less important when she's rocking her hips against me and moaning.

Her wetness soaks into the fabric of my pants, and the scent of her arousal is maddening. I fist a hand in her hair and tug, exposing her neck. I scrape my teeth against the pale, fragile skin there and then suck, marking her as mine.

She gasps my name—my real name—and I'm addicted to the way it sounds coming from her lips. I let her use me, grinding against my cock until her breath stutters and she comes with a cry.

Fina leans against me for a few moments, breathless and satisfied. My cock twitches with need and she reaches down to undo the fastener of my pants, but I gently grab her hand and bring it to my lips instead.

"I want this to just be about what you need," I say, my voice still thick with arousal.

"But what if I need—"

I interrupt her with a kiss and when we part there's a slight downturn to her lips.

"I know you're trying to help me so I won't argue—at least not this time." Fina extricates herself from my lap and grimaces down at the wet stain she made on the front of my pants. "Oh god, that's embarrassing."

"Nonsense. I'm never washing these pants again."

"Alien pervert." She wrinkles her nose, and I chuckle at her reaction.

"I guess it's pretty late...I should go. Let you change out of those pants," Fina whispers after a moment.

"Or you could stay." I blurt out the words. "I won't do anything but cuddle and sleep, I promise." I hold my hands away from her, demonstrating my restraint.

Her lip quirks. "How honorable of you. What if *I* do something?"

My cock throbs against my wet pants. "Then we'll see how long my resolve to do the right thing for you holds."

# 36

## ✦FINA✦

Despite my teasing and the ache that's still present between my legs, I don't end up trying to put any more moves on Maerlon tonight. He's considerate, finding me a toothbrush and a soft sleep shirt of his while I shower. I catch him watching me with a goofy little grin on his face as we get ready for bed. It's such a pleasure seeing this side of him that I don't have a chance to feel awkward about the impromptu sleepover.

We whisper and cuddle until far too late into the night cycle. When my eyes can't stay open any longer, he wraps me in his arms and holds me there until I fall asleep. I normally have trouble sleeping in a new place. But tucked against his warm body, feeling the steady rise and fall of his breath feels safe. Before I drift off to sleep, I wonder what it'd be like to spend every night with him.

I wake up before the alarm to something long and hard pressed against my backside, and I sleepily grind against it before I can stop myself. Maerlon sighs in his sleep and nestles his cock closer to the aching heat between my legs. As good as it feels, I need to go back to my place before work, so there's no time for messing around.

The alarm buzzes just as I'm about to pull away and get out of bed. Maerlon lets out a groggy groan before shutting off the alarm, then tugs me against his chest and kisses my head. "I almost thought you here in my bed was a dream. It feels too good to be true," he murmurs sleepily. His hard length presses insistently against my ass, but he doesn't acknowledge it.

"I'm very much real. In case my snoring and morning breath didn't shatter the illusion." I try my best to ignore the way my pussy clenches with need as I lie here with him so close.

"I'm glad you stayed, Fina," he whispers.

Maybe there's time for a bit of under the covers action after all...

The secondary alarm I set just in case I slept through the first one goes off. I sigh and haul myself out of bed before I can let Maerlon's romantic words seduce me.

As good as it felt to spend the night at Maerlon's place, it was impractical. I barely have time to go change back at my apartment before I have to head to the office. By the time I get to CiaXera, I'm ready for a nap.

I shouldn't spend the night again unless I prepare ahead of time. But that would involve leaving things at his place. Isn't that moving way too fast? I wonder how much I can cram into my purse without it looking like I'm assuming I'll spend the night when I visit him.

I don't want to assume anything. Past experience and a whole lot of romance vids tell me that doing too many relationship-y things too fast is off-putting to a partner. Paul freaked out at me when I told my parents we were dating before he was ready to be "official". His commitment phobia conditioned me to be cautious. Maerlon seems different, but it still makes me hesitate.

Maerlon must sense me thinking about him, because he shows up at my office a few minutes after I arrive, laden with one of those amazing coffee-like drinks and a breakfast wrap. The sight makes my stomach flutter—and then rumble audibly. In the rush to get to work, I didn't have time to eat.

He gives me that cute, nervous smile where the tips of his sharp teeth are just barely showing. I'm growing obsessed with seeing his softer expressions and I beam back at him, unable to hide my pleasure at seeing him.

"Brought you something to help start your day," he says, placing them on my desk, carefully avoiding a stack of datapads.

"You're a lifesaver, thank you! I hope you don't think I expect you to keep bringing me breakfast every morning, though."

"I know you don't." His lip quirks at my disclaimer. "Giving your partn—giving someone food is a sign of affection for my people. Much like your baking."

"Well, in that case, I won't argue." I move over to wrap my arms around his neck and pull him down for a quick kiss. I want to add some tongue, but that's probably not appropriate for work. I spent the morning looking for CiaXera's policy for dating coworkers, expecting a lot of paperwork and a discussion with Employee Resources. But it turns out we don't need to declare anything since our departments don't interact directly.

"How do seladin feel about PDA? Should I not be kissing you here?"

"I don't know what PDA is, but you can kiss me wherever you want." His tone sounds far too sexy for this early in the day.

I raise an eyebrow at him. "Dirty." His eyes glow brighter for a moment, which I'm coming to realize is the seladin version of blushing. "PDA is a public display of affection. Personally, I'm okay with kissing and hugs, but if you grab my tit at the office, that's a bit much."

"I'll do my best to resist the urge." He addresses his words to the swell of my breasts instead of my face, a hungry grin on his lips. I nudge him playfully and give him another quick kiss before he has to head off to his office.

OVER THE NEXT couple of weeks, we fall into a rhythm of meeting for dinner a few nights a week, either at Maerlon's place or mine. On the weekends, we're able to spend the day together, exploring the station, and spending time with Mezli and Paul. Those two have turned into a bizarre duo, with her acting as his guide to alien dating and nightlife on Spire. They taunt each other and argue incessantly, but at least Paul's adjusting to station life without me. It'd be awkward to be his only guide to the station, knowing his feelings for me aren't entirely gone.

Speaking of feelings, I haven't had any more sleepovers with Maerlon. Mostly because I'm too scared to ask if it's okay, and he's too worried about encouraging me to move too fast. His insistence on "protecting my heart" makes me feel safe.

But it's also driving me crazy.

I know he still feels guilty for misleading me, but it's getting ridiculous. I'm daydreaming about how close I was to just shoving him down on my couch, ripping off his pants, and riding him last night when Mezli gives my arm a sharp flick.

"Hey! Quit daydreaming about seladin dick and tell us what you think of this one," she says, shoving her comm in my face. On it, there's a Syzygy profile with a highly-altered photo of a light purple ankite who is "looking for someone who's always ready for an adventure."

"Mezli, even I know that's a fake profile. They're probably a scammer looking to steal credits, not hearts. On the off-chance it's real, that's not a great fit," I say, shaking my head at the screen. "No offense, Paul."

Mezli scoffs and yanks the comm screen back. "Fine, I'll just have to go out with them to vet them."

Paul rolls his eyes. "That's what she says about all of my matches!"

They bicker as they scan through more profiles. God, I'm glad I found Maerlon. Syzygy is a nightmare.

"What about this guy? He's a hot seladin and has his own ship!" Paul looks over the profile and seems intrigued, so I resist the urge to point out that a seladin with his own ship probably means he won't be hanging around on Spire much.

"Speaking of which, how's that seladin cock treating you, Fina?" Mezli's loud voice carries across the cafe we're sitting in.

I sputter and end up dripping some of my drink onto my top. "Dammit, could you not yell stuff like that while we're out in public?" I look around sheepishly at the people staring at us now.

"That's not an answer. You look like you want to hop on his dick every time I see you together, so I'm guessing it's good." She grins at me. "Oh! By the way—if you go out with this guy, don't swallow. Fina learned that the hard way," she says, turning to address Paul.

Paul's eyebrows shoot up. "What happens if you do?"

"I had, uh...a reaction to it. It made me hallucinate. Maerlon thought it was an allergic reaction, but felt more like being drugged."

"It also made you extremely horny, don't forget that," Mezli chimes in.

"Wow, good to know." Paul looks embarrassed to be chatting about his ex's experience with trippy jizz. I know I am. He doesn't ask any follow-up questions, but Mezli's still stuck on the subject of Maerlon.

"Is it good? Or *really* good?" She gives me a knowing smirk.

My face falls and she gasps, clutching two hands to her chest. "Oh shit, it's bad?!"

"No! It's just...he offered to help me take things slow after what happened."

Paul wrinkles his brow in confusion—I haven't told him about the SimTech stuff—but I push on. "It was really sweet at first. I appreciate that he wants me fully comfortable with him. But I'm going crazy! I don't know how to tell him I'm beyond ready now."

"Damn, that's a lot." Paul looks like he wants to say more, but ends up just shaking his head.

"If you want to say something, say it!" I snap at him. Paul refusing to give me his opinion and then acting self-righteous if he ends up being right reminds me why we stopped dating. He looks shocked, and I immediately feel bad. "Sorry, I shouldn't get upset with you. Just...if you have an opinion or idea, I'd rather you tell me than keep it to yourself."

Paul places his hand on mine and squeezes it. "I think you need to tell him what you told us. You overthink things. A lot. If you're ready, be very blatant about it."

"Yeah! Tie him up and have your way with him!" Mezli says. "Or just show up at his place naked."

Paul chuckles at the suggestion. "I hate to agree with Mezli, but nudity certainly would send a clear message."

"Neither of you seriously think I'd do something like that, do you?"

Mezli considers for a moment. "The Fina of the past? No. But the brave, badass babe Fina? Absolutely."

Though I hate to admit it, she has a point. I've changed since coming to Spire. And I can't expect Maerlon to be honest with me if I'm not open with him. I have tell him what I need.

# 37

## ✦ MAERLON ✦

The past few weeks have been incredible. Some of the best of my life. I've spent them getting to know Fina and falling more and more in love with her.

They've also pushed my willpower to the limit. I've never wanted someone so desperately. I end up taking myself in hand multiple times a day to keep my desire for her at bay. It's unsatisfying, but I promised her I'd make us go slow. Each time I see her, it gets harder to restrain myself. The needy looks and breathy sighs she makes whenever we touch don't help.

I've looked up human courtship rules to find an appropriate length of time to wait, but find conflicting information. Some things specify an amount of dates, while others say there's no rule. A few even say no sex until marriage. *Vash-ka*, I think I'll die if she wants to wait until marriage. If that's the case, we'll need to have a bonding ceremony as soon as possible.

Is it wrong that the idea of marrying Fina appeals to me? They say that when you find someone to share a soul bond with it resonates in you. Seladin fortunate enough to find that partner often perform the bonding right away. I can't mention any of this to Fina, though. I don't want to scare her away. K'thress looked at me like I was crazy when I told them about soul bonds. Their incredulity was hurtful, but Fina's would be devastating.

Tonight, she's out with Mezli and Paul, so I'm home alone with my besotted thoughts. I'm glad she's out with her friends; I've been monopolizing her time for weeks. That doesn't mean I don't still crave her presence. More than once, I've stopped myself from messaging her to ask her over later. I need to give her space so that I don't smother her with my affection.

To keep myself occupied tonight, I'm working on my secret project—a portrait of Fina using the supplies she gifted me. I'm out of practice, but it's nice to paint again. And even nicer that I don't have my mother nearby to give me her opinions on my work. For years, I hid my paintings from my mother. I knew she would find my art too imprecise, and therefore a waste of time. It takes effort to push her critical voice away and allow my creativity to come forth. Fina didn't realize what a gift it was encouraging me to paint again—to let that unshackled side of me free once more.

An hour into painting, the door to my loft buzzes. Immediately, I hope that it's Fina. I set my brush down and turn the easel to face toward the wall, then quickly smooth my hair back before answering the door.

"Maerlon!" My younger sister stands in the doorway, holding her arms out for a hug.

I pull her in and her strong arms squeeze me tight. It's been so long since I've seen her in person. What is she doing here?

"Dezlon, is everything okay? Is Rhysti okay? Did she kick you out again?"

Her brow furrows. "What? No, she didn't kick me out! That one time wasn't even her kicking me out. The clearance codes on our ship got messed up, and I got locked off of it."

"That's not how she tells it." Once, Dezlon called me in the middle of the night cycle to come pick her up from the docks after getting locked off her ship wearing only her underwear. I can't resist teasing her about it any chance I get.

"*Hilarious*. Everything is fine. We just needed to make an impromptu stop on Spire and I wanted to drop by before we take off again. I messaged your comm a few times to warn you."

"I turn my comm off when I'm painting to limit distractions. Sorry about that. Come in! Can I get you anything? Stars, it's good to see you!" I'm babbling while my brain tries to catch up with her presence here.

Dezlon gives me an appraising glance as she follows me inside. "I can't stay long, but some tea would be great."

I nod and head into the kitchen. She trails behind me and when I turn back toward her, she's still giving me an odd look.

"You're painting again?"

"Yeah, I started it up a few weeks ago. Finally felt inspired." I smile, thinking about how happy Fina looked when I told her I loved her gift.

"You're different. Happy. Relaxed." Dezlon's eyes narrow at me in suspicion. "Who are you and what have you done with Maerlon?"

Is it that obvious? Was I so miserable looking before? "Can't I be happy to see my sister?"

She narrows her eyes even more.

"Stop looking at me like that! Go sit down. I'll bring over the tea when it's ready."

"Okay, okay. But I'm onto you." She wanders into the sitting area and I hear her make a small, surprised sound.

"Everything okay?" Last time she visited, she knocked over one of my plants, so it won't surprise me if she's broken something again.

"Absolutely," she calls back. There's an amused cadence to her voice which spells trouble.

I brace myself for whatever she's done while I wasn't looking as I grab two mugs of tea.

*Esh'et.*

Dezlon is staring at my painting—an incomplete depiction of a violet-haired woman in a gauzy, transparent gown. It's Fina, bathed in the moonlight of a bioluminescent glade.

I drew inspiration from an ancient seladin ritual where an acolyte is bound and offered as tribute to the god of night. Since the night we met, the fantasy of tying Fina up has played on repeat in my mind. At least I haven't gotten far enough in the painting to add the ropes to Fina's body. But the canny look Dezlon gives me over her shoulder as I approach tells me she recognizes the ritual even without them.

"When you mentioned inspiration, you didn't say you had a muse." Dezlon takes her mug of tea from me with a smirk. "Is this your human? Fina?"

Right. I haven't spoken to Dezlon since I told her about my predicament with Fina. "Yes. We've been dating for a few weeks. Before you ask—yes, I came clean. She knows I'm the person from SimTech. You and Rhysti were right. She's not scared of me like I was worried she would be."

Dezlon snorts in amusement. "You say that like you're surprised. I'm always right, especially when it comes to matters of the heart. How else would I have ended up with a goddess like Rhysti?"

"True, she's way too good for you," I reply dryly.

She glances back at the painting. "And Fina isn't too good for you? Because if this is accurate at all...*vash-ka*, she's sexy. Objectively speaking, of course. I'm happily bonded to the most beautiful nexxit in the galaxy."

"Quit looking at my partner like that!" I turn the canvas back toward the wall so she'll stop staring at it.

"Oh, so she's your partner? That sounds serious." Dezlon heads over to the couch and plops down.

"She—it's complicated. I care for her deeply. We're taking things slow, but I think she's my soul—"

My door buzzes, interrupting me for the second time tonight.

Dezlon's eyes dart to the door. "Expecting company?"

"No. But that didn't stop you from showing up. I'll be right back." I set my mug down and answer the door.

This time it *is* Fina. She steps inside and holds a hand up to signal she wants to speak. Her face is flushed, and she looks slightly out of breath.

"I know I shouldn't come over uninvited. But I can't take it any longer. I need you, Maerlon. *All* of you." She presses a button at the neck of her cloak and it retracts into a small pouch and falls to the floor.

My mouth falls open, and a choked gasp escapes me. She's completely naked.

"Fina, I—"

She doesn't let me finish my warning, launching herself at me and tugging me down to press her mouth to mine in a desperate kiss. I groan, the force of the kiss threatening to drown out all reason, and I pull away before I get swept away in her.

"Fina, wait—"

Her eyes fill with water and she turns an even brighter shade of red. "Oh god, I'm sorry, I shouldn't have…"

"Who's your friend, brother?" Dezlon appears beside me with a shit-eating grin on her face.

## ✦FINA✦

OH GOD, I'm naked and Maerlon's sister is here. Did she hear what I said?

Maerlon instantly moves to block my body from his sister's line of sight, but I catch an amused smirk on her face before he does.

I bend down and pick my cloak back up, cursing as the unfurling mechanism catches on the first few attempts, and then hastily wrap it around myself.

"I'm so sorry, I tried to warn you but…" Maerlon trails off.

He tried to tell me, but I attacked him like some sex-crazed lunatic. I peek out from behind Maerlon and give him and his sister a chagrined look.

"You must be Fina," she says to me and then turns to grin at Maerlon. It's remarkable how much they resemble each other—they could almost be twins. "I'm Maerlon's sister, Dezlon." She bows and I return the gesture, making sure that my cloak doesn't gape open as I do.

"N-Nice to meet you. I've heard great things about you," I say back, unable to meet her eyes.

"Nice to hear that he's so fond of me. Though you wouldn't be able to tell by the way he's glaring at me." Dezlon pokes Maerlon in the side.

She's not wrong. He's bristling and keeping himself interposed between me and her. I move to his side and place a hand on his arm, even though I'd much rather go hide away somewhere.

"I'm glad to see his ridiculous ruse at SimTech didn't scare you off." Dezlon's tone is teasing, but Maerlon stiffens at her words. He scowls at her and then gives me a pained, apologetic look.

I stroke his arm where I'm holding onto it, trying to let him know that I'm not upset by the topic. "He's wonderful. I'm lucky to have met him—even if it was a misleading introduction."

Dezlon nods in agreement. "Stupid decisions aside, he's great."

It warms my heart to see how much she loves him. "He's the best."

"I'm not the best. Fina is," says Maerlon matter-of-factly.

"It's almost sickening how cute you two are." My face heats, and Maerlon's eyes brighten as Dezlon assesses us. "So are you going to make Fina stand half-naked in the entryway or what?"

I clutch my cloak around myself more tightly, the reality of the situation hitting me again like a slap across the face. "Oh no, I don't want to interrupt! I'll be on my way."

Maerlon frowns down at me. "You don't need to leave."

"Yeah, I can catch up with him another time," says Dezlon with a polite smile.

There's no way I'm going to ask Maerlon to kick out his sister because I showed up uninvited. I've already embarrassed myself enough tonight. "Really, it's fine. You never get to see each other. I'll message you later, okay?" I go up on my toes to kiss his cheek, but get more of his chin because of his height.

He looks conflicted and like he wants to argue, so I step out the door before he can. It slides closed behind me automatically and I rush to the elevator. Once inside, I slip my dress back on and hope there aren't any security cams catching my naked ass.

Fuck, that was mortifying. So much for making a grand gesture. Remind me to never take Mezli's advice again.

# 38

## ✦ MAERLON ✦

It takes me a moment to snap back to my senses after watching Fina abruptly leave. Dezlon crosses her arms over her chest, waiting to see what I do. I want to race after Fina and convince her to stay. To kick my sister out and then spend all night showing Fina how much I loved her boldness. If not for inconvenient timing, I'd be worshiping her at this very moment.

I don't do that though. Dezlon is my blood, and I don't want her to think she's unwelcome. It's true that we never see each other. Fina was kind to recognize that.

"Well, that was...I'm sorry, I didn't know..." I'm unsure of how to get back to our conversation after that shocking interruption.

"I mean this respectfully, but what *fa-shar* nonsense are you up to that your partner showed up at your door, begging for you to sleep with her? I hope it's a roleplay thing and not you leaving that gorgeous human unsatisfied."

"I'm not talking to you about my sex life!"

"Maybe you should. I have a lot more experience with ladies than you do," Dezlon shoots back, her eyes sparkling with amusement at my embarrassment.

"*Vash-ka*, not that it's *any* of your business, but I don't have any problems...satisfying her. I told her we could go slow after what happened at SimTech. I don't want to screw things up when she's giving me a second chance."

"Seems like you took that a bit too far, huh?" Her voice is less teasing and more sympathetic now, but it still stings.

I sigh and run my hand through my hair. "I just want her to be happy. To be the one that makes her happy. I frayed the tethers of our soul bond with my deceptions and I will do anything to keep them from breaking. Yes, I've been over-protective, but it's because I love her and I don't want to ruin things."

She moves closer and pulls me into a hug. "It brings me joy to know you've found someone to soul bond with. I know how much it means to you. How long you've dreamed about it." She squeezes me and lets me go. "With all the love in my heart, I have to ask—why in the void are you still standing here talking to me? Go be with her!" She shoves my chest emphatically.

"I didn't want to be rude to you..."

"Oh, shut up. I have better things to do than hang out with your *fa-shar* self." She grabs her bag and gives me one more smirk, stopping at the door. "A word of advice—don't just stick your cock in her right away. She's a lot smaller than you, so you need to be patient and get her really worked up."

I scowl at her in annoyance and mortification. Does she think I know nothing? I've waited this long to be with Fina—I'm not going to lose control and shove inside her like an inexperienced fool. I start to tell Dezlon that, but she's already darting out the door with a devilish cackle.

I sigh and take a moment to steady myself. Fina said she needs me. My cock's already stiff at the thought. Gathering my courage, I race out the door.

## ✦FINA✦

So much for seducing Maerlon.

I drop my purse on the kitchen counter with a tired sigh and check my comm. No new messages from him. He's probably still dealing with the fallout of my impulsive ass showing up and flashing him and his sister. I'd imagined meeting his family during one of my more besotted daydreams, but it went very differently in my head.

I couldn't get out of there fast enough. As I rode the transit back to my apartment, a nagging voice kept telling me I should have stayed. But I'd already met the limit of my bravery for the night just by showing up naked and begging him to fuck me.

There's a graphic, highly descriptive message from Mezli suggesting what I should do to Maerlon tonight. Oh god, she can never find out what happened. I'll never hear the end of her jokes about it if she does.

With nothing but my humiliation to keep me company tonight, I decide to put on my nightgown and crawl under my covers to hide until sleep takes me. As I'm washing my face, my doorbell chimes.

Who the hell is bothering me at this time of night? I scrub off the suds and wait, hoping they'll go away. The chime goes off again, so I creep over to check the door monitor.

It's Maerlon. My mind spirals with panic. Is he upset with me? Did he come here to chastise me for my recklessness? Is he going to break up with me?!

The doorbell goes off a third time, and I scramble to answer it, heart in my throat. The door slides open and Maerlon steps in before I can greet him.

"Maerlon—"

I barely catch his intense, determined expression before he's on me, hauling me into his arms and pressing a fevered kiss to my lips. I squeak in surprise and cling to his neck as he carries me over to the bedroom door, kicks it open, and then tosses me on the bed.

Hunger blazes in his glowing eyes as they rake across me. I'm speechless, holding my breath, waiting to see what he does next. In a lightning fast movement, he leans over, grabs the neck of my nightgown with both hands, and tears it down the center as if it were made of tissue.

"Maerlon!" I gasp as he tosses the ruined nightgown away. My whole body sings with anticipation, and wetness pools between my thighs.

He inhales sharply and rubs his palm against the enormous bulge in his pants. "Do you still need me, Fina?" He squeezes his cock through the fabric and then hovers his hand at the clasp of his pants. "Do you need all of me?"

I'm frozen in place as I watch him. "Y-yes, god. *Please.*"

He tugs his shirt off over his head and then slides his pants down off his hips in a slow drag. I hold my breath, watching as his cock springs free, hard and already leaking. Maerlon fists his length and gives it a leisurely stroke. "Tell me what you need." The deep, commanding tone makes me shiver.

"You. I need you," I say shakily.

He gives me a wicked smile as he kneels down and grabs my legs to pull me so that my hips are at the edge of the bed. His powerful hands push my thighs apart so I'm spread wide before him. I suck in my breath as he nips at my inner thigh. A finger drags against my slit and I squirm, my pussy clenching. His tongue replaces the finger as he gives me a long, teasing lick that makes my breath shudder out of me.

I'm so desperate for him and it's not enough. I want him inside me. "Please, I want—"

Maerlon lifts his mouth and looks up at me from between my legs. "I know what you want, but there's no rush. We've got all night. I'm going to make you come until you're truly begging for me."

A delicious shiver runs down my spine at his words. Part of me wants to protest that I've been waiting long enough, but then his mouth is on me again and all rational thought goes out the window.

His long, slick tongue teases at my entrance, dipping inside. A thick finger plays with my clit, rubbing tight circles around it as he fucks me with his tongue. The way he licks so deep inside of me feels incredibly alien and I squirm, unsure if I want to get away from the sensation or encourage it. Maerlon lets out a low, throaty groan and presses his other hand on my low belly, pinning my hips in place. The pressure there adds depth to the sensation, and a choked moan rips from my throat.

Time seems to melt away as Maerlon devours me. Normally, I'd worry that I was taking too long or that he's getting bored, but his enthusiastic growls and moans let me get swept away in the feeling of his mouth on my pussy. My release coils slowly, getting tighter and tighter until my whole body is shaking with need.

"Oh god, *Maerlon*."

His nails dig into the soft flesh of my belly and that prick of pain is what I need to tumble over the edge. My legs tighten around his head as waves of pleasure crash over me. Maerlon slows his movements but doesn't stop completely. He moves his tongue to my sensitive clit and flicks it, making me cry out and buck my hips.

I can sense his smile against my pussy as he grips me tighter and continues to flick and circle my clit. Arousal builds again, and after a few minutes I'm whimpering with need. Maerlon slides two fingers inside me, pressing them firmly against my inner walls, then sucks on my clit.

"It's too much...fuck, I can't," I cry, even as my hips rock against his face.

Maerlon groans against me and continues his assault, devouring my pussy and rubbing his thick fingers inside of me. He sucks on my clit again and I'm seeing stars and coming harder than the first time.

He slowly builds me up to release one more time, making me scream his name until I can't take it anymore. I lay on the bed, dazed and panting, as he finally gets up from between my legs. His face glistens, which would embarrass me if he didn't look so wild with desire.

He kisses his way up my belly to my breasts and my pussy clenches again as he teases one of my nipples with his tongue. I sit up and pull him into a kiss before he decides to go down on me again.

Not that I'm complaining about how much he loves eating me out. No one's ever been so dedicated to my pleasure and I feel selfish that he's had no release yet. It makes me desperate to do the same for him. I've waited for weeks and I'm not letting him distract me any longer.

Maerlon palms one of my breasts lazily and hunger fills his gaze when our lips part. "Stars, you taste so good. I could eat your sweet cunt for hours and still not be satisfied."

"I'm pretty sure you already were down there for at least an hour. I have no clue how your tongue isn't cramping up from overuse."

"My tongue is still very capable. Shall I show you?" He slides down my body, but I roll away with a squeal.

I look down at the painfully stiff cock jutting up between his thighs. "Why don't you let me show you how capable mine is instead?"

Maerlon's eyes flare brighter and he swallows heavily. "*Vash-ka*, yes. I haven't stopped thinking about the feel of your tongue on me since…" He trails off, looking at me with a mixture of need and concern.

"I've thought about it a lot, too. How I had to stretch my lips just to fit the tip inside." As I speak, I push him back on the bed. "I've touched myself, remembering the sounds you made when I took you deep into my mouth."

I move over him, pressing kisses against his taut abdomen until I reach his cock. It's already coated in his slick lubricant, the head flushed dark gray and his balls tight. He looks ready to explode at any moment.

I lick a testing swipe, circling the tip. Maerlon gasps and his cock twitches, but he maintains his control.

"I've even thought about swallowing your release again and letting that bright, overwhelming heat wash over my senses until all I can think about is *you*," I whisper, giving his cock another teasing lick.

He releases a shuddering, raspy moan at my words. "Fina, you can't."

I smile up at him for a moment, then wrap my lips around the head of his cock and sink down as far as I can take him. I don't plan on actually doing that—getting high off him tonight. I want to have all my senses under my control this time. But fuck, I like the idea of it. Of feeling so overwhelmed by my need that I lose myself in him.

I slide my mouth off of him and gaze up into his eyes. "Don't worry, I won't. Not tonight, at least. I want you to come inside me."

He growls as his hand flies up to tangle in my hair, guiding my head back down to his cock. I take him in my mouth eagerly and my arousal builds when he thrusts up as his hand gently presses my head down onto his length. I almost choke a few times, but it feels so damn good for him to take what he needs.

It doesn't last long. His hips stutter and he quickly pulls me off of him. "I'm going to, I can't—" He roughly pumps his cock a few times and then he's coming all over my tits and neck in hot, thick spurts.

He places a possessive hand on my chest and looks at my breasts, dazed. I gasp as he rubs his cum over my tits, like he wants me to be coated in his essence. It's filthy, but excitement pools low in my belly as he does it.

"*Esh'et*, Fina. You're too good," he murmurs between heavy breaths.

If he were a human man, it might disappoint me he came before I even felt him inside me. But after watching him touch himself a few weeks ago, I know he's just getting started.

# 39

## ✦MAERLON✦

When I arrived at Fina's apartment, I hadn't planned on the desperation that slammed into me as soon as she opened the door. Possessed by the need to have her, to make her mine, to show her just how much she affects me, I let myself go. But now that I've released my restraint, I don't know how to stop. The heady scent in the air, the sweet taste still coating my lips, and the heat of her plush body next to mine all sing through me. Calling for me to take her over and over. Urging me to claim her body like she's claimed my soul.

Fina covered in my seed touches something primal in my mind. It screams at me to bury myself inside her and fill her over and over until it floods out to mix with the wetness between her thighs.

She sits next to me on the bed, watching me with wide eyes.

Waiting to see what I'll do next. I enjoy her gaze on my bare skin. Knowing that she sees me for who I truly am and that she desires me just as I am. Knowing that I don't need to hide anything from her.

I lean back against the headboard. My cock is already surging back to life, eager to be inside Fina.

"Wow, that was fast," she remarks, watching it with rapt attention. Her breath quickens as I stroke my length and I hold her gaze.

"Do you see what you do to me, Fina? I've been hard and aching for you every time we're together. Every time we touched, every little breathy sound you made when we kissed, every time I smelled your arousal—it was maddening. I want this to be good for you. I want everything for you. But I don't know how much longer I can control myself." The words spill out of me as I continue to pump my cock while Fina stares at me with need.

I'm not exaggerating. I'm seconds away from pinning her down on the bed and rutting into her like an animal.

"You don't need to hold back anymore," Fina whispers. She straddles me, guiding my hand from my cock to her hip. I groan when I feel her hot, slick cunt pressed against me and she sighs, echoing my need. I will myself not to lift her up and spear her on my cock, gripping her hips so tightly that I'm worried about bruising her pale, delicate skin.

She tilts her hips and her cunt slides against me, practically begging for me to bury myself in her. She's so wet that we slip against each other with ease. Then her mouth is on mine, her tongue eagerly pressing into my mouth to tangle with my own. She moans and rocks her hips again.

"What do you want? Tell me. I need to hear you tell me." Rough need bleeds into my voice. I want this, but I need to know for certain that she wants it too.

"You. I want you. *Please.*" Fina's eyelids flutter and her head falls back as my cock drags along her slit and teases the little nub at the apex.

It's not enough. I need her to say exactly what she wants. "What do you want from me?" I growl, holding her hips tighter and thrusting up to meet her movements. We both gasp when the head of my cock slips inside her, but I pull back.

She whimpers at the loss. "I want you inside me. I want you to fuck me so hard I can't breathe."

What remaining threads of control I had left snap at her words. I surge forward, pushing Fina down onto her back. I fit the tip of my cock against her entrance, but I hesitate. It seems impossible that it will fit inside her.

"Yes. God, yes, give it to me." Fina spreads her legs wider to encourage me.

Slowly—so slow it's almost painful—I sink into her. She's wet and willing and my slick already coats my cock, but she's still so tight it takes my breath away.

Fina inhales sharply and I stop. I'm only halfway inside her and she already looks stretched to her limit.

"*Esh'et*, I'm so sorry. Did I hurt you?"

She shakes her head and brings her legs up to wrap around my hips, and I slip in even deeper. "No, you feel—fuck, I need more."

With a shudder, I thrust the rest of the way in and she gasps when I'm fully seated inside her. *Vash-ka*, I've never experienced anything like this—this overwhelming bliss of being consumed body and soul by her. I almost come right then and there.

We both adjust to the sensation and Fina stares up at me with wonder, and something more. Something so intimate it makes my heart clench.

*L'thris a talla.* The ancient seladin words confessing an all-consuming love echo in my mind, begging me to say them aloud. I told Fina I loved her before, but these words mean so much more. They mean she is *everything* to me. I thrust inside her in deep, long strokes to the rhythm of the words my mind chants. The confession bubbles to my lips and I kiss her before it can burst free.

She gasps and sighs beneath me with each movement, the hot clasp of her threatening to be my undoing. I'm already far too close to coming and need her to get there before me. I slip a hand between our bodies and start stroking the sensitive spot on her cunt.

She whispers my name like a prayer and her channel clenches tighter around me. "More," she begs, her hips rising to meet mine.

I pump faster, thrusting my hips in sharp, savage motions. It's too good. She's too good. I look at where we're joined. Fina's abundant thighs cradle me and her soft belly jiggles deliciously with each thrust. Everything about her body is supple and giving, just like she is.

"*Vash-ka*, I...Fina, I..." The chant in my head grows louder and more insistent. *I love you. You are my heart. L'thris a talla.*

"Maerlon!" Fina chokes out my name in a frantic cry and her cunt ripples around me as she comes. She grasps onto me tightly as I pound through her release, chasing my own.

She kisses me, needy and heated despite her climax. I'm barreling toward my release, but desperately cling to this moment. Our mouths part and Fina looks up at me, pupils wide.

I feel a spark, the undeniable tether of our soul bond joining us, and see it reflected in her eyes.

"I love you." Fina's words are barely more than a whisper, but they hit me in the chest like an phaser blast. My hips stutter and I come with a roar, spilling inside her with blinding hot pleasure. She takes all that I have to give so perfectly. She is *mine*.

"*L'thris a talla.*" I murmur the sacred words of love against her neck, confessing that she owns my heart and soul.

## ✦FINA✦

Maerlon's lips press against my neck and he mutters words my translator doesn't pick up. His hips still and he holds himself over me, still gasping from his release. His hair hangs down, obscuring his face from my view. I can't see his expression. I can't tell what he's thinking.

Nothing but the sound of our heavy breathing fills the air. The cruel prickle of anxiety creeps up my spine in the silence.

I told him I love him. I didn't fully understand that I did until the words tumbled out. At that moment, everything told me how *right* he is for me. It was more than just the feeling of him inside me—he fills a hole in my heart I didn't even know I had.

It seemed so clear. But now he's not saying anything.

I reach up and brush his long, silky hair aside, searching his face for something to reassure me. Maerlon looks utterly wrecked. His eyes are so bright they're almost hard to look into, and his lips are swollen and parted.

I feel him hardening inside me when our eyes meet and the hint of a feral smile curves onto his mouth. He pulls back slightly and then pushes into me in a slow, dragging thrust that makes my breath hitch. His fanged grin grows and heat pools in my belly. I want to beg him to fuck me again, but need to know what he's thinking first.

"If I said something that you're not ready for, please tell me…I didn't mean to make things awkward." I force myself to bring it up before I can talk myself out of it.

Maerlon gives me a confused look, and my face heats. Is he really going to make me spell it out for him?

"What could you possibly have said that I wouldn't want to hear, my heart?" He rolls his hips again, and it feels like he's even harder than before.

Shit, did he not hear what I said? I'm too scared to say it again now.

"I'm your heart?" I ask instead, hoping those words hold more meaning than a generic endearment.

"Yes," he whispers, face filled with affection and desire. "*L'thris a talla.*"

There are those words again. "Le thriss ah tahla? What does that mean?"

Maerlon's eyes soften and he strokes my cheek, his thumb pausing to trace my lower lip. "Ah, it means 'keeper of my heart' or 'most beloved'. Though...it means more than that—it's something my people only say to those we share a soul bond with." He leans down and kisses me with such tender devotion that my whole body sings. "I'll work every day to deserve your love, Fina."

Oh, *wow*. "A soul bond? Is that like a mate?"

"Yes, and no. It's not rooted in a biological imperative, like nexxit and aespian mates. Or even a sense of someone being destined for you, like shikzeth believe. It's more...knowing deep inside you that you fit with someone. It's also not limited to one person, but many seladin go their entire lives without finding even one true soul bond."

"O-oh. And you've found that with me?" My heart skips a beat as I process his words.

He hesitates, searching my face. He swallows hard at whatever he finds there and then speaks. "Yes, Fina. I have. I wouldn't have said anything...I don't want to pressure you if you don't feel the same. But I promised not to keep secrets from you. And that's my truth. My soul is bound to yours. I am yours, if you'll have me."

"I—wow, Maerlon, I—" I stumble, unable to find the right ones to express the depth of my emotion. Of how much his words mean to me.

"You don't have to say anything. I understand." He looks crestfallen and he starts to pull back.

Panicked, I grab his hips and hold him in place. "No, you don't understand! Of course I'll have you. I don't know if humans can soul bond, but I feel...I feel safe and cherished when I'm with you. Like you see me. God, that seems crazy to say. We haven't even known each other that long. But I feel it. I love you, Maerlon."

He whispers my name, and our lips meet, both our hearts pouring into the kiss. My hips rise and he slides deeper inside me. We both gasp at the sensation.

Heat returns to his gaze, and he moves inside me with deep, heavy strokes. "Do you feel this, Fina?"

I'm so close already, but it's not quite enough. "Yes. I need more."

Maerlon pulls out, and I groan at the loss. But before I have time to complain, he speaks.

"Get on your hands and knees. Show me what's mine."

# 40

## ✦FINA✦

Maerlon's command sends a thrill through me. Something deep inside me needs that—to let go of my anxieties and just exist. To allow myself to experience pleasure and take what he has to give me without second guessing things.

God, maybe I'm kinkier than I thought. Definitely something we'll have to explore further.

I roll over and a little yelp of surprise escapes my lips when he grabs my hips and tugs them up, raising my ass in the air. I feel exposed in this new position, even though he's already spent hours with his face between my legs. My pussy clenches in anticipation and I freeze in embarrassment as some of his cum drips out of me.

He runs his fingers along my pussy, gathering our mingled

release on them. "You look so perfect like this." He presses his fingers inside me, pushing his cum back in with them. "I'm going to fill your pretty cunt until my seed is dripping down your thighs," he says as he starts to fuck me with his fingers.

I rock back on his hand, his words making any shame I felt melt away as I chase my pleasure. "Do it," I gasp. "Fuck me, Maerlon."

In one swift motion, he replaces his fingers with his cock, hilting himself fully inside me. He doesn't give me a chance to adjust this time, but I don't need it. I'm so ready for him.

He sets a brutal pace, his hands sinking into the flesh of my hips as he pounds into my pussy with rough strokes. At this angle, he feels even bigger, and each thrust hits something deep inside me that knocks the breath out of me.

My face presses into the pillow and I moan, reaching a hand down to rub my clit. Over and over, he thrusts into me until I'm shaking. "Don't stop. Oh god, I'm going to come." I don't recognize the desperate, raspy sounds coming out of me.

"Give it to me. Come for me," Maerlon growls, and he reaches underneath me to grab my breast and pinch my nipple.

I shatter. My orgasm wracks my body in a violent surge. It's almost too much. Maerlon keeps thrusting as I clench around him, groaning at the sensation.

Despite my release, my body screams for more. I know I'll be sore later, but right now, I couldn't care less. All I want is to feel him as deep inside me as possible. I press up onto my hands, giving myself leverage to push back onto his cock. We both inhale sharply at the sensation.

"Fuck, you feel so good," I gasp.

Maerlon wraps a hand in my hair and tugs just enough to send a spike of pleasurable pain through me, bowing my back.

"You're *mine*, Fina," he says with a snarl, and speeds up his thrusts. All I can do now is hold on as he slams into me.

"I'm yours." My whole body feels delightfully warm, and the air sparks with the electricity between us. It's all so bright and I need *more*. A far away voice in my mind realizes that the sensation is beyond what I would normally feel, but I'm too absorbed in it to care. With a choked sob, I come again. Lights dance behind my eyes and I feel like I'm floating away from my body.

Maerlon's movements become erratic and he follows me, pumping hot ropes of his cum into me like he promised he would. Each spurt makes my spine tingle, dragging out my orgasm. I press back against him, wanting to milk every last drop out of him.

He shudders and stills and when he pulls out, a flood of our releases slides down my thighs. I already feel empty and I whimper, rolling over to gaze at him as I caress my breast.

"You're insatiable," he chuckles, watching me. "Do you need more?" His husky voice dips lower.

I feel like I just ran a marathon. My pussy throbs in protest at the idea, but desire still courses through me, hot and insistent. Something is making me desperate for more.

*Oh shit.*

"You came inside me," I murmur, bringing a hand down to stroke my clit.

"Mmm, yes. Do you like it when I come inside you?" Maerlon rasps, running his hands down my thighs as he watches me touch myself.

"God, yes," I whimper, my release building fast. Faster than normal, because…"I think it affected me. Not as much as when I swallowed. But everything seems hotter, and even though I know I should take a break, I want more."

His hands still their movement and his expression fills with worry. "*Esh'et*, I didn't think about that. I shouldn't have—"

"I wanted it. I'm just as much to blame. But I feel fine. Great, really." I emphasize my last point with a soft moan as I touch myself. "Just don't come inside me this time?"

*Yes, that's a sensible solution.*

"Fina..." He still looks concerned, so I sit up and kiss him deeply. When I bite his lower lip, he hisses and pulls back, eyes filled with the same sharp need that mine undoubtedly are.

"I want you inside me again. *Now*."

WE END up with him taking me two more times before the high fades, finally leaving me satisfied. And fairly sore.

Maerlon insists on helping me clean off, carrying me into the shower and gently washing me. When he delves between my legs with the washcloth, the movements stoke my desire once more. The little breath I release when he brushes over my clit is all he needs before he's got one of my legs up on his shoulder as he licks me to a gentle, languid orgasm.

I try to return the favor, but he just laughs and kisses me softly instead. He even insists on drying me off. It feels a little silly, but I let him. He runs the towel over me with a tender devotion that I never dreamed I would experience.

After working together to change the sheets—something Maerlon protested, wanting to sleep surrounded by the evidence of our joining—he holds me, stroking my hair. Despite how exhausted we are, we stay like this, talking and sharing our hearts' secrets until the simulated sunlight of the station peeks through the windows. When sleep claims me, I smile, knowing I'm in the arms of the man I love.

# 41

## ✦ MAERLON ✦

*3 months later*

"Shit, we're going to be late! I'll never hear the end of it from Paul." Fina scurries around her apartment, makeup half-done and a hastily wrapped robe hanging askew off one shoulder.

I watch her, suppressing a guilty smile. I'm a large part of the reason she's running so behind getting ready for tonight's event. When I saw her step out of the shower in a cloud of steam, her lush body glistening and wet, I couldn't help myself. We ended up back under the water for far longer than the station-recommended water usage, while I feasted between her legs. Then I pressed her against the tile wall and lost myself inside her. Twice.

She moves past me into the bedroom. When I go to follow, she presses a hand to my chest and shakes her head. "No way! Go wait on the couch while I get dressed."

"I just want to help you," I murmur, leaning in to kiss her neck. Even after a shower, I can still smell the sweet, heady scent that is pure Fina.

Her breath hitches, but then she's pulling away and glaring at me half-heartedly. "You've already 'helped' enough."

I chuckle and smack her ass as she turns to head into her closet. I love the indignant look she gives me, her cheeks reddening as she pushes me out and closes the door behind her.

With a glance around the living area of her apartment, I busy myself tidying up while she finishes getting ready. Fina leaves a trail of chaos behind her when she's anxious. I note that the luminescent blooms I gifted her have outgrown their current container—I'll have to re-pot it soon. The plant flourished under her care, despite her insistence that she doesn't have a "green thumb". I'm still not sure what that has to do with anything. I like her pale pink skin.

Soft curses emanate from the bedroom. I want to check on her, but she told me to wait out here. My heart will call me if she needs me.

Tonight's party is celebrating the Coalition embassy's opening. After months of feverish preparations, the Xi Consortium officially instated the human embassy on Spire. Countless hours of work went into preparing for the Coalition's ambassadorial contingent and smoothing out any PR issues this change to Spire created. Fina's work played a large part in successfully selling the benefits of humanity's presence on the station to the locals.

A twinge of guilt nags at me. I shouldn't have let myself get so carried away earlier. I know how much tonight means to Fina. That's part of the issue though—I'm so proud of what she's accomplished and the glow of her achievements makes her even more irresistible.

Tonight's important for another reason, too. One I'm not sure if Fina is aware of or would want to recognize. It's the half year anniversary of the first time we met. Mezli told me countless times how important anniversaries are to humans and while I hesitate to trust her advice, I like the idea of celebrating the milestone. I reach a hand into the pocket of my formal jacket, pressing against the small pouch inside to check that it's still there.

Fina emerges from her bedroom and I hastily pull my hand out of the pocket, smoothing the jacket down. My pulse quickens looking at her. She's wearing a black, strapless gown with a deep neckline showing off her perfect breasts. There's a high slit over one leg that makes me want to use it as a guide to tear the whole thing off of her. Her hair hangs down over one shoulder in cascading violet waves that beg me to run my fingers through them. *Vash-ka*, she looks...

"Don't tell me, I know it's not great, but there's no time to get changed," Fina mutters, not meeting my gaze as she reaches to grab her purse from the table beside me.

My hand darts out, and I grab her wrist, pulling her closer. She gasps softly and I lean down to bring my lips to her ear. "You are going to kill me, wearing a dress like that. No one will be able to keep their eyes off you," I whisper, loving the way she shivers as my breath tickles her neck.

"O-oh. Well...good," she says breathily, leaning into my touch as I run a hand down her spine to rest on the small of her back.

With a reluctant groan, I release her and step back. "Ready to go? We don't want to be late."

Fina makes an exasperated noise at me and I hold back my laughter as we head out the door.

DESPITE ALL ODDS, we manage to arrive only a few minutes late to the party. Though it looks like half of Orion district has lined up for the chance to gawk at the newly arrived humans. The line stretches down the walkway almost all the way to the transit station. I catch many of the people in line staring at Fina as we weave past them to the doors of the event hall. A few give me envious glares.

They should be jealous. Fina is a goddess and I'm the luckiest person on Spire to be by her side.

The buzz of conversation and soft, stringed music fill the air of the large ballroom. We only have a moment to take in the elegant atmosphere before Paul comes to greet us. He looks handsome and polished in his fitted, midnight blue suit, but his expression betrays his stress.

"Fina! Maerlon! Good, you're here. You both look amazing." Paul gives Fina a friendly hug, then moves to hug me but hesitates. He still acts worried around me, as if I'm going to suddenly tear his head off because of his romantic history with Fina. But I like Paul and want to help him look good tonight, so I bridge the distance between us and give him a firm embrace. I swear I hear Fina giggle and when I pull back, Paul looks flustered, his brown skin flushed darker.

"We wouldn't miss it! You look wonderful, I love the suit. Anything we can do?" Fina asks.

"No, everything seems to be going well. A lot bigger crowd than we expected, though. Everyone here from the Coalition is getting a crash course on being Spire's latest spectacle." Paul looks over at a cluster of humans over by the bar, who peer out at the room with trepidation.

"Try to relax and have some fun tonight, okay? You deserve it,"

Fina says, placing her hand on his arm and squeezing it reassuringly. Paul's eyes dart over to me when she touches him and I stifle a laugh. Am I still really that intimidating? I know a part of Paul still loves Fina, but her heart belongs to me. Plus, I know Mezli will kick his ass if he tries to make any moves on Fina again.

Paul sighs in frustration. "I will if my date ever gets here. Have you seen Mezli? God, why did I let her convince me to bring her to this?"

Poor man, he should have asked someone more reliable to be his companion tonight. Someone who doesn't act like she's on the verge of killing him half the time they're interacting.

"No, but she's always late, so I wouldn't take it too personally," I say, attempting to reassure him.

A yellow-haired human with wide hips catches his eye and gestures for him to join them. "Well, duty calls," says Paul with a slight frown. He plasters on a smooth smile and heads over, calling out a greeting to the human.

For the next hour, acquaintances and previous coworkers from the Coalition ambassadorial office bombard Fina. She handles each interaction with grace, though I know she's nervous about speaking with people she hasn't seen in a long time. She never expected to have her old life follow her here. Everyone I meet remarks upon how good Fina looks and I heartily agree, doing my best to be as non-threatening to some of the more skittish-looking humans.

When she seems overwhelmed by a pair of embassy pages grilling her about how she found an alien partner, I step in and pull her away to the dance floor. I'm immediately swept up in the warmth of Fina's nearness and her welcoming scent as we move to the music. She stumbles a few times on her tall heels, but I hold her steady and only wince slightly when she steps on my toe. I'd gladly suffer much more to have her in my arms. Knowing that I'm the one that gets to press her close and savor the way her soft body molds against me. Showing everyone that she's mine and I'm hers.

Fina's voice startles me out of my reverie, close to my ear so that only I can hear her. "As nice as this is, there's something else I'd like to do tonight."

I press my hand into her low back, drawing her closer to let her feel how much I like the idea. "Oh? What's that?"

She gives me a mischievous smile. "It's a surprise. Do you trust me?"

I lean down and press a kiss to her lips, lingering there longer than appropriate for the setting. "Always."

# 42

## ✦MAERLON✦

A frown pulls at my lips when we arrive in Sagittarius district and head in the opposite direction of my loft. The expression deepens as Fina tugs me behind her into the glowing neon strip of nightclubs and bars.

"You want to go to a club? Really?" I'm unable to hide my skepticism. If that's what she wants, I'll do it. But that isn't the romantic atmosphere I'd envisioned when she suggested we sneak away from the party.

"Nope. Something better. More appropriate for the occasion," she says cheerily.

Something more appropriate for the occasion?

I follow her, my gaze sliding down to watch her bottom jiggle enticingly as she walks. I almost bump into her when she stops and spins around to give me a hesitant look.

"Okay, so we don't have to do this if you don't want to. We can just go back to your place. This is probably a terrible idea. I just thought it might be fun. You know what? I'm sorry. I don't want to make you uncomfortable, so we can just go." Her anxious stream of words confuses me until I glance up and realize where we are.

The sign above the very familiar building reads "SimTech Suites". A wave of my own nerves washes over me, but it quickly fades and gives way to amusement at Fina's worries. If she's okay, then I'm happy to indulge in whatever activity she has in mind.

I wrap an arm around her waist and smile down at her, affection flowing through me. "Tonight's the half year anniversary of when we first met. You've brought us back to where it all started. This is the perfect way to celebrate."

Fina's eyes sparkle back at me, and she relaxes. "You remembered?"

"How could I ever forget the day my life truly started?" I pull her in, pressing our mouths together in a languid kiss.

"God, I love you."

"I love you too, *l'thris a talla*. Now, shall we go inside so you can show me what naughty things you want to do that require a pleasure sim?"

## ✦FINA✦

It's odd being back at SimTech. And even stranger when an unfamiliar voice greets us from the holo-receptionist. Maerlon's hand rests on my back, rubbing small circles with his thumb as I check in for our sim reservation. He does that when I'm nervous—it's his way of anchoring me to him and letting me know he's by my side. The holo-receptionist—Almarsi—is friendly and professional. They send us back to our room with no extra chatter.

As we follow the illuminated path, I nudge Maerlon. "I didn't realize before talking to that tech just how flirty you were, even when we first met. Were you like that with all the customers?"

"Hah! Not at all. But it's not every day I meet a human. You were adorable, standing there all nervous, apologizing for everything. And when I saw you in that tight pink outfit, all curves and softness that begged to be touched, I was lost." He slides his hand down from my low back to cup my ass, emphasizing his point.

Even after the months we've been together, I still get flustered by how much he desires me.

The door to the suite opens and we enter the empty room. Heat pools low in my belly as I anticipate my plans for the simulation. I booked the suite ahead of time and provided the simulation details so I could keep it a secret from Maerlon until the last possible moment.

"Just let me know when you're ready for your simulation to begin, Ms. Kress," Almarsi calls out through the audio comm.

"Sure, give us just a moment." My heart races at the sudden reality of what I'm about to do.

Right. I've got this. I'm allowed to ask for what I want and if he isn't interested, it'll be okay. My self-motivation mantras run through my mind as I take a deep breath and force myself to look into Maerlon's eyes.

"Okay, so...that first night we met, you gave me...you told me a safeword. What if we used that tonight? For, you know...if you...*tiemeupandmakemedowhateveryouwant*." I mutter the last words so quickly that they're incomprehensible.

"I didn't quite get that last part. If I what?" Maerlon asks, bemused.

"If you make me—if you tie me up and I can't—fuck, you know what I mean!" My face flames and I cross my arms over my chest.

Maerlon's eyes blaze with heat and he takes a step closer so that he's towering over me. "You want me to dominate you, Fina?" he asks in a low growl.

"...Y-yes."

"Yes, what?"

Oh god, he's going for it already. I've fantasized about this for so long. We've talked about it too, but I've been too shy to really ask for it. I'm not sure what he wants me to call him though—sir reminds me too much of the military. Daddy feels weird...but there's a seladin word that has a similar connotation.

"Yes...*kha-shar*," I answer tentatively, feeling silly. I should have practiced the pronunciation ahead of time.

The low purr in his throat makes me feel a lot more serious.

"Good girl," he murmurs and *fuck*, I didn't realize how hot it would be to hear him say that. "Remember, your safeword is 'aquamarine'. Say it and we'll stop, no matter what."

"O-okay, got it. Aquamarine." I say back to him, wondering why he chose that word when we first met. But with how he's looking at me, now's not the time to ask.

"Tell the tech that we're ready, my heart." Maerlon gives me that smile with a hint of fang he gets when he's trying not to look too excited.

I call out to the technician to start the sim. After a few seconds, the familiar blinding light fills the room. When it fades, Maerlon inhales sharply. Hopefully, that's a good sign.

I knew I didn't want to use that sex dungeon setting from before. I was worried about bringing up bad memories. So instead, I drew inspiration from one of his paintings. He told me about the seladin ritual that inspired it and since then, many of my bondage fantasies have centered on it.

We're in a clearing within a dark forest, surrounded by bioluminescent plants that shed dim, multicolored light. Glowing motes float through the air as a breeze rustles the leaves. In the center of the glade rests a circle of stone pillars surrounding a raised altar and an x-shaped cross. I'm no longer in my dress from the party. Instead, I'm clad in a sheer white gown wrapped in thin gold ropes that criss-cross over my breasts and hips, creating a harness-like bodice. Maerlon's suit has also disappeared, leaving him in only a loose-fitting pair of dark pants.

I take in the ethereal beauty of the setting, trying to calm my nerves. *Please let him like this.*

I should have asked beforehand, but I wanted to surprise him. I'm not sure that was the right call. There's a tense set to his jaw when he finally looks at me.

"We can do something else if you don't like it. I'm sorry, I just wanted it to be special for you. I should have checked that it was okay."

"You never cease to amaze me." Maerlon drags his gaze up and down my body, pausing where my nipples strain against the fabric. He swallows heavily. "It's perfect."

The way he's staring at me, I'm not sure if he means the simulation or my appearance. I'll take either as a win.

"Do you know what happens in this setting?" He stalks around the pillars, keeping his distance as he surveys me. "You're offering yourself up to me. To let me bind you and use you however I want. To submit to my most primal desires. Is that what you want, Fina?"

"Yes. I know. I want it all." My voice shakes with the adrenaline and desire coursing through my veins. It's all I've been able to think about since he showed me the painting.

Maerlon moves to stand by the altar. "Come here."

I walk toward him slowly, the speed of my breaths increasing with each step closer. A breeze flows through the clearing as if it's also obeying his command, rippling through my gown and hair. When I'm finally standing before him, I watch him breathlessly, waiting for his order.

"Kneel."

I sink to my knees before him immediately and am rewarded with his hand threading through my hair. I lean into the touch reflexively and his grip on my hair tightens. "Don't move unless I tell you to," he growls.

My pulse races at his tone. I still my movements and peer up at him. "Yes, *kha-shar*."

I watch with rapt attention as he drags the loose pants down off his hips and steps out of them. In my kneeling position, his cock is right at eye level and my mouth waters at the sight of him. Here, in this facsimile of the lush forests of ancient Sela, he looks like a god. And I'm his willing acolyte, ready to worship him.

Maerlon brings his cock to my lips and rubs it against them. I want to dart my tongue out to lick the smear of his slick off my lips, but don't know if that counts as moving, so I stay frozen.

"You look so beautiful on your knees. Open your pretty mouth for me, my heart."

I open my mouth and he slides the tip of his cock inside. I taste his unique, heady flavor on my tongue and let out a little moan as he presses in further, holding the back of my head in place.

"That's it. My obedient *fa'sli*, sucking my cock with those perfect lips." He groans, pumping his hips, gently fucking my willing mouth. My translator lags with one of the words, so it takes a moment for me to realize he just called me his "eager slut". There's clear affection in his tone despite the filthy things he's saying, and the combination makes me throb with need.

I moan around his cock and let him guide my movements, trusting that he knows how deep he can thrust into my mouth without making me choke too much. Arousal soaks my thighs, and when the breeze kicks up again and his nostrils flare, I know he can tell how affected I am by this.

He works himself inside my mouth until my jaw begins to ache and tears fill my eyes. I *love* it. It feels like I could come just from the possessive way he takes his pleasure from me.

When I run my tongue along the ridges and bumps near the head, he curses. "*Vash-ka*, you're doing so well. Do you want me to spill down your throat?"

My eyes widen. He doesn't come in my mouth—not since the first disastrous night I went down on him. He's been too nervous to try again despite my assurances I'll be fine now that I know what to expect.

Maerlon yanks my head off of his cock and waits for my answer, his breath coming rapidly. He's already close to his release.

"Yes, *kha-shar*. Come in my mouth. I need to taste you." I'm surprised at how needy I sound.

He lets out a choked growl and then he's fucking my mouth again, fisting my hair as he pumps in shallow, rapid thrusts. With a low groan, he comes and the hot stream fills my mouth. I let most of it spill out of my mouth and down my chin, but when he pulls out and more spurts across my lips, I look into eyes and show him the remaining release on my tongue before swallowing.

"*Vash-ka, Fina.*" He groans at the sight.

A pleasant buzz and warmth begins to infuse my senses, just

enough to make my whole body tingle with increased awareness and need. When Maerlon runs a thumb across my lips, rubbing in his seed, I whimper involuntarily, wanting so much more.

# 43

## ✦MAERLON✦

Fina kneels before me, her hands clasped behind her back in a way that thrusts her breasts against the wispy, sheer fabric of her gown. She looks up at me, her eyes sparkling like the ocean at sunset. Her pupils have dilated, and she does her best not to move as the cool breeze tickles at her bare skin.

The haze of my frantic release fades, letting me come out of my lust-filled fog to better assess the situation. A hint of panic creeps into my mind—will my seed affect her too much? I don't want to push too far tonight. I need her to be able to tell me if she wants to stop.

"How do you feel? Tell me your safeword if this seems like too much." I hold her chin so she meets my eyes.

"I feel amazing, Maerlon—*kha-shar*." The seladin word for

"master" sounds incredibly erotic in her breathy, sweet voice. My cock twitches and hardens again.

That doesn't tell me if she's still lucid enough to continue, though. I decide to test her with something I know she finds unappealing. "You look so sinful like that. I bet you'd let anyone who came in here come in your *fa'sli* mouth. Should I ask the technician to add others to the sim so they can use you like I have?" The thought holds no appeal, but I try to sound like it would please me.

Fina's eyes widen and then she frowns. "No, *kha-shar*. I only serve you," she squeaks, looking worried I'll punish her for denying me.

"No? You're here to serve my every need. Use your safeword if you truly don't want that." I need to double-check that her "no" wasn't just part of an act to rile me up.

She slumps slightly. "...Aquamarine. Sorry, I don't—"

I rest my hand on her cheek and caress it with my thumb, worried that I've broken the mood with my concern. "Shh, I just wanted to make sure you're still all there, my heart. Should we continue?"

Fina visibly relaxes and nods. "Yes. Please, *kha-shar*."

"Stand," I command.

She wobbles slightly as she rises, and I grip her arms to steady her. A small gasp escapes her lips at my touch and when I let my sharp nails dig lightly into her pliant flesh, she inhales sharply and the scent of her arousal grows thicker in the air.

With a firm grip on one of her arms, I lead her over to the cross behind the altar. Lengths of gold silken rope that match the knotting cage across her body rest atop it. My pulse quickens—tying Fina up is a fantasy that's run through my mind since the first night we met. I even learned how to bind a human safely, just in case she ever asked me to. That she trusts me enough to surrender her control like this intoxicates me.

With a slight tremor in my hands, I pick up a rope and lift her arm above her head, and begin tying it to the cross behind her. I let my fingers brush against the sensitive skin of her wrist as I wrap the ropes, lingering when I feel her shiver. I savor the process of binding her hands and then her ankles, taking my time to let her feel every step of the process. Loving the way her skin prickles as the smooth rope and my fingers slide across her delicate skin. Each careful loop and knot is a heady reminder of Fina's willing surrender to me.

When I'm done and have checked in again to make sure nothing is too tight or cutting off circulation, I take a step back. The sight leaves me breathless.

Fina's chest rises and falls rapidly as she watches me, unable to move. She's spread out in an x, her plush, abundant curves barely covered by her ethereal gown. I want to see more. I want her completely bare for me.

Her breath hitches as I move in close again and my hand goes to her neck. I let it rest there lightly and hold her gaze. There's no fear in her eyes, only need and anticipation.

"Mmm, my beautiful *fa'sli*. Look at you, all spread out for me to savor." I slide my fingers down to the neckline of her gown, letting the tip of a sharp nail scrape across her skin. My talons snag in the tissue-thin fabric and I use them to tear the gown down the center. I yank it off her body when I reach the bottom, leaving her with only the decorative rope cage that hides nothing.

Running my hand along the inside of her thigh as I stand back up, I pause when I get to her cunt and let my hand cup her there. Fina lets out a needy little gasp and tries to tilt her hips into my touch.

"What do you want, my heart?"

"Please." She whines and squirms against her bonds deliciously. I'm already becoming addicted to the sight of her like this. My cock feels harder than it ever has before and I'm leaking my slick in anticipation.

"Please what? Tell me exactly what you need." I slide my hand up across her rounded belly and ghost it between her breasts, avoiding touching them for more than a second, even though I long to. Every time I touch her, I marvel at how soft she is. Everything about her body calls to me, telling me to make her mine.

"Touch me." She wriggles again, and the movement jiggles her breasts temptingly.

"I am touching you," I say, stroking down her side. "Or do you mean somewhere else? Say it."

"God, I need you inside me, please." Her voice is husky as she locks her eyes with mine. "Use me, *kha-shar*."

Any plans I had for teasing her with my fingers and tongue evaporate. I need her *now*.

I slide a hand between her legs and find her already wet and ready. "Is this what you need? Your cunt is dripping for me, begging to be filled without me even touching you."

"Y-yes, fuck. Please," Fina whimpers.

With a quick motion, I position my cock at her entrance and thrust inside. She lets out a low, desperate moan and something inside me snaps. Her cunt grips me perfectly, so tight and hot. I need *more*.

I can't hold back, thrusting into her deep, so hard that it shakes her whole body. She cries out each time I pump into her, urging me on with guttural, broken sounds. My release crests far too fast. I bring a hand down to rub at the sensitive spot she calls her clit, while my other hand cages her throat.

"Is this what you wanted? For me to use your tight little cunt for my pleasure?" I don't know where the filthy words streaming out of me come from, but they send a full-body shiver through her. She cries out my name, her channel squeezing me like a vise as she comes undone.

I follow her over the edge. All that exists is the hot, wet clasp of her cunt as I pump my seed inside her with a roar. "*Mine.*"

When I reluctantly pull out of her, I glance down to make sure she's okay. She's panting and flushed all over and for a moment, I worry it was too much. I lean in and kiss her, looking for reassurance.

"*Yours,*" she whispers when our lips part. My chest squeezes with love and the certainty that she truly means it.

# 44

## ✦FINA✦

Maerlon fucks me twice more, once still tied to the cross and then once more bent over the stone altar. In between, he teases me with his fingers and mouth until I'm begging to come. By the time the session end warning chirps, my whole body feels shaky and thoroughly used. And god, that feels *amazing*.

Tonight was better than I could've imagined. Experiencing this with Maerlon—trusting him and letting him control me—was exhilarating. From the starry-eyed way he looks at me as he gently wipes me off and we re-dress, I know he feels the same way.

We leave SimTech in pleasant silence, Maerlon's arm around my waist, supporting me on my wobbly legs. As soon as we're out on the walkway, he scoops me up into his arms. I squeak in surprise and circle my arms around his neck. A few passersby glance at us curiously.

"I can walk, you know," I say with a chuckle.

Maerlon shakes his head and begins carrying me toward his loft. "Let me."

I sigh and resign myself to being bridal carried for the duration of our trip back to his loft. He weaves past club patrons and blaring holoscreen ads with ease, making sure not to bump me into anything. He insists on carrying me even when we reach his building, and I roll my eyes at his behavior.

"Okay, we're back. You can put me down, weirdo." I poke him in the chest as we step into his loft.

He chuckles and carries me over to the bed, setting me down with care.

"You're up for more? Already?" I ask, amused by where he put me.

He strokes a hand across my cheek. "There wasn't time for me to take care of you properly."

Despite everything it's been through tonight, my pussy throbs with a hint of need at his tender caress. "You took care of me four times!"

Maerlon gives me a self-satisfied grin that tells me he's well aware of that. He leans down to kiss me softly and then moves to sit on the bed behind me, running his hands over my shoulders. "Not that kind of care." His fingers knead into my shoulders and I let out an involuntary groan. "Unless you need it," he says in a lower voice, nipping at my neck.

"Mmm, maybe. But first I want to get this fancy dress off and take a shower. And then a massage—that feels wonderful." I lean into his touch.

"Anything you want, my heart."

I stand and start to undress, kicking off my heels and throwing my dress over a chair. Maerlon goes to take off his suit jacket and pauses, a strange expression on his face.

"Everything okay?" I ask.

"Yeah, I just forgot something. I got you something for our anniversary. After what you arranged, it's nowhere near as perfect a gift for the occasion. But here," he says, pulling a small velvet pouch out of his jacket pocket.

My heart flutters with affection. "You didn't have to get me anything!"

"Just open it." He sounds nervous.

My heart beats faster. Oh god, is it a ring? Is he proposing?!

I open the pouch and pull out something small and metallic from inside.

"It's a...key?" I'm unable to hide my confusion. The key looks worn and is probably some sort of antique, which is nice, I guess. But I think I'm missing something.

"Yes. I read that humans often give someone a key to their home when they care about each other. You already have the access code to my loft, so I got you that."

I blink down at the key and then back at him. "That's very sweet, thank you."

He sighs and runs his hand through his hair. "I'm not explaining properly. I meant it as a token to signify an offer. To live together. It doesn't have to be here if you prefer your place. Or we could find something new. I just want to spend all my days and nights with you, Fina. If you'll have me."

I stare at the key, and my eyes fill with tears. God, I love him.

His face falls, misinterpreting the water welling in my eyes.

"*Esh'et*, I'm an idiot. You're not ready for that step. I'm sorry, I shouldn't have presumed."

"Yes. Let's do it. Of course I want to live with you!" I tug him into my arms and plant a happy kiss on his lips. I wipe away my tears, amused that he thought I was upset.

"You do?"

"Yes! I love you, Maerlon." I kiss him again, lingering longer this time and slipping my tongue into his mouth to deepen it.

He groans and presses my body closer.

I pull away with a giggle. "Shower and massage, remember?"

"Right." He's still giving me a hungry look that says the shower will turn into him fucking me against the tile walls.

I finish getting undressed and head into the bathroom. "You know, for a second, I thought you were going to ask me to marry you. You seemed so worried and nervous," I say teasingly as he joins me.

Maerlon freezes mid pants-removal. He gazes at me with intensity and then, after a long pause, speaks. "If I had, what would you have said?"

Now it's my turn to freeze. What *would* I have said?

I love Maerlon. He makes me feel so cherished and supported. I've thought about Maerlon as my life partner. A lot. About if we'd have a human wedding ceremony or a seladin soul bonding ritual or some kind of hybrid. The logical side of me says it's too soon to make that kind of decision. But something deep inside of me knows he is mine, like I am his.

"Yes. I would have said yes. Why? Are you proposing now?" My heart feels like it's going to beat out of my chest.

He steps closer, almost tripping over the pants around his ankles. For once, I'm the one to steady him. I can't help but laugh and he makes a low growl, tugging me into his arms to press me against his chest. I look up at him, breathlessly awaiting his answer.

"Yes," he replies. "I know in my soul that I belong to you. I am yours for as long as you'll have me, Fina. *L'thris a talla.*"

# EPILOGUE

## ✦ MEZLI ✦

Damn, that date was a bust.

With a slight wince, I down the rest of my too-hot tea and set the mug on the cleaning pad. The spicy-sweet flavor is meant to be savored, but my date didn't last long enough for the liquid to cool. I shouldn't have waited for them to arrive. At least then I wouldn't have completely wasted the twenty minutes that passed until they deigned to show up.

Not only did they get there late, but then the ankite jerk said a total of two complete sentences. They didn't even interact when I asked some of my best first date questions.

On top of everything, my appearance obviously didn't impress them. I don't give a shit what some stuck up ankite thinks about me, but at least attempt to be polite!

*Goddess.* When they left after barely ten minutes with the excuse of an "emergency", I didn't bother to fight it. What a waste of time. Plus, they didn't even offer to pay for my tea.

Honestly, it shouldn't surprise me. At least they looked like their profile pics. The last few dates I've gone on ended up being totally different people than shown in their pictures. I've even had a few scam bots. But no matter how pretty an ankite my date today was, it doesn't make up for a lack of chemistry and basic manners. I'd much rather have a date who looks like shredded *mlesp* but who can banter with me than one who looks pretty but is like talking to a VI. And not a particularly well-programmed one, either.

Ugh, that's what I get for going out for tea instead of drinks. If I meet at a club and the date is a dud, I can find someone else to have fun with. And isn't that the whole reason I'm here on Spire?

My comm makes a twinkling chirp, letting me know I've received a message. It's from Paul—the fourth one I've gotten today reminding me of the time, location, and dress code for tonight's event. He's urging me to not be late. A spiteful part of me feels tempted to show up late just to mess with him. I know he's super stressed, but damn, I got it after the second message.

Paul's lucky that I'm willing to give up a prime weekend night to be his date to the human embassy opening. Doubt there will be fun singles there. Just a bunch of nervous humans and aliens there to gawk at them. I'd take it as a challenge to seduce one of the humans, but Paul made me swear not to. Something about not traumatizing his coworkers. None of the non-humans will spare a second glance for me, no matter how hot I look. They'll be there for the crop of exotic new arrivals.

All this cuteness is totally wasted. Unless...

Maybe tonight's the night I finally make a move on Paul. When we're not at each other's throats, we're flirting. I know he's attracted to me, even if he pretends otherwise. He's certainly appealing, with his smooth, light brown skin and his dark eyes. I bet he'd look even better tied up in my bed while I torture him until he begs for me. The cocky ones are always the ones that beg the most.

I've held off on propositioning Paul because of his shitty history with Fina. But now that he's finally admitted how much he mishandled their relationship, my horniness outweighs my vengeful nature. We could make something casual work as long as it's clear that it's just physical. I know he's curious about alien sex, but has had no luck on Syzygy. What better night to experience all the Xi Consortium has to offer than the celebration of the human embassy opening? And now that Fina's firmly entrenched in her whirlwind romance with Maerlon, I don't feel bad about getting with her ex.

The more I think about this idea, the more I like it. Perhaps I can salvage today after all.

I tread my well-worn path on the walkways of Orion district back to my apartment, mind filled with potential seduction tactics. The lame ankite from earlier is already ancient history.

Once home, I don't waste any time. I put on my favorite dress—the one I save for special occasions, when I need to make a striking impression. It hugs my body perfectly and the semi-translucent, shimmering fabric is just daring enough to be sexy without being indecent. I pin my hair up to show off my neck and sharpen my painted nails to points.

When I look at myself in the mirror, I give myself a little shimmy and a wink. Damn, Paul's one lucky human. He won't know what hit him.

A dull thump from the sitting area of my apartment snaps my attention away from my dazzling reflection. Dammit, did the neighbor's flesstra sneak in when I came in earlier? That little shit is always trying to get in my loft and chew my shoes. If it wasn't so cute, I'd call station pest control on it.

"Shaila! Come here, you rascal. I know you're in there. Quit messing with my stuff!" I call out into the sitting area, poking my head out the door to scan the space for the flesstra.

A heavy hand clasps over my mouth. I squeal against it in surprise, but the hand muffles the sound. Another hand grabs two of my wrists and pins them behind my back. I scratch out wildly with my lower hands and the intruder grunts in pain, but holds tight.

*Fuck*! My mind frantically tries to recall the self-defense training course I took years ago, but nothing but blinding panic and adrenaline comes forth. My attempts to twist out of this assailant's grasp are futile, and when I try to stomp on one of their feet, they easily avoid it.

The intruder makes a frustrated huff and holds me tighter. "Calm down! I'm not here to harm you. I just need to talk." Their voice is melodic and even. Like they're trying to soothe a wild beast.

"Fuck you, you broke into my home! Let me go!" I shout pointlessly against the large hand over my mouth. I scrape my sharp teeth against their palm and in their moment of surprised pain, I twist around to look back over my shoulder at the person holding me.

*Goddess, preserve me.* My eyes widen in surprise and my panicked pulse races even more. It's the ankite from my tea date. Did they follow me home?!

Fuck, Fina keeps telling me I should be more careful. Now it's too late and I'm going to get murdered by some creepy asshole. Please, Goddess, or anyone who's listening—I promise I'll stop being so reckless. Just let me get out of this alive.

Angry, bewildered tears stream down my face as I continue to struggle, feeling what little strength I have utterly fail me.

"Please. I just need to talk. If you calm yourself, I can explain. Well, we can explain," the ankite says smoothly. They glance over toward my living area and with dread I notice two other people sitting on my couch. Another ankite and a...human?

I might be able to fight off one person, if I could still my mind enough to be smart about it. But *three*? I stop struggling, sagging in their grip in defeat.

The jerk holding me keeps their bruising hold. "Are you going to listen?"

I can't even remember their name. They said so little during our date. What kind of fucked up game are they playing? Maybe if I can distract them and get them to talk long enough, I can try to get a message out to Paul or Fina.

As if reading my mind, my stalker yanks the comm device off my wrist and shoves it into their pocket. The muffled, angry noise that escapes my mouth earns a tighter grip on my wrists. They shake their head in warning.

I force myself to be still again and am surprised when they release their grip. I shove away from their grasp with a gasping curse, tempted to scream out for help.

It's useless. By the time anyone came to see what the commotion was, I'd probably already be dead.

"What the fuck are you doing here? Why did you follow me?" I hiss at the intruders, rubbing my wrists and backing away from my assailant.

"We needed to speak with you, Mezli. Or should I say Princeps Mezlitrasta val Frye?"

My heart stops when I hear my full name. Who the hell are these guys and how do they know who I am?

**Want more Space for Love? Sign up for my newsletter to get an exclusive bonus story where Fina and Maerlon return to SimTech for some extra-spicy times.**

# AUTHOR'S NOTE

Well, hey there! If you're here, that most likely means that you read my book and liked it enough to be curious about the author. Or, you hated it and wanted insight into what wretched creature could create such an abomination. Either way, you have my heartfelt thanks and appreciation for choosing to spend your precious time with my words!

If someone told me a year ago that I'd decide on a whim to write an alien romance novel, I would have laughed. Not because of the subject matter—I'm no stranger to unusual creative endeavors and I'm unabashedly horny for monsters. I'd have laughed because writing a book requires you to sit down and actually write the damn thing, instead of just imagining it. I've never been the best at turning dreams into reality, yet here we are. In no small part due to the looming threat of dying without accomplishing anything. But mostly because this silly story really wanted me to tell it!

Huge thanks to my beta readers, Angelina, Courtney, Holly, Lauren, and Sara. Your feedback was immensely helpful and there's

# AUTHOR'S NOTE

no way I could have made this book without your insights. I love and appreciate you so much! Special shoutout to Cassi, who helped catch some errors that slipped through the cracks, and to all of my amazing ARC readers for their support and encouragement.

Through this whole process, I've discovered that I love writing and have so many more stories I want to tell. Even if no one ever reads them. Though, if you liked this book, I wouldn't be mad if you shared it with a fellow romance lover.

Speaking of writing more, I already have plans for other books set in this galaxy. Mezli's story, Space for More comes out on February 20th. If you want something other than hot aliens, I have a monster romance series—Monsters of Moonvale! Maneater is a cozy, high-heat monster romance novella set in the 1980s featuring a lanky cinnamon roll witch MMC and, a curvy, confident succubus FMC. Behold Her is a spicy paranormal romance featuring a plus-size FMC and a monster MMC that blends dark themes with humor and heart to create a spellbinding story of transformation and love.

Thanks again for reading and for your support!

## ABOUT THE AUTHOR

Emily loves cozy, emotional, and spicy romances with a monstrous twist. When she isn't musing on the merits of doting, dominant monsters, she reads an obscene amount of romance novels, and cultivates her eccentric recluse persona.

Made in the USA
Columbia, SC
21 January 2025

51378144R00195